Libby was in danger.

She'd unceremoniously dumped him, cruelly told him that she had no feelings for him. The way she'd returned that ring just now… She'd treated their engagement as if it had meant nothing at all. He clenched his fists. She'd dumped him, and still the thought of anyone hurting her made him nearly wild. Not that he was still attracted to her. Definitely not. His primitive caveman self simply hadn't caught on to the fact that she was no longer his, that's all. That explained his decision to call out of work for a few days so he could stand guard beside her.

This was a matter of honor, nothing more.

Dear Reader,

I entered Mills & Boon's 2011 New Voices Competition armed with a first chapter and a vague outline. I knew how the book would start and end, but the middle? That was a little fuzzier. But as I uploaded that first chapter, reeling with a mixture of terror and optimism, I vowed that I would finish this book.

Something about Nick and Libby's story hooked me from the beginning. They are idealists navigating a dangerous world. Writing about them made me realize that I love romantic suspense because it reminds us that we can choose to be loving, selfless and brave in the face of our greatest fears. If we happen to fall in love with someone equally heroic along the way, well…I can't think of anything better than that. I hope you enjoy your time with Nick and Libby as much as I did.

This book was the winner of the 2011 New Voices Competition. (Yes, I still have to pinch myself when I say that!) This book is for all of you who supported me through this amazing journey, and for my fellow contestants, whose criticism and talent challenged me to be better.

With love and gratitude,

Natalie

NATALIE CHARLES

The Seven-Day Target

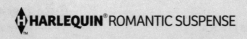

HARLEQUIN® ROMANTIC SUSPENSE

Recycling programs
for this product may
not exist in your area.

ISBN-13: 978-0-373-27820-6

THE SEVEN-DAY TARGET

Copyright © 2012 by Allison McKeen

Printed in U.S.A.

Books by Natalie Charles

Harlequin Romantic Suspense
The Seven-Day Target #1750

NATALIE CHARLES

Natalie Charles is a practicing attorney whose day job writing is more effective for treating insomnia than most sleeping pills. This may explain why her after-hours writing involves the incomparable combination of romance and suspense—the literary equivalent of chocolate and peanut butter. The happy sufferer of a lifelong addiction to mystery novels, Natalie has, sadly, yet to out-sleuth a detective. She lives in New England with a husband who makes her believe in Happily Ever After and a daughter who makes her believe in miracles.

Natalie loves hearing from readers! You can contact her through her website, www.nataliecharles.net.

For Ryan. You are my rock.

Chapter 1

Nick was climbing in his car to drive back to Pittsburgh when his phone registered the voice mail. It was Dom. The message was short and characteristically brief: "Hey, Nick, I heard you were in town for a few days. I found a body. We need to talk." So much for quick escapes.

The forecast called for rain in the afternoon, but the clouds were already gathering. They blotted the sky in a shapeless gray mat, swollen thick with moisture. Nick parked at the far end of the lot without more than a brief thought to the threat. What did he care if he was caught in the rain on his way out of town? That would be appropriate. A dark end to a dark visit.

His footsteps fell heavy in his ears as he paced toward the building. An architect had attempted to disguise the facade of the Arbor Falls police station, to make it more in keeping with the surrounding historic architecture. The result was a single-story brick building with black shingles that exactly resembled a police station posing as Victorian Era construction. It had been like that since day one, a real-life version of a game Nick used to enjoy as a kid, where he would pick out the object in a picture that didn't belong. As he approached the station today, he felt a kinship with that building and all of its ungainliness. A sympathy shared amongst those who don't belong.

Before he left Arbor Falls nearly three years ago, he'd spent years plotting his escape. This is where he grew up, sheltered from the rest of the world in a too-small town in too-Upstate New York. He felt no fondness for the collection of office buildings that the locals referred to, without irony, as the downtown area. He didn't miss the narrow roads that curled like black snakes through the valley. He'd buried this life long ago. Nick scratched at the skin below his collar. One more stop, and then he could leave it again.

He pressed his palm against the glass door and strolled inside without more than a brief wave to the familiar faces working behind their desks. Everything was still the same. The same cracks splintered across the parking lot asphalt. The same ivy clawed up the side of the building. The same anemic faces aged behind the same industrial gray metal desks. He silently thanked fate for leading him away from Arbor Falls. Had it not, he'd have suffered a similar stagnation.

"Nick Foster. It's good to see you again, man." Domingo Vasquez rounded his desk when he saw Nick in the doorway. "How's the FBI treating you?" He extended his hand.

Nick accepted Dom's handshake with a smile and a

firm grip. "The coffee sucks and the red tape is even redder than it is here."

"Now, you can't talk about red tape in the Arbor Falls P.D. anymore. In case you haven't noticed, I *am* the red tape." Dom pointed to his name plate. Sergeant.

Nick and Dom had been partners for almost four years when Nick was still on the police force. Dom had never aspired to anything, but then again he didn't need to be ambitious. He was good at his job, and the promotions followed. "Congratulations, Sergeant."

Dom's eyes were glossed by a new wariness, his brow lined by the weight of his responsibility. "I didn't ask you to come down here to congratulate me. Let's walk."

Nick followed Dom down the hallway. The cinderblock walls were coated in a fresh layer of institutional green paint. New paint on an outdated building didn't make the building look new, it just called attention to its problems. Air circulation was one, and the smell of the paint would haunt the hall for weeks. All of the windows in the station were sealed shut.

The familiarity of the surroundings coaxed memories to the surface. He'd walked this hallway too many times to count, imagining his escape to a more exciting career where he wasn't spending Saturday night busting drunk teens for cow tipping and watching them puke in the holding cell. He'd scratched each day he'd served in this station into some corner of his memory and walled it off when he'd left. Nick had a list of significant obligations that could draw him back to town. Holidays. His mother's birthday. Weddings for close friends. He didn't return to Arbor Falls any more often than he had to. Returning felt like someone chipping away at that wall.

This weekend he'd returned to pay his final respects to a man who'd despised him. He'd known Judge Andrews for twenty years. He could still smell his breath tinged with a musty odor and hear the rattle of a cough the man seemed to have fought for decades. As he'd stood in the back of the church staring at the oak casket, Nick had tried not to also hear his voice. Twenty years, and each one was spent in love with the judge's daughter. That had earned Nick plenty of words.

"You be careful, son." The judge could deliver his statements like a fist to flesh. "My Libby is going places. Don't get any ideas."

A challenge if he'd ever heard one, and Nick had gotten ideas, all right. He'd dated Libby, then he'd asked her to marry him. After only six months she'd broken the engagement. "I don't want to marry you. I don't love you." Her voice had been edged like a razor blade, the words designed to slice. She'd learned from the best.

That was almost three years ago. At the judge's funeral, he'd stood in the back of the church and watched Libby and her sister clutching each other in grief. He didn't know why he was there. If he was looking for forgiveness for the man who'd wronged him, it didn't come. He'd slipped out the back of the church without offering condolences to the family. Libby wouldn't want to see him, not ever. The feeling was mutual.

Dom flicked on the light switch in the conference room. The fluorescent bulb sputtered and hummed but eventually cooperated. "We had a murder overnight. Found the body a few hours ago. I know you work violent crime for the FBI, so I wanted your opinion."

"You told me over the phone that you suspect you're dealing with a serial killer."

Dom paused. "It's only one body."

"But?"

Dom thrust a stack of files across the table. "But we've got a young prostitute who appears to have been manually asphyxiated. No big deal, right? Happens all too often. Well, the sick prick severed three fingers while she was still alive."

Tension pulled at Nick's forehead as he opened the first file and viewed the gruesome crime scene photos. He'd worked in violent crime long enough to have developed a mollusklike shell against the gore he saw on a regular basis, but every now and then, a case would still turn his stomach.

He frowned. "A prostitute, you said? She's wearing a business suit."

"Yeah. Looks like she was dressed postmortem. Like her hair? It's a wig. The girl was blonde."

Nick's pulse quickened inexplicably. "A fetishist, maybe. Nothing the FBI would take an interest in. Not now, anyway."

He didn't like the darkness in Dom's eyes. "I'm not thinking about the FBI. I'm thinking about you." He slid two plastic evidence bags across the table. "We found this letter by the body. The bastard promises six signs over six days followed by another murder on the seventh. Then he was kind enough to leave sign number one. A picture of your girl."

Nick's heart arrested as he looked at the image of Libby Andrews. She was coming out of the courthouse dressed in a navy blue skirt suit. Her black hair was pulled back from her face and she was looking at the camera through dark-rimmed glasses. He hadn't seen her in glasses in years. Hell, he hadn't seen much of *her* in years, aside from her father's funeral. The photograph was typical Libby: sexy buttoned up in a power suit, a look those in the Arbor Falls P.D. referred to as "Ice Princess." "She's not my girl," he mumbled. Hadn't been for years. Louder he said, "This looks like it's been ripped from the paper."

"*The Journal.* Last Tuesday, April tenth, page one. It's from the Brislin trial. You know, the state senator who was found guilty of felony corruption charges. Libby was the prosecutor."

Of course Nick knew all about it. Even living in Pittsburgh, he maintained ties to Arbor Falls, and he'd have to have been living under a rock not to have known about that trial. Brislin was considered to be a shoo-in for the United States Senate until Libby got ahold of him.

He pushed the evidence bags and the files back at Dom. "I don't know what you want from me. It's your case. Take care of it."

The crease between Dom's eyebrows deepened. "Six days, Nick. That doesn't give us much time."

"And what do you want me to do about it?" He fought to maintain control of his voice. "I live five hours away. I have other responsibilities. Does she know?"

"Not yet. I sent a car over to her house. The officer rang the doorbell a few times, but she wasn't home. Must've stayed somewhere else last night. She didn't answer her phone. I was going to head over to the District Attorney's office this afternoon, tell her myself."

"Damn it, Dom. You haven't told her?" His stomach

churned. Libby's life was in danger and she didn't even know it yet.

"She hasn't been home." Dom's jaw tensed. "We only found the body early this morning. We're still processing the evidence. We're doing the best—"

"Don't tell me you're doing the best you can." Nick felt electricity surge through his body. "What's your plan to protect her?"

"We have a car parked outside of her house now. We can have another one there tonight."

"It's not good enough."

"Nick, get real—"

"It's not good enough, Dom." Nick pushed away from the table. He was due back at work tomorrow morning. His case load was heavy and there'd be hell to pay if he took time off. "And what am I supposed to do about this? She hates me."

Dom had folded his arms across his chest and was standing with the air of someone who'd decided to play the role of neutral messenger. "You're a good man," Dom said slowly. "You'll do the right thing."

Nick ground his teeth together. "I'll tell her myself," he said.

Dom nodded. "I thought you might want to do that." The fluorescent light flickered as he gathered the files and evidence bags. "It should come from someone she trusts."

"Yeah, it should," Nick mumbled as he zipped his jacket. "But instead, it's gonna come from me."

Libby had already circled the block three times when she turned the corner of Marbury Street and noticed a man standing in the middle of the only empty parking space. The driving spring rain dripped from his black umbrella in rivulets, gathering in the already sizable puddle at his feet. Her lips went cold. He'd owned that umbrella since, well, forever, and he was wearing the black windbreaker jacket she'd bought for his birthday. Libby swallowed a sudden knot in her throat.

Nick.

His face was characteristically inscrutable as she approached. It wasn't until he stepped backward onto the sidewalk that she realized he'd been saving the parking space for her. A thoughtful gesture, and yet his mouth was fixed in a tight line, and the hand that gripped the umbrella was white on the knuckles. His gesture hadn't been warm and fuzzy. Libby turned her eyes to the road in front of her, taking unusual care with her parking.

Damn her nerves. Her fingertips had turned to ice hours ago in anticipation of this meeting, and all the calming breaths in the world weren't going to slow her pulse. She fumbled for her purse and pretended to look for something inside, buying a few precious seconds to steady herself. Then she looked up and saw Nick standing by her car door, holding the umbrella. Waiting for her. She took a deep breath and opened the door.

"I saw you driving around." He held out a hand and gripped her forearm, steadying her as she climbed out of the car. "Watch out for that puddle," he murmured.

"Thank you."

He led her to the sidewalk, keeping one hand pressed lightly on her lower back. His fingers rested awkwardly against the base of her spine. He cleared his throat. "I thought we could grab a coffee. It's that time of the day when I start to drag."

"I don't have much time." The words flew out of her mouth too quickly. For a flash of a second he looked injured and Libby's gut twisted with guilt. She'd agreed to the meeting, and she was going to be civil. "Coffee's fine," she continued. "I have time for coffee."

"Good." He didn't smile.

A cold breeze penetrated to her bones and Libby pulled her trench coat tighter. Nick held the door to Coffee On Main and waited as she brushed past him and headed for a small round table in the corner, relieved to be in the dry warmth of the little café. This was where she'd studied for the bar exam, drinking coffee until her hands trembled. Six years ago she'd known every staff member by name and she'd committed the menu to memory, but she hadn't been back since then. The walls were painted the same reddish-brown, obstructed in spots by flyers advertising local concerts and household furniture for sale. Libby rested her hands on the wooden table, which felt faintly tacky.

Nick shook off the rainwater that had pebbled on his jacket sleeves, filling the empty space in Libby's line of vision with his broad shoulders. When he was finished he flicked his fingers, scattering droplets on the floor. He reached into his jacket for his wallet. "Skinny cappuccino with a double shot of espresso?"

"I've quit coffee. I'll just have a cup of Earl Grey."

She sat back in her seat and leaned an arm across the table, feigning a casual indifference to the meeting. Nick stood in place with his hands in his pockets. It was on the tip of her tongue to ask him in a rude tone whether he had something he wanted to say to her, but she caught herself just in time, her face hot with realization. "Oh, you're waiting for me to pay you."

"It's not a date," he said curtly.

"No, it's not." Clearly. She unclasped her bag and removed several dollars from her wallet. "That should cover it. Keep the change."

He lifted the corner of his mouth in a condescending smirk. "I don't need your charity."

She narrowed her eyes. "Then put it in the tip jar." She snapped her pocketbook shut and turned away.

She watched his reflection in the window as he took long strides to the counter. He was pleasant to the barista, but his back was rigid, almost as if he were on high alert, waiting for an attack of some kind. Then he turned a frostbitten glare at her and she momentarily lost her sense of place, gripped by the emptiness in his stare. She'd long wondered if Nick still hated her for ending things the way she had. It seemed the answer was yes.

Libby tugged at the hem of her skirt. If he wanted to hold on to his anger, that was his business. During the years they'd dated and the months of their engagement, she'd never been unfaithful to him. She'd gone to college and then law school, and she'd built her career, and she'd never excluded Nick from any of it. In contrast, he'd joined the FBI and demanded that she move to Pittsburgh with him. Give up her family, sell her house and leave her job—leave everything in New York and all that she'd worked so hard for and start over, all because that's what Nick wanted. Even now resentment coiled in her belly.

She considered the markings on the table, edging her

fingernail across a deep, dark groove as she remembered their last argument. The problem was that Nick put himself first, and the FBI was just one example. Nick pursued his goals even when that meant leaving a path of devastation behind him. Even if she'd left her home and her job to follow him to Pittsburgh, he would have eventually left her once he'd realized what an obstacle to his happiness she'd become.

She felt a pinch of guilt about keeping her biggest secret from him. She'd meant to tell him the truth, she really had. It's just that the words had lodged in her chest. Instead, in that final, awful argument, she'd told him she didn't love him. Maybe that was also the truth.

Libby chewed at her thumbnail, but then stopped. She was being better about that. She was quitting caffeine, which made her shaky and disrupted her sleep, and she was not chewing her nails. The past few years had been difficult ones, but she was working on pulling herself together. Seeing Nick again was a matter of taking her medicine. Toughen up and get it over with, and afterward she would feel better.

She shifted in her seat and studied him. He still looked the same. No, maybe he looked a little different. His golden-brown hair was longer than she remembered and slightly messy, and his cheeks held the beginning shadows of a beard. He definitely hadn't shaved that morning. He looked broader in the shoulders, as if he'd been working out more. Had she expected him to be broken down and lost without her? To look gaunt and haunted? To the contrary, he'd never looked better. Something about that stung.

Nick returned to the table and sat down across from her. "You look well."

"You, too."

His dark eyes were as intense as ever but softened by an unfamiliar sadness. Even in the dim afternoon light streaming through the window beside their table, Libby could make out the flecks of gold around his pupils. She sat up straighter. "You called me."

At the office, no less. He'd sounded frantic about something and scolded her for keeping her cell phone off. "What if someone needed to get in touch with you?" he'd asked.

She'd been *this* close to hanging up on him, except that she was so stunned that he was calling her after not talking to her for nearly three years. She'd clutched the phone with white knuckles, remaining on the line out of sheer curiosity, nothing more. "What do you want, Nick?"

She'd heard him sigh. When he'd spoken again, his voice had lost some of its edge. "To talk, Libby. Can we meet somewhere? Today?"

The morning was impossible. She had to be in court, and no matter how much Nick had tried to persuade her, she didn't want anyone else covering her hearings. So they'd agreed to meet in front of the park on Main Street, and Libby had imagined a quick, cordial meeting followed by a rapid getaway in her car. She wasn't interested in whatever Nick wanted to discuss.

She silently cursed the weather. Of course it had rained. Of course! And they'd had to move their meeting indoors, where awkwardness would be distilled to cups of tea and coffee and served piping hot. Curse her luck.

"I'm glad we're meeting," she said brightly. She wasn't lying. She was trying to be pleasant, and that was different. "I have something I wanted to talk to you about, too."

"You do?" He arched an eyebrow. "You've piqued my interest."

"It's nothing, really." Libby reached into her coat pocket and wrapped her fingers around the black velvet jewelry case that held the engagement ring Nick had given her. After she'd broken off their engagement and he'd left, Libby had called and left a message on his cell phone, asking what she should do with the ring. He'd responded with a text message: Keep it.

What did he expect her to do, pawn it? He knew she wouldn't. He knew that she would bury that ring at the bottom of a drawer, lest she see it and think of everything that had gone suddenly, terribly wrong in their lives. He was just being difficult. Besides, the modest diamond must have cost Nick over two months' salary. Even if returning the ring hadn't been a matter of burying the past, the gesture would have been a matter of clearing her conscience.

She'd intended to return it. She'd packed it in a padded envelope and brought it to work, where she'd stuck it at the back of a filing cabinet. She'd intended to get his address in Pittsburgh, but she'd realized that once she'd hidden the ring, she didn't want to retrieve it, not even long enough to mail it away. Half of her prayed someone would just steal it and resolve the problem for her. She'd almost forgotten about it until he called that morning.

She clasped the small case in her fist. The feel of the velvet triggered an ache in her heart, and she wondered why she couldn't have left well enough alone and pawned the ring, or sold it on the internet. Never thought about Nick again.

"I just…" Her voice trailed. She just had no courage. "You seem well."

"Yes, I am." He cleared his throat. "I was sorry to hear about your father. He was a good man."

"Thank you." Libby released the case and brought her hand to her lap, relieved for the moment to have something else to talk about, even if that something was her father's death. Even if Nick was lying. He'd hated her father, and the feeling had been mutual, but she would set that aside. Today, the goal was civility.

"I heard it was pancreatic cancer. I heard it was sudden."

"You heard correctly. He died eight weeks after the diagnosis." She leaned forward then, bringing her elbows to rest on the table. "The funeral was Friday."

The pointed tone of her voice betrayed a question that she hadn't intended to ask, a sharpness that she hadn't known she felt. She had no right to have expected him to attend services for her father, yet she'd been hurt that he hadn't been there. They'd been engaged. He should have been there. Then again, Nick had always been selfish.

She clamped down on her lip, biting back her criticism. *Civility.* It was just that she'd been thinking lately that she couldn't quite get used to all of the emptiness that had filled space in her life where loved ones used to be. Her father, for example. She imagined that one day she'd accept the fact of his death, but today and yesterday and every day since he'd died, she'd thought about calling him on the phone.

Nick looked down at the table. "You admired your father. He's the reason you became a lawyer."

Libby spun a tendril of her hair around her finger. "I keep thinking that he never saw me on trial. He was so busy all the time, and then he was sick." She let the hair fall. "I know. It sounds minor."

His mouth twitched. "It doesn't sound minor." He stiffened again and brought his hands together, looking as awkward as she was sure he felt.

Nick was another example of someone who used to be in her life. Someone she used to love…or so she thought. He looked out the window and Libby admired his profile. His nose was slightly crooked from the time he'd broken it in middle school, when an older kid had sucker punched him and Nick responded by giving him two black eyes and bringing him to the ground. By the end of it the kid who'd started the fight had been crying.

Libby had been near her locker when the brawl started, and she'd stood by and watched them rolling in the hallway: two boys rabid with hormones and rage about some cheerleader who'd been flirting with Nick. The older kid should have known better. Lots of girls flirted with Nick, and he flirted back, and none of it meant anything.

He turned to face Libby and her heart skipped. She hoped he hadn't seen her staring at him. The barista walked over with their drinks and settled the steaming mugs in front of them. Libby gratefully wrapped her hands around her mug. Damn her icy fingers.

She was aware of a flailing in her chest as she weighed whether to give him the ring now, or later. "So.

You asked me to meet you." She sat forward expectantly. "What do you have on your mind?"

First things first. The ring could come later.

He shifted in the wooden seat. It was uncomfortable as hell. The chair. Libby. The small table that was too short for his knees and wobbled so badly his coffee had already splashed over the side of the mug. All of it felt like a colony of ants marching up his limbs.

Libby was ancient history as far as he was concerned. Been there, done that, and it hadn't turned out well. He could still see her face the day she'd told him it was over, tight and unmoving. He'd seen her practicing her opening and closing statements in preparation for trial, and the face was the same. *I don't love you.* Her lips had tightened and the pronouncement had upended his world.

Maybe she was a good actress because he could have sworn she loved him. People who don't love each other don't feel the things that he felt when they made love, and people don't just fall out of love with each other overnight. Except…yes, they do. Because he was pretty sure that he'd fallen out of love with Libby that same night, when he'd realized that it was possible to know someone for nearly twenty years and to have no idea who they were.

That didn't mean he wanted to hurt her, though. Telling her that she was the target of a stalker or possibly a serial killer? It ran ice through his veins.

He rubbed at his face with both hands. "I don't know where to begin."

Damn if he didn't hate talking to victims. He'd rather get a root canal without anesthesia. Libby wasn't helping. When she'd stepped out of the car and he'd seen her again, he'd almost forgotten to breathe. She'd always reminded him of a Siberian forest, with silky black hair falling like bare branches against the new-fallen-snow perfection of her skin. Now as her ice-blue eyes watched him with increasing concern, he realized that if he'd hoped that time and distance would mitigate the effect her beauty had always had on him, he was disappointed. Libby was as stunning as ever.

"You're making me nervous," she said, twisting her hands in her lap and peering around the café. "Just tell me."

He inhaled deeply. "I saw Dom Vasquez this morning. There was a murder last night."

Her hands flew to her face. "Someone I know?"

"What? No, no, I'm sorry." He ran his fingers through his hair and shook his head. Damn, he was no good at this at all. "It was a young woman over on Peterborough. Rita something…I forget. She had a record. Prostitution and drug possession."

She exhaled. "Oh. I'm sorry to hear about her. I just… I don't understand." She turned her gaze to him and he felt his heart squeeze. "The way you were talking, I thought it was someone I knew. I thought we were meeting about something serious."

"We are. It's serious. I just don't know how to tell you." If he could only get the words out the right way. He took another deep breath. "I think your life is in danger."

She blanched. "What do you mean?"

"Whoever killed that woman last night left a letter threatening someone else, and beside that letter, he left a picture of you."

Libby sat perfectly still for a few moments. Then she whispered, "There must be a mistake. What did the letter say?"

"I have a copy." Nick pulled a photocopy from his jacket and handed it to Libby. "He promises to take revenge for some injustice, but he doesn't say what."

As she read the paper, he noticed her fingers trembling. "What is this? Six signs over six days? What does that even mean?"

"We don't know. Dom is trying to figure that out now. It's a priority."

He reached over to grasp her hand in a gesture he'd intended to be reassuring, but was instead hopelessly clumsy. Her fingers felt cold, and she didn't appear to register the contact at all. He watched as she untangled her hand from his, calmly folded the letter and handed it back to him. "I don't want to see this again."

They fell into an eerie silence as she looked past him and out the window. For a moment Nick was concerned that he'd mismanaged his responsibility, given her a violent shock. Then she took a sip of her tea and he realized that this was Libby's characteristic stoicism, nothing more. She repressed emotion better than anyone he'd ever met.

"Dom's planning to have a patrol car stationed outside your house. I don't want you to be alone."

She brushed her hair behind her ears, still looking out the window. "Where did you say the killer found the picture of me?"

"I didn't. But he used one that ran on the front page of *The Journal* last week."

"In my ugly glasses?" She smiled. "I tore my contact

lens. Must've gotten worked up while thinking about my closing argument."

Good lord, was that a joke? "Libby. This is serious."

"Is it?" Her eyes flashed. "Or is it some crazy who found a picture of a woman in the newspaper and wants to get attention?"

"We have to assume it's serious. You know that."

She set her jaw and stared straight out the window. "You know, I wish you hadn't told me this. I preferred the awkward silence."

He kept looking at her as if he were watching for some kind of reaction. What, was he waiting for her to dissolve into hysterics?

She was a prosecutor. Her job was to enforce the law, and that often required her to put people in jail for a long, long time. She didn't worry about ruining political careers or dividing families because such concerns were irrelevant to the question of whether a person had committed a crime. But she wasn't stupid. She knew that she'd made a lot of enemies.

"I've received threats before," she said. "A few from jail, a few from the families of those I've prosecuted. I can usually tell them by the envelope. Handwritten, addressed to Attorney Andrews. I just hand them over to the police." She shrugged. "The threats are all empty. They send the letters to the District Attorney's Office, not my home. Besides, it makes sense I'd be targeted now since I've been involved in some high-profile litigation recently. You probably haven't heard, living in Pittsburgh."

"Senator Brislin. I've heard about it. He was going to run for the U.S. Senate."

"Yes, well. Not anymore. He's going away for a few years. Seems he had a penchant for trading his political influence for free hot tubs and ski weekends in Vail." She took a sip of her tea. It was already lukewarm. She pushed it aside. "Things like that trial make me an easy target. I'm sure the good senator has a lot of friends who hate me."

Nick narrowed his eyes. "You heard me correctly, right? Vasquez found this threat next to a dead body. This isn't someone blowing off steam."

"Yes, I heard you." She balled her fists in her lap. "But what am I supposed to do now, Nick? Hide myself away? Live in fear?" Her voice cracked, but she didn't care. "You tell me that my life is in danger. What's that supposed to mean?"

He sat back in his chair and she felt a flush of satisfaction. He didn't know what she was supposed to do, either. "I need you to be careful. And I'd like to hang around for a few days to keep you safe."

"Like my personal bodyguard?" She sighed and folded her arms across her chest. "Is that really necessary? I work in a public place, surrounded by cops."

"And you live alone." His voice was firm. "This is not the time to be proud, Libby."

"Do you mean proud? Or do you mean a tight-ass?" she snapped. Nick froze, and she bit her lip. So much for civility.

He parted his lips and then pressed them firmly together again, looking as if he'd been about to say something but then thought better of it. "I'm not any happier about this than you are. But the Arbor Falls P.D. can't watch you twenty-four hours a day, and I don't want you to be alone."

She leaned forward until her elbows rested on her knees. "You really think I'm in danger?"

"I do. And I think I should stay with you."

"Why?" She tilted her head at him. "Why stay with me, when I have a cop parked outside my house and a bunch more at my office?"

He held her gaze. "Because I protect people, and you need protection."

She looked away and started chewing on her thumbnail again. This time, she didn't bother to stop. "I don't think that's a good idea. I'm seeing someone. I don't want anything to get…confused."

Was it her imagination, or did Nick straighten in his chair? "There's no reason things would get confused." He shifted in his seat and then eyed her. "I didn't know you were in a relationship. Does he live with you? I don't mean to pry, but if you're not living alone—"

"He's not my boyfriend." She said the words quickly, without thinking. David wasn't her boyfriend. Not technically. At least, they hadn't had that discussion yet. "We went on a few dates. His name is David. We don't live together, and he's in Zurich this week."

She watched Nick for signs of relief, then kicked herself. What did she care if Nick was relieved that she wasn't committed to anyone? They'd both moved on. And yet he seemed to relax his shoulders a little…or was she imagining things again?

"So you're alone." He fixed her with an intense gaze. "I don't want you to be alone. I want to stay with you."

Libby picked at the wooden table. She wasn't convinced that she was in any immediate danger. A killer hadn't contacted her directly, he'd left a newspaper clipping in a random victim's home. Neither was she convinced that hosting Nick in her house for a few nights was a great move. She eyed him. His black jacket was open to reveal a gray V-neck T-shirt that hinted at the chiseled muscles beneath. As he shifted, she caught a glimpse of his holster. Nick was looking dangerous on a number of levels.

Her temple started to pound. She'd set Nick free. She'd collected the pieces that had been broken with their engagement and she'd rebuilt herself stronger. She was proud of her career and her life since Nick. Inviting him back into her world would only tempt her, and being with Nick was too complicated.

Then again, what if he was correct and her life was in danger?

She reached into her pocket and fingered the jewelry case. *Just give it to him.*

"Libby?" Nick was still watching her. "What do you think?"

"I think I have to be in court to argue a pretrial motion." She placed the jewelry box between them and tried to ignore the look in Nick's eyes: anger dusted with hurt. "I'm cleaning out old things. This belongs to you."

He sat back in his seat as if the sight of the case repulsed him. "I told you a long time ago that I don't want it."

"And neither do I." She shrugged on her trench coat and reached for her bag.

"But you kept it. You kept it all these years." He

said it with a quick snap, his words betraying a depth of raw hurt.

Libby halted. "I meant to return it."

"Ah, sure. When the time was right and the gesture was calculated to hurt the most."

She swallowed. "I'm due in court. Thanks for the tea."

"You paid for it."

"Then thanks for nothing." She slung her bag over her shoulder and headed out of the café where the air was clearer and the rain had almost stopped.

She inhaled deeply and felt the scattered thoughts in her head organize. How ridiculous to think she was being targeted by a homicidal maniac. Things like that didn't happen in real life, and they certainly didn't happen to people like Libby.

She didn't bother to turn around as she stalked to her car and turned the key in the ignition. But as she pulled away, she saw Nick watching her from the sidewalk, his hands tucked into his jacket pockets. A tightness gathered in her chest at the thought that she'd succeeded, that he'd turn around and drive right back to Pittsburgh. Decide she wasn't worth the effort.

There was that ache in her heart again.

Chapter 2

Libby paused before entering her office. Nothing out of place, no surprises or strange packages on her desk. She exhaled and realized that she'd been holding her breath since she'd come out of the stairwell.

She felt shaky inside her own skin and she had to get a hold of herself. Nick was overreacting, that was all. What was it her father had said? Nick shoots first and asks questions later, and that's an ass-backward way to live. She hadn't appreciated his insight at the time, but he'd been right. Her father had always been right about Nick.

In hindsight she could see why the relationship was doomed from the start. As the daughter of a prominent judge, Libby had a privileged upbringing. She'd enjoyed countless dinners at the country club, rubbed elbows with powerful men and women at political fund-raisers and enjoyed a private school education. Her father had taught her and her sister the importance of good manners and grace. Nick had had no such opportunities, and her father took note. "Have you noticed," he'd casually remarked one evening, "that Nick holds his fork like a barbarian?"

Libby had bristled with a mixture of defensiveness and mortification. Before their next dinner she'd taught Nick how to hold his fork properly and smiled over her glass at her father when Nick executed the European style like a pro. But later her father had remarked how funny it had been when Nick had used the dinner fork for salad. "You come from different worlds," he'd said. "It's only natural that he'd feel out of place in ours."

The differences ran deeper than table manners. Libby could happily spend a weekend curled on the couch with a book while Nick played rugby with his friends. He had an almost bottomless supply of energy, excelled in most sports and hated school. She had no patience for basketball but could recite entire soliloquies from several Elizabethan and Jacobean playwrights. Mutual affection carried them far, but their paths would have inevitably split.

She switched on the light to her office and hung her coat on the standing rack in the corner. She wouldn't pretend that she hadn't gotten goose bumps to think about a killer leaving her photo at a crime scene, but she'd read the letter, and there were no overt threats made against her. She'd take extra precautions, that's all. She could stay with her sister. Cassie was a single mother who'd just given birth four weeks ago. Libby had stayed at her place last night, and maybe she'd invite herself over again tonight. Cassie would be grateful for the help.

She halted. And what if Nick was right, and someone was after her? Would she be placing her sister and nephew in harm by staying with them? Libby felt the familiar stirrings of a headache. No more thinking about absurd possibilities. She'd sleep in her office if she had to.

She rounded her desk and stared at the piles of work. With a heavy sigh she sat in her chair and reached for the top pile, *State v. Bailey*. Mr. Bailey was charged with first-degree murder, and he could walk if she didn't try to figure out a way to save the day at the suppression hearing that afternoon. She pulled a court decision from the file and grabbed a highlighter and pen.

"Busy, Libby?" Greg leaned against the door frame to her office, clasping a thick stack of papers. "A few of us are going to moot Kate. She's got an appeal coming up."

Greg LaFrance was a chief attorney in the Appellate Bureau. He was always trying to recruit other attorneys in the office to practice appellate court arguments. His efforts were so notorious that one or two colleagues readily admitted to hiding when they heard his footfall. Had she not been so distracted, Libby may have done the same.

She looked up momentarily and then returned her gaze to the case she was reading. "Sorry. I'm due in court at three."

"Too bad. We're going to have to find another judge to play the hard-ass."

Greg was grinning, but Libby gritted her teeth. She placed the pen in her hand on the desk firmly and looked up at him. "What's that mean?"

He blinked. "Sorry?"

"You called me a hard-ass." She folded her arms. "I want to know why."

Greg cocked his head to one side and looked at her as if she'd completely lost her mind. She didn't appreciate that at all. "Are you serious?"

"Yep. Let's hear it. Why am I a hard-ass?"

Poor Greg looked as if he was bargaining with some deity to make the earth open up and swallow him whole rather than answer that question. He was probably her closest friend in the office, but their friendship was limited to pleasantries about plans for the weekend or politics. They didn't have lunch or coffee or crack jokes at the photocopier. Most days Libby was far too busy for chitchat. But now? She wanted to know why he'd just used that awful term, the one that made her muscles tense with irritation until her shoulders practically rose to her earlobes. The one that she'd been called too many times to count.

"I didn't mean anything by it, Libby," Greg said gently. He thumbed the stack of papers and rolled them into a loose cylinder. "I'm sorry, I shouldn't have said that."

"Do people think I can't take a joke?" she demanded. "That I don't have a sense of humor? Is that what that means?" Even as the words hung in the space between them, the irony wasn't lost on her. *Good one, Libby— demand to know why he thinks you can't take a joke. That'll show him you're not uptight.*

His eyes were wide, and he tapped the cylindrical papers against his stomach in agitation. "Of course they don't think that. We've always had lots of fun together. Or we used to. You've been busy lately."

She raked her lower lip with her teeth as she thought.

"Is it because I don't go out to happy hours anymore? You know I don't like those social things, Greg. I'm not good at small talk." Much as she'd tried, Libby had never felt comfortable making idle conversation.

She realized she was imploring him to validate her, and she didn't know why she cared about her reputation around the office. She was a great prosecutor—what else mattered?

"You're all business, Libby. There's nothing wrong with that. We admire you." Greg ran a finger under his collar to loosen his tie. The gesture made her feel like a big jerk. She'd made him uncomfortable. "Everyone wants you to moot them because you ask the tough questions. You see the things that we miss. That's all."

He shifted to his other foot and looked away, and Libby felt a pang in her chest. She was taking out her problems on Greg, and that wasn't right. She relaxed her arms. "I'm sorry, Greg. I'm having a bad day."

"Is it because of your father?" Greg's forehead creased with concern, and Libby felt even worse for the interrogation she'd just put him through. "You know, I appeared before Judge Andrews many times. He was a good judge. Fair. Smart. My dad died a few years ago, and I've been thinking about him a lot." Libby waited for him to say more, but he let the thought drop.

"Thanks, Greg. And I'm sorry about your father." Strange, she didn't remember his father's passing. "How long has it been?"

He sighed. "It was three years in January."

Libby tightened her mouth. That explained it. That would have been just about the time she went to the doctor and her entire world fell apart. She'd gone to find out why her periods were so irregular, and he'd informed her she couldn't have children. "Early menopause," he'd explained with clinical detachment, "as a result of the cancer treatment you received as a child."

That news had sent her into a tailspin. Libby had dreamed of having a large, loving family and the pleasant chaos that would bring to her normally orderly life. Noisy holiday dinners. Busy weekends. Laundry piles. The opposite of her rigid upbringing. She'd grieved never knowing what it felt like to carry a life inside her, or decorate a nursery. She'd grieved the little hands and feet. She'd spent sleepless nights sobbing that she'd never be called Mommy, gripped with an ugly self-pity that she couldn't shake. Shame had been a constant companion, and she'd indulged in long self-evaluations before the mirror, taking inventory of everything that was broken and wrong with her. First cancer, then *this,* as if cancer alone hadn't been adequate punishment for some unknown sin.

Nick had been in Quantico. She'd never told him. She'd meant to, when the time was right and he'd be receptive to hearing that his fiancée couldn't give him the children he'd always wanted. Until then she'd tucked her secret in a corner of her mind, only to discover that the longer she kept it hidden away, the stronger her grip on it became. An infertility diagnosis meant their relationship was doomed. But if she never told him the truth, he couldn't reject her, could he? Instead, she could reject *him,* make the breakup look like her idea. She'd found a measure of comfort in controlling the source of her heartache.

All along, she'd assumed she'd been carrying on as

usual during the daytime, keeping her personal business personal. Greg's revelation now filled her with a new sense of shame. She'd been so self-absorbed that she'd been oblivious to the suffering of others.

"Time flies," she said carefully, and then lowered her gaze to his feet. She hadn't sent a card or flowers. She hadn't even asked him how he was doing. How could he still stand to be in the same room with her?

"It sure does." His tone was wistful, but after a brief pause, he brightened. "Hey, if you ever want to talk sometime… I know you're busy, but if you can break away from your files for a little while for lunch…"

"Thanks, Greg."

He tapped his knuckles on the door frame and gave her a sad smile as he left. Libby clasped her head in her hands. She had screwed up with Greg, big time. She would make it a point to do something nice for him soon. Maybe she'd even take him up on that lunch offer. Her treat.

A knot formed in her stomach as she glanced at the clock. She had a hearing in less than two hours and it promised to be a rough one. Unlike Greg, Judge Hayward had *not* been a fan of her father, and Libby often had the sense when she appeared before her that the judge was making her pay for some crime her father had committed a long, long time ago, when he had been a prosecutor and she a public defender. Maybe Libby was just being sensitive; in a way, it seemed perfectly natural that a public defender would have different politics from a prosecutor.

She returned to reading her case, highlighter in hand, and was jotting down some notes on a piece of paper when she heard a woman in the hallway outside her office shriek, "Nick! Long time no see!"

Libby froze. No. Just...*no*.

Surely she'd been greeting a different Nick. Surely Nick Foster, who'd worked closely with the prosecutors in the District Attorney's Office during his time as a member of the Arbor Falls P.D., had not been so brash as to follow her back to her office. Then she heard his voice. "Good to see you, Sheila. I thought I'd surprise Libby."

For a frantic moment Libby considered diving under her desk. She settled on popping a breath mint just as he strolled into her office. "Well, well," she said coolly. "Let me guess—you're heading back to Pittsburgh, and you thought you'd say goodbye?"

"You've always been lousy at guessing games." Nick paused and looked around the office. "You hid your visitor's chair."

"The state took them back as part of some budget-saving measure." She sighed and turned back to the paperwork on her desk. "There was a giant yard sale on the town green."

"Liar." He walked to the gray filing cabinet in the corner, looked behind it and removed a chair. "What's the matter, Libby? Don't you want visitors?"

"Visitors occupy space I don't have." She didn't make eye contact as he plopped the chair directly in front of her desk and sat down. Then she looked up and sighed dramatically. "Did you need to do that?"

"This is where visitor chairs go," he explained as he pulled out his BlackBerry and checked his email. "In most offices, at least. In yours I guess they go behind

the filing cabinet." He winked but was rewarded with
a scowl.

"I'd throw it out a window if they opened," she muttered.

He'd followed Libby to the office, watching for any
pursuing cars. State police officers were stationed at the
District Attorney's Office as a matter of routine. They
stopped him at the door, but Nick flashed his FBI cre-
dentials and informed them of the threats against Libby.
"If you see anything suspicious, anything at all, give me
or Sergeant Dom Vasquez a call."

The stairwells had been secure, as had the eleva-
tors. Nick walked the four flights of stairs to the fifth
floor and surveyed the surroundings. The office was
as busy as he remembered, and nothing struck him as
unusual or concerning. Despite all of these assurances,
Nick couldn't get his pulse down.

Libby was in danger. She'd unceremoniously dumped
him, cruelly told him that she had no feelings for him.
The way she'd returned that ring just now…he'd had to
fight his anger. She'd treated their engagement as if it
had meant nothing at all, and he suspected she'd been
unfaithful. Well, sometimes he suspected it. Most often
he repressed his suspicions because the thought of Libby
with another man made him want to do something de-
structive. Something he would regret and have to pay
for. Then again Libby was principled above all else.
She drove the speed limit and did things the hard way.
"Cheating" wasn't in her vocabulary. No, he decided as
he watched her, she probably hadn't cheated.

He clenched his fists. She'd dumped him, and still the
thought of anyone hurting her made him nearly wild.

Not that he was still attracted to her. Definitely not. His primitive caveman self simply hadn't caught on to the fact that she was no longer his, that's all. That explained his decision to call out of work for a few days so he could stand guard beside her. His supervisor had threatened to discipline him for taking vacation on such short notice. Let him. This was a matter of honor, nothing more or less. Territorial paleolithic stuff.

Nick frowned to himself as he checked his Black-Berry, sorting through the day's messages. He was relieved to see that his inbox contained nothing of real importance, although one of his larger cases was moving forward quickly. There was another message about his upcoming transfer. He was required to spend a three-year rotation in a major FBI office, and he was hoping to be placed in Washington, D.C. He'd learn his placement soon.

He returned the BlackBerry to his pocket and rested his arms on the chair, which had seen better days a long, long time ago. "You know that the arm of this chair is split?" He ran his thumb over the crack. "You should ask for a new one."

"It's not in the budget. They'd just hand me a roll of duct tape."

He watched her as she read. Hardworking, serious Libby—had she always been that way? He didn't think so. She'd always been smart and studious, just like her father, but she'd balanced her seriousness with spontaneity. Nick would never have wanted to date a woman who'd shut herself off the way this Libby seemed to.

"Wanted to date"—who was he kidding? "Fallen

completely in love with" was closer to the truth. Blindly, stupidly in love.

He couldn't tell what she was reading, but she was intent. She chewed her lip when she was lost in thought; he'd always found that adorable. Nick leaned back and exhaled, suddenly feeling like he was sitting on a stack of thumbtacks. "I don't know how you do it."

"What?" She didn't bother to look up.

"Sit still like this. All day. My skin is crawling." He rubbed his arms, partly to prove his point and partly because he hadn't meant it as a figure of speech. His skin felt like it was covered in something vile.

"Mmm," she responded. "You don't need to stay, you know. Shouldn't you be busting a drug cartel or something?"

"I busted them all before I left. And I told you I don't want you to be alone."

"And I told *you* that this is nothing but empty threats." She retrieved a paper from her file and studied it. "Anyway, I was thinking of staying at Cassie's, just to be safe. She just had a baby, and she could use some help with the nighttime feedings."

His eyebrows shot upward. "I didn't know Cassie was seeing any—"

"She's not," Libby replied quickly. "She's on her own. That's why she likes it when I can stay over to help out."

She flashed him a look that warned him off any questions, but Nick didn't care enough to pursue the issue. Whatever happened to Libby's little sister wasn't his business. He fished out his BlackBerry again. "What's the name?"

"Hmm?"

"The baby. What's the name?"

"Samuel." Libby's face softened. "Samuel James. That was my grandfather's name."

"I know."

She must have forgotten herself, because she looked up at him and smiled before returning to her paperwork.

His gaze hovered on her pale, slender fingers. Once he'd surprised her at work after hours, just after their engagement. She'd closed the door and kissed him, running those fingers down the front of his shirt to his belt buckle. He'd watched her tug the leather loose, fixated on the sight of her manicured fingernails as she'd felt his arousal, then boldly freed him from his pants. Prim and proper Libby. So concerned about appearances. A lady by all accounts. But that night she'd slid off the flimsy excuse for panties she'd been wearing under her skirt and tossed them at him. Then she'd seated him in her chair and given him a naughty smile as she flung first one long bare leg across his waist, then another—

He rose from his seat and walked to the window. He was not going there.

As if she could read his thoughts, Libby looked up, her lips pinched in prim disapproval. "Maybe you can step out into the hall. I have a lot of work to do before the hearing."

Nick nodded silently and slipped out the door. He needed some air, anyway.

"You're late." Officer Frank Hawkins was standing in the hall outside the courtroom, his arms folded across his chest and his eyes narrowed at Libby in obvious contempt. His gaze darted to Nick. "You a new prosecutor?"

"Nope. Just a friend of Libby's."

More like a shadow, if shadows could be so irritating as to demand to drive you to a court hearing. No need to argue semantics in front of Hawkins, who made Libby's blood pressure rise like nothing else. Hawkins was no stranger to the attorneys in the District Attorney's Office, and this wasn't the first time she'd had to defend his questionable police practices. If she didn't know any better, Libby would think that Officer Hawkins loathed the very laws he was charged with enforcing.

"I'm not late. I'm five minutes early," she said in a brusque manner as she walked past him and headed for the courtroom. "I was preparing for this hearing."

Hawkins grabbed her roughly by the arm. "Wait, shouldn't we discuss this first?"

Libby glanced down at the hand gripping her arm and said in a stern, level voice, "Officer Hawkins, I'd appreciate it if you'd refrain from touching me."

"Answer my question."

Nick spun on his heel and pinned Hawkins with a glare. "Take your hand off of her."

Hawkins blinked twice but dropped his hand.

"Thank you," Libby said. She turned to Nick, "Can you give us a minute?"

He hesitated. "Okay, but I'm going to be right over there. I'll be watching." The warning was delivered to Hawkins with another glare.

After Nick was outside of earshot, she turned to face the officer. "What do you want to talk about?"

He scratched at the back of his head. A nervous habit, she supposed, or else he had a violent case of seborrhea. "Shouldn't we go over my testimony?"

She shrugged. "What's there to go over? I interviewed you last week. I'm going to ask you a series of questions, and I want you to tell the truth."

There he went again with the scratching. His jawline was red with a painful-looking razor burn that extended down his neck. Between the bumps on his neck and the scratching at his head, he looked miserable. But, she mused, he probably didn't look as miserable as he made those around him feel on a regular basis. Libby eyed him carefully, trying to conceal her distaste.

"I thought we were supposed to meet. You know, to practice before the hearing."

"You've testified many times before, Officer Hawkins. I don't see..." Libby paused. "Wait. Are you asking me to help you lie?"

His eyes shifted and he placed his hands on his hips. "Of course not."

Her eyes narrowed. "Then what, exactly, would we be practicing?"

Hawkins leaned closer, unintimidated. "I'm trying to help you and your office out, Andrews. Keep a cold-blooded killer and an abusive husband locked away."

Libby laughed. The nerve of this man. "Help me out? You've made my job *infinitely* more difficult. Thanks to your overzealous police work, I'm certain Judge Hayward is going to toss this entire case."

His face darkened. "You wait a damn minute—"

"All right," Libby huffed, all five feet five inches of her glaring at all six feet of him. "You want to review your testimony? Let's review it. You responded to a domestic dispute and then, without probable cause or a search warrant, proceeded to conduct a search of the house. You found a handgun with a filed-off serial number in a closet. Turns out that handgun is linked to an unsolved murder."

"I cracked open a cold case," he growled.

"You broke the law. You had no business searching that closet, and if the defense attorney succeeds in suppressing that handgun, we have no case." Her voice was flat. "Do you understand? A murderer could walk because of your actions, and if you think that I'm going to help you to cover up this…*mess,* you are sadly mistaken."

Hawkins was dangerously still, and he seemed to channel the focus of a cobra immediately before striking. "Well. You've made yourself clear." His upper lip rose to reveal his teeth. "Judge Hayward is expecting us, *counselor.* We don't want to keep her waiting." His voice dripped with acrimony.

Libby pulled her shoulders back and lifted her head. Hawkins was a creep who'd shown contempt for the rule of law. Judge Lucy Hayward was a former criminal defense attorney who distrusted law enforcement officials. Sparks were about to fly. She'd do what she could to defeat the motion to suppress, but this would be an uphill battle. The judge was bound to chastise them both for this particular embarrassment.

"No," she agreed. "We don't want to keep the judge waiting."

Nick hovered by the door as the judge entered. The courtroom was mostly deserted except for a few men in dark suits, probably attorneys waiting for the next argument to be called. The court reporter dutifully typed names as counsel identified themselves. A young man in a gray suit sat somberly in the otherwise vacant jury box with a pen and notebook in hand, prepared to take notes. A law clerk or an intern. A marshal stood by the jury box. Nick slid onto a wooden bench in the last row. From here he could see everything that happened during the proceeding and he could respond if necessary.

His gaze returned to Libby. He'd never watched her argue before. She was poised as she addressed the judge, but Nick thought he detected an underlying discomfort. The way she was moving, stiffly looking through the accordion file in front of her, made him suspect that their conversation at Coffee On Main had bothered her more than she'd let on. Then again, most people would have been bothered to find out that their photograph had been left beside a dead body. She'd never been one to be typical.

Nick's focus was drawn to Officer Hawkins, who was sitting behind her. He kept looking at his watch as if he had more important things to do. Nick had worked with a few bad cops, the kind that give law enforcement officers a bad name. Hawkins struck Nick as a loose cannon.

As the argument commenced, Nick realized this was a suppression hearing. The defense attorney had asked the court to throw out evidence discovered as the result of an unlawful search. Nick had testified at a few such hearings himself, first as a police officer with the Arbor Falls P.D. and more recently as a special agent with the Bureau. If an officer didn't have a warrant or a damn good reason for conducting a search, then everything discovered in that search was tainted. Fruit of the poisonous tree. When evidence was inadmissible in court, entire cases were lost.

"I'd like to call Officer Frank Hawkins," Libby announced, and the scowling officer marched to the witness stand.

Libby waited while Hawkins raised his right hand to swear and affirm that the testimony he was about to give was the truth. She arranged a small stack of papers before asking Hawkins to state his name for the record.

Nick felt a tightness in his gut as she spoke. Her voice wavered. She was nervous.

The testimony seemed straightforward. Hawkins had responded to a domestic dispute and found the wife of the accused badly beaten while the accused was flying high as a kite on a drug cocktail. "Did you see any drugs in plain sight?" Libby asked.

"No."

"Did you see any weapons in plain sight?"

"He struck her across the back with a floor lamp."

"But no guns or knives?"

"No." The officer paused. "But she told me he had a gun."

The response caused Libby to halt her questioning entirely. Hawkins had just surprised her. She continued. "By *she* do you mean the victim? The wife of the accused?"

"That's right. She told me he had a gun hidden in the closet and that it was loaded. I checked the closet and sure enough, there it was. Right on the top shelf."

"In plain sight." Libby's voice was flat.

"Yep." Hawkins flashed his eyebrows before sitting back in his seat and folding his arms across his chest.

"A moment please, your honor." Libby retreated to her files and shuffled through them, then set them aside. She was rattled. She lifted an envelope and puzzled at it before setting it on the corner of the table. Finally she looked up at the judge. "Your honor, may I approach?"

"You may." Judge Hayward turned so that her back was to Hawkins as Libby and the defense attorney approached her. They spoke for several minutes, but Nick couldn't hear any of the conversation from his place in the courtroom. When she was done speaking, the judge's face was dark. Libby and the defense attorney returned quickly to their respective tables.

"It has come to my attention that the witness has changed his story," Judge Hayward announced. "I can only conclude that he has done so in response to this motion to suppress, and I will not tolerate such abuses from officers of the law. Therefore, I am granting the motion. The gun is inadmissible."

"You bitch!" Hawkins was standing in the witness box, pointing at Libby. "You're gonna pay for this."

Nick sprang to his feet, but the marshal had already restrained Hawkins. Judge Hayward pounded her gavel. "I'm holding you in contempt. Get him out of here!"

"You screwed the whole case!" Hawkins continued to shout as the marshal dragged him out of the courtroom. "I hope he kills you next!"

Nick was at Libby's side, his arm around her shoulders. He could feel her trembling. Judge Hayward continued to bang on her gavel. When Hawkins was out of the courtroom, they heard him shrieking down the hall. After a minute, the room was silent again.

Libby and Nick were still standing as the judge announced that she was taking a brief recess to collect herself and that she would be back in fifteen minutes.

"Libby," Nick began after Judge Hayward had left, "are you—"

"No. I'm not."

Now he noticed that her teeth were chattering. "You're a prosecutor. You had an ethical obligation to tell her the truth." He stopped himself from rubbing her arms. That would have been an old habit.

"What?" She looked at him blankly. "No, I know. I don't care about Hawkins. It's that." She pointed to the envelope she'd placed on the corner of the table. "Nick, that's not mine, but it was in my file."

His heartbeat quickened, and he patted his jacket. He always carried a few sets of latex gloves, just in case. He put them on and picked up the envelope. "Did you open it?"

She shook her head. "I only saw it a few minutes ago. But it's addressed to me."

Indeed someone had scrawled *Elizabeth Andrews* in block letters on the front. The envelope was unsealed. Nick tucked his finger under the flap and peered into the pocket. He frowned. "Looks like a photo," he said.

"Oh, God." She turned away.

Nick looked around. There were still people scattered in the courtroom. He turned his back to them and carefully slid the photograph out of the envelope. The image was blurry, but after a moment it came into focus. A layer of perspiration beaded on his forehead.

"What is it?" Libby's voice quivered.

"It's a photograph of the murder victim," he said. "And it says you're next."

Chapter 3

Libby forced herself to look at the photograph, to take in the image of the poor woman. The sick bastard had framed the picture like a head shot, capturing the ligature marks on her neck and the vacant stare of her blue eyes. On the back he'd written "Your next" in red block letters, followed by a number two. He should have written "You're next," but that was the least of anyone's problems.

"Yeah, that's her, all right." Vasquez's expression was grim as he considered the photo. "Where did you say you found this again?"

"It was shoved into one of my files." Libby wrapped her arms around herself. Vasquez's office was stuffy and warm, but she couldn't seem to shake the chill that had settled over her in court.

"That means that the suspect gained access to your

office," Nick said. "The D.A.'s Office is monitored by video surveillance."

"We'll take a look at the videos," said Vasquez. His face pinched with concentration as he turned the evidence bag that protected the photo in his hands. "The image is digital. We'll analyze the ink used, see if we can trace it to a printer make and model. That could be helpful once we locate a suspect."

"Handwriting analysis will be impossible," Nick mumbled. "He used a thick marker and block letters. What do you make of that number two?"

"There was a reference to six signs in the first letter. Six signs over six days." Vasquez placed the letter on his desk and rested his hands on his trim waist. "So I guess this is sign two?"

Libby rubbed at her forehead, which pulled with tension. "Six days." She was going to be sick.

"We're going to get him," Nick said, gripping her shoulder. "I'm going to be right by your side. I told you I wouldn't leave."

There was something wild and fiery in his eyes as he swore to protect her, and he intensified his grip as if to underscore his commitment. A few hours ago she'd hoped he would leave her alone, but now she clung to his promise with a frightened desperation. He wasn't leaving. She wouldn't be alone. "Thank you." Her voice was barely a whisper.

"So this is sign number two, and sign number one was the photograph left beside the victim." Vasquez spat a foul word as he folded his arms. "What are these signs about, anyway?"

"Some sick game he thinks he's playing with us."

Nick sat in the chair beside her. He was close enough that she felt the heat radiating from his body. "Serial killers get off on torture, and what is this but psychological torture? Mark my words—he's watching us very closely. He wants to see Libby in a state of fear, and he wants to see us panic. If these details land in the paper, so much the better."

"We're not giving him that satisfaction," Vasquez growled. "It'll be a cold day in hell."

Libby looked at Nick. "So this is a serial killer, then? That's what you're thinking?"

"We're looking through our files to see if this most recent crime compares to any other cases," said Vasquez. "The crime had bizarre elements that make me think it's possible this is some sort of fantasy fulfillment."

"And killing me is the fantasy?" The realization washed over her like a rush of icy water. The black wig on the victim, the navy blue business suit. "I wasn't chosen at random. I was selected for a reason."

"We don't know that, Libby." Nick's voice was calm. "This could still be random, or you may be a target because of your work on the Brislin trial."

"Do you have any enemies?" Dom asked.

Too many to count, it seemed, but she didn't want to admit that. "Probably. Officer Hawkins just threatened me in court this afternoon. Well, I guess he didn't threaten me directly, but he said that he hoped someone already accused of murder would kill me next."

Nick eyed her. "Spoken like a true attorney. Hawkins threatened you, Libby."

"Hawkins, huh?" Dom said. "Between us he's been a real problem. He's going through a divorce and there's a nasty custody battle. He's become something of a liability. I can't see him as a murder suspect, but we'll check him out."

"He should be easy enough to find. He was thrown in the holding cell at the courthouse," Nick said. Dom's lips thinned.

Libby felt a wave of nausea as something occurred to her. "That file wasn't just in my office." She pressed the bridge of her nose between her thumb and forefinger and closed her eyes. "I took it home with me a few days ago to review it." Oh, God. Had he been in her home?

A silence fell over the room, and when she opened her eyes again, Nick and Dom were watching her. Dom finally said, "Who has keys to your house?"

"My sister. That's it."

"Did you notice anything unusual at home? Any signs of entry?" Nick placed his hand on her back and lowered his head to peer at her.

She shook her head. "No, nothing. I would've called the police."

"Did you leave windows open? Forget to lock a door?" Dom was perched on the edge of his desk.

Leave her windows open? Geez, she wasn't stupid. "No, of course not. I'm a prosecutor. I see the awful things people do to each other every day. I have an alarm system. And yes, it works, and yes, I turn it on."

She slumped forward. This was a nightmare. Less than twelve hours ago the biggest problem in her day had been the fact that she was seeing Nick again. Now she was wondering whether she had days left to live. How had her existence managed to unravel to this point?

She was aware of Nick's hand moving in circular

strokes across her back. His hand felt too warm, his touch too good, to move. She allowed him the contact.

"We don't know that he was in your house," Nick said softly. "It could have been your office, or your car, even."

She nodded. She could handle someone rifling through her office files, but the thought of a psychopath violating the sanctity of her home was too much to bear. Libby pressed her forehead against the palms of her hands. "So now what?"

"We're going to check for fingerprints, and our lab is processing the evidence from the crime scene already. The medical examiner is conducting the autopsy tomorrow. Believe me when I say that we're taking this matter very seriously. In the meantime you're going to go somewhere safe."

"Somewhere safe," Libby echoed. "Does that mean I can't go home?"

"We'll go home and get your things." Nick removed his hand from her back. "But I think it would be best if you stayed somewhere else for a little while."

"He must be following me, right? Do you think he knows I stayed at Cassie's last night?" The thought that she'd unknowingly put her sister and her young nephew in harm's way made her stomach ache. "Are they safe?"

"They will be," Nick assured her. "We'll make sure of it."

"They?" Dom asked.

"Cassie and her baby," she said.

"Dom, maybe you can send someone over to park in front of the house and keep an eye on them. From what I understand, Cassie's all alone."

"Of course."

Libby shook her head. "I don't want Cassie and Sam in that house. It's not safe."

"We'll get them somewhere safe, then. Let me work it out with Dom. I want you to focus on keeping your cool."

"Keeping my cool?" There was a shrill peak to her question. Her entire life had changed in the span of the afternoon, and he was telling her to stay calm? "That's easy to say when no one's leaving photographs of murder victims in your files."

"Libby." Nick wrapped both of his hands around hers and looked into her eyes. "I know you're hurting, and when you hurt you like to take control. I'm telling you that you're better off controlling yourself and leaving the rest to us. Can you trust me?"

She studied his face, running her gaze from one dark eye to another. *Controlling.* That had been a buzzword in that last fight they'd had. Nick complained about Libby's need to count the calories she consumed and to regiment every minute of her day. Could she help it if she hated surprises? Organization was the hallmark of success, and frankly Nick could stand a little more neatness in his life. Did he expect her to go blindly along with his plans for her now of all times, when she was feeling so out of control?

"I'm not a victim," she said. "I'm your partner. If you can promise to work on treating me like an equal, I can work on trusting you."

After a moment of consideration Nick nodded his head. "Okay. We'll work on it."

They left soon afterward, walking in silence to the parking lot. Libby stared at the front seat of Nick's beat-up coupe. There were scattered junk food wrappers and balled up napkins on the passenger floor. It was nothing short of a miracle the vehicle wasn't crawling with rodents. "Should we just leave my car at the office, then?" She lifted a napkin by its corner and tried not to wrinkle her nose.

Nick swiftly cleared the floor and threw all of the wrappers into a paper bag. "The lot is monitored by security cameras. It will be safe." He took the napkin from Libby's hand and added it to the bag.

"I don't know. This guy seems pretty bold."

He sighed. "Do you want to drive separate cars? You know what, don't even answer that, because it's not going to happen. He knows your car, but he may not know mine, and we need every advantage over this bastard we can get."

Fair enough. She climbed into the bucket seat and inhaled. The car smelled like Nick—soap and aftershave with undertones of something musky and masculine. Also French fries, but he sometimes smelled like that, too. She felt a nostalgia for better times, when Nick had been her entire world and she'd been his.

She shivered, and Nick turned on the heat without asking. Then they drove in silence to her house, riding along the same roads that Nick always used when he drove her. Libby had avoided that particular route for years.

As the car rolled to a stop in her driveway, Libby reached to open the door. "Wait," Nick said, lightly touching her arm. "I want to make sure it's safe first."

She waited as he walked around the house, presumably checking for signs of a break-in. When he disappeared into the backyard, she glanced around her, watching for the slightest movement or shadow. Her mouth was dry and she gripped her house key in her fist like a weapon. She'd use it if necessary.

After a few minutes he returned to the car and opened her door. "All clear."

"Thanks," she said. "You're better than an alarm system."

He felt cold grip the inside of his stomach as he walked up the front steps to Libby's house. This was where he'd finally rid himself of the heavy burden of being in love with Libby Andrews since middle school. Funny the way she'd helped him do it so effectively.

She turned to him as she opened the door. "Come in, I guess." She swallowed, clearly uneasy.

Nick caught his breath. There she was, the sweet vulnerable girl he'd fallen in love with. He'd never forget the first time he saw her, walking to school with her books clasped against her chest, talking with her best friend. She'd worn her black hair short then, and it curled slightly around the back of her ears. He'd wondered why he'd never seen her before but then he'd learned that she'd been out of school the previous year with cancer. Non-Hodgkin's lymphoma. She never wanted to talk about it, and when she discussed that period at all she simply referred to it as "the time I had cancer." But even today he'd noticed the scar that was seared above her left breast, which was visible every time she wore a blouse that buttoned down. That, she'd once grudgingly explained, was where the doctors had placed the port to administer the chemotherapy. "They told me I needed the port or else the drugs would have ruined my veins.

Or maybe that's the way I understood it." She'd changed the subject after that, and he'd never pushed her to say more, respecting that the topic was a painful one.

Her sister, Cassie, had only been ten years old at the time, but she'd talked openly to him about it. "Libby was bald," she'd said. "My mom had to shave her head one night because clumps of hair kept falling out. I remember Libby crying for hours, and my mom, too. I think that's why she's always kept her hair long since then."

Libby had no reason to cut her hair short, anyway. It was thick and black, richly wavy, and it fell halfway down her back. It smelled sweet, like vanilla. Gorgeous hair that fell like silk ribbons when it was wet. Hair like that should never be short.

Walking across the threshold of her home boiled something in his stomach. He'd helped her choose the paint for these walls, and he'd refinished the hardwood floors himself. The day she'd moved in, they'd eaten pizza on the living room floor. He thought he'd buried these memories when he'd walked away from Libby that last time. He'd never intended to return here.

He raked his fingers through his hair, trying to clear his thoughts. Protecting Libby wasn't a choice. He couldn't allow someone he'd once cared about to be alone under such terrifying circumstances. He understood terror. He still had the scars from his father's beatings and so did his mother. Nick had stood by as a child when his father stumbled home, stinking of alcohol and cigarette smoke, and looking for a fight. He still woke in the night imagining the sound of her body being thrust against the wall, or the "strum" of his father's leather belt as he pulled it through the belt loops and clicked it against his palms, stalking toward Nick's bedroom. His mother had kicked his father out of the house, but she couldn't keep him away forever. The routine had continued for years, interspersed with brief periods of reconciliation and sobriety.

Then Nick had gathered the courage to fight back. One evening, when his father had come calling, Nick was waiting. He didn't know how many of his father's bones he'd broken. All he knew was that he'd brought his father to the ground and warned him that if he ever came back to the house, he'd do worse than that. That time his father had listened.

Law enforcement was more than a job, it was his calling. He'd spent the rest of his life protecting women and children from abuse. Libby was just another victim, and when he'd helped to capture the bastard who was threatening her, he'd leave and he'd never think about her again. The thought strengthened him.

"So, everything's messy." She was a little breathless as she spoke.

Nick glanced around the house. Her countertops practically glistened; the window treatments were arranged just so. She'd placed fresh flowers in a vase on the kitchen table, an arrangement of pink-and-yellow tulips. He opened his mouth to compliment the selection but then halted, because those flowers were probably from David. Her new beau. He turned his back to them.

"Your home is beautiful, as always."

She grimaced and hurried to place a stray coffee cup in the dishwasher. "Where are we going if we're not staying here? A hotel?"

"I thought we'd go to my place."

She froze. "In Pittsburgh?"

"I meant my parents' place. My mom and stepdad are in Florida. They won't be home until the middle of May. You know how it is. The temperature has to reach a consistent seventy degrees before my mom will set foot in the Northeast."

Libby nodded slowly. "Your mom is doing well, then? And your stepdad?"

"Yes, they're well." He walked to a cabinet and helped himself to a drinking glass. "And Bio Dad has been sober for a while now. We talk sometimes." A real father was a supportive role model to his children. A biological father contributed DNA. Nick had a strictly biological father.

She filled Nick's glass with water and handed it back to him. A silence settled between them. "I guess I'll pack."

"I'll go with you."

"No. I don't need you to watch. I have to pack personal things." Her cheeks flushed and she looked down demurely.

"I'll stand outside your door, then. I won't look."

"Oh, for God's sake—"

She was interrupted by a knock on the door followed by the chime of the doorbell.

Cassie. She'd completely forgotten that she'd promised her dinner. Nick made a macho show of looking out the window, one hand on his gun, before giving Libby the nod to open the door. She tried not to roll her eyes at him.

Cassie's normally wild blond curls were even wilder,

if such a thing was possible. She was bouncing on her toes as she held Sam, who was crying impressively. "I swear I'm going out of my mind," she said. "He's been crying for the past half hour. Babies are supposed to sleep in the car, right? Well, not Sammy—" She froze. "Oh, my God, Nick!"

Cassie gave him a one-armed hug. Libby had almost forgotten how close they were, but Nick had been part of Cassie's life for so long that he'd been like an older brother to her.

"Cassie. And this is Sam? Congratulations."

She made a noise like a severed laugh and handed the baby to Libby. "Thanks. I'm so overwhelmed right now. Sleep deprived. I don't know what I'd do without Libby."

Libby held the bawling infant closely and bounced gently on her toes with him. "He looks even bigger than he did yesterday," she told Cassie, knowing that her sister worried incessantly about his weight. Sam had been premature and had spent his first two weeks in the neonatal ICU.

Cassie half listened as she babbled excitedly to Nick. Libby took the opportunity to walk back into the house with the baby. She nuzzled her nose against his scalp, inhaling his sweet scent of powder and warm milk. She loved the way he grasped her finger tightly when she held it out to him. She loved everything about him.

A pang struck her under her rib cage. Didn't it figure that Cassie would get pregnant unexpectedly, without even trying, while Libby, the sister who'd always loved babies, was still reeling after learning that chemotherapy had left her infertile? Libby had been so filled with rage at the universe that she hadn't fully accepted her nephew until he was born. Then, the first time she saw him in the incubator, the tubes and monitors covering his body, she'd talked to him and he'd turned to her. It had taken her until that point to realize that he wasn't some cosmic irony. He was a miracle. And he was quieting in her arms.

"He had to burp. Now he's feeling better." She placed him in the little swing Cassie had brought over a week ago.

"Oh, thank God." Cassie heaved a sigh. "Maybe he'll sleep for a while."

Libby took her sister gently by the forearm. "I can't do dinner, Cass. I need to leave the house. Can you come upstairs to help me pack? I'll explain."

Cassie's eyes widened in concern. "Yeah, okay. Is everything all right? Can Nick watch Sam?"

Nick nodded and sat by the baby swing. He watched the baby drift into sleep, Sam's lower lip jutting out in a pout. Something sad rippled through Libby as she watched the scene and remembered how much Nick wanted children. His own father had been terribly abusive, and she suspected that to Nick, having children represented a way to compensate for his own father's failures.

He reached out a hand, tentatively stroking Sam's cheek with his fingertips and murmuring an apology when the infant stirred. She swallowed a tightness in her throat. Nick would be a great father. She hoped he'd get the chance some day.

Cassie dropped a four-letter word. "My God, Libby. This is like something out of a movie. This can't be happening."

"It seems it is." Telling Cassie about the events of that afternoon left Libby feeling sober, almost as if she were relaying someone else's nightmare. "But I don't want you to worry, I just want you and Sam to go somewhere safe. Away from me."

Cassie threw her hands into the air as she plopped herself onto Libby's bed. "How can you tell me not to worry? And God, Libby, where is safe anymore? You think he knows where I live?"

"I don't know, but let's not take chances. I don't know how long he's been following me or to what extent, but I don't want to make anything easy for him."

This is where Libby excelled, in the role of patient counselor. She could speak calmly to her sister and assure her that everything would be fine, and she could momentarily forget about her own problems as she lost herself in trying to resolve Cassie's concerns. Later she would come back down to the reality that someone was stalking her, but now? She could simply focus on Cassie's wide eyes and the frown between her eyebrows. They were only two years apart in age, but her little sister had always been younger than her years where Libby was concerned.

"Hey, it's okay, Cassie." Libby sat beside her on the bed and wrapped her arms around her shoulders. "You know I'm a target because of my work. Earlier today a police officer started shouting threats at me because I informed the judge that he'd fabricated his testimony. This happens. The police are all over it, *believe* me, and it's possible that they'll find a fingerprint or see something once they review the video surveillance footage from the D.A.'s Office."

"And Nick is here. That makes me feel better." Cassie sniffed back tears.

"Yes." Libby stood stiffly and walked to her closet. She needed to pack.

She flung the closet door wide and selected a few outfits for work. Her fingers grazed the clear plastic bag that held her wedding dress and Libby paused. She hadn't thought about that dress in ages. The perfect dress for their perfect June wedding: a strapless gown that was fitted to her waist before collapsing in elegant layers of chiffon. The perfect dress to match the perfect cake, the perfect flowers and the perfect meal. She'd thought of every little detail for that day, a hundred ways to announce to the world that she and Nick were in love.

Libby tightened her jaw and closed the closet door. Nothing was perfect.

She turned to her dresser and opened her jewelry box. Libby didn't wear much jewelry and she didn't have anything of real value except for a small silver charm bracelet that had belonged to her mother. Even then, the bracelet was more valuable for sentimental reasons and she couldn't imagine leaving it behind knowing that the killer could come back to her house. She clasped it across her wrist.

As she looked up, she caught Cassie watching her in the reflection of the mirror. "You know, if someone like Nick swore to protect me no matter what, I'd be swooning. Especially if I'd told that person point-blank that I didn't love him."

"Cassandra—"

"Do you realize what he's doing, Libby? He left his job,

took a leave of absence, to be at your side. Do you know what I'd give for someone to be that devoted to me?"

Cassie's voice clipped as she fought her emotion. She'd never told Libby about Sam's father and Libby had never asked, but more than once Cassie had suggested that the father had rejected her. Libby may have envied Cassie's ability to have a child, but her heart broke for the circumstances under which it had happened.

"Please keep your voice down. Of course I appreciate all Nick is doing. I hope that when this is all over we can continue to be friendly." She lifted a stack of light sweaters from her drawer and refolded them before tucking them into her suitcase. "He's doing what anyone in his position would do."

"Don't be so sure. You treated him like crap."

Libby spun around. "Cassie!"

"He thought you walked on water and you dumped him for your career. How much courage do you think it took him to get into that car and to drive over to meet you, knowing how much you could hurt him again? And knowing Nick, I'll bet he did it without a thought."

A raw ache pulsed across Libby's chest. She'd told Cassie that she'd broken up with Nick because he would have made her leave her job, knowing how shallow the excuse had sounded. She could handle shallow more easily than the pity she would have seen if she'd told Cassie the truth: that Nick was better off without her. Breaking off their engagement had given him a chance to have the family he'd always wanted. She'd done him a favor.

She turned her back to her sister. "Nick left *me*. He moved away and put his own career first." Libby pursed her lips and continued to fold her clothes. "None of that matters, anyway. I don't love him, and he doesn't love me. We've both moved on."

Cassie paused. "Maybe I'm being unfair to you." She sat back against the pillows. "But I was sad when you two broke up. You always made each other happy. He makes you better than you are. You do the same for him."

Libby shook her head. "I'm not having this conversation."

"Fine." Cassie rolled onto her side. "It makes no difference to me. Do you think you'll be packing for twenty minutes? I just want to get a nap in. I can't handle all of this right now. Any of it."

Libby didn't respond. She watched her sister drift into sleep, quickly and deeply. *Me neither,* she thought. *Any of it.*

Chapter 4

Cassie shivered as she pulled Sam out of the car and sped toward the little house she rented. The lights were off and the neighborhood was silent. Her fingers trembled as she slipped the key into the front door. Sometime after leaving Libby's house the reality had struck her: someone was after her sister, and she could be a target. Her blood thundered in her ears.

She locked the door behind her and wondered why she'd never listened when her father had told her she should get a dead bolt and an alarm system. "Dad, we live in *Arbor Falls,* where the most heinous crime is trespass to livestock." She should know; she'd tipped a few cows in her day. Dad had always been worrying about her and Libby, ever since Mom had died. Mostly he'd worried about her, because Libby was self-reliant. Libby was the daughter who was going places while Cassie... how did he put it? Required a guiding hand. She turned her gaze to Sam, still asleep in his car seat. *Well, Dad, maybe I needed more guidance than even you thought.*

He'd met his grandson before he'd died, at least. He'd held him in his arms and kissed him without lecturing her about how a boy needed a father in his life. She didn't want to hear it anymore, and she didn't want to have to tell him that Sam's father didn't even know about him. In a way that had been Dad's final gift to her, to keep his opinions to himself.

She looked at the clock. Sam had been sleeping for about an hour, and she probably had another hour or so before he woke and wanted to eat again. Long enough to get some things packed and head off to God-knows-where. Wherever people go when their sister is being stalked, she supposed. She knew she had to leave, but her legs felt like lead as she wondered if it was always this quiet in the house. Quiet enough to hear your own blood rush through your veins. She listened to the house settle, suddenly afraid to turn on the lights, because what if he was here now? What if she wasn't alone?

She turned at the sound of gravel grinding as a squad car stopped at the curb in front of the house. The door slammed, a tall figure approached and, moments later, he began pounding on the door. With a quick glance to make sure the baby was still asleep, Cassie cracked the door. "What?"

She didn't mean it to come across so rudely. Then again, she didn't care about her manners at the moment.

"Ma'am? I'm Sergeant Domingo Vasquez with the Arbor Falls P.D. I'm here to escort you to a safe location."

He flashed his badge and Cassie turned on the porch

light to get a better look. He seemed official, dressed in a uniform and carrying a gun. Not that she'd be able to tell a fake cop uniform, but she'd be able to tell a fake cop *car,* and the car looked legitimate. She opened the door wider. "My son's sleeping. Don't wake him up."

The sergeant entered through the doorway and Cassie winced at the sound of his loud footsteps. A quick reminder to be quiet, for God's sake, was on the tip of her tongue, but then she got a full look at him. Six-four, she'd guess. Broad-shouldered and muscular. He wasn't about to tiptoe anywhere.

"Pack up." His voice was clipped. "I want you out of here immediately."

She snorted. Who did this guy think he was? "Look, you may be a big deal at the precinct, but this is my house, Sergeant. I call the shots. And may I remind you that I have an infant, so it's going to take me longer than 'immediately' to pack."

"Well, I don't have all night. I'm doing this as a favor, but I'm not running a charity here." He placed his large hands on his hips, and heaven help her, but Cassie's gaze followed those hands south.

She snapped her gaze back to more appropriate territory. Dark hair. Olive skin. Full lips, and the top one was edged by a small white scar. Yeah, he was hot all right, and he had a bucket of arrogance to go along with it. "Thanks, Prince Charming. Why don't you pull up a seat and lose the attitude. Did I mention I have an *infant?* I'm running on hormones and four hours of broken sleep, and I promise that's a more lethal combination that that gun and your trigger finger. So I'll be done when I'm done."

Her heart was pounding and her face was hot as a rush of anger pooled below the surface of her skin. How dare he come in here and order her around! And how dare he eye her like that: coolly, and with a hint of smug amusement as if she was trying to be funny. She was *not* being funny.

"You don't need to call me Prince Charming. Just 'Dom' is fine." Then he said the damnedest thing. "How can I help you?"

His voice was calm, his tone authoritative. Just like that, Cassie felt the beast raging within her flinch. She began to stammer a response but then just stared at him. Speechless.

He took a step forward, moving his large body with a remarkable elegance. "I can watch the baby," he continued. "Or I can help you to get things together. Just tell me what you need."

He was studying her with his dark almond-shaped eyes, peering at her from beneath thick black lashes, and Cassie's heart skipped off-kilter for a beat. Damn him and his cavalier ways. She'd always gotten weak in the knees around a man in uniform. She took a breath. "Can I ask you a favor?"

His brow creased. "Sure."

"Do you think you could turn on all of the lights in here? This house creaks sometimes and I don't have an alarm system. I just want all of the lights on."

He smiled softly. "I can do that."

She waited while he walked around, patiently switching on the lights in each and every room. She could follow him by the creaking of the floorboards beneath him. She'd never noticed how noisy this old house could be.

He returned after five minutes to announce, "Your house is well lit, señorita."

"You went in my closets. I heard you." Her cheeks were hot. Those closets were filled with cobwebs and shame: wrinkled clothes on wire hangers and cardboard boxes stuffed with odds and ends. Old stuffed animals with missing eyes. Tattered concert posters she couldn't bear to throw away. Years of junk, formidable evidence of the chaos that was her life. And he'd just seen it all.

"I didn't look, except to make sure they weren't hiding anyone. I even checked under the bed. And the crib."

She bit her lip. What's done was done, and she wasn't sure why she cared so much in the first place. He was a hot cop…big deal. He'd escort her somewhere and then he'd be gone, and none of this would matter. "Okay. Whatever. Thanks."

He hesitated. "Do you want to go pack? I'll wait here or go with you, whichever you prefer."

She wiped her palms on the front of her skirt, wondering how far she could push her luck. "Can you sit here? With Sammy? I'll just be a few minutes."

He waved his hand to indicate that she should go ahead, and she headed into the bedroom. The urge to shove him out of the house had been replaced, leaving in its stead a swirl of butterflies in her stomach. After all, turning on the lights for her was kind of an apology, wasn't it? And it was too nice to have a gentleman in her house to kick him out so soon.

She opened a duffel bag, scooped up armfuls of clothes and dropped them inside. She chuckled as she thought about the way her father might react if he saw that. He'd stand there and watch her remove each and every article, refold it and return it neatly to the bag. He would *not* have allowed hot Sergeant Vasquez to escort her anywhere. Dad had made a career of law enforcement, but he'd never trusted the police.

She grabbed another armful of clothing, shoved it tightly in the bag then tugged the stretching zipper closed. She tossed Sam's clothes into a diaper bag, then remembered how many outfits he soiled in a day. She packed a second bag for him just to be safe. Cassie emerged from the bedrooms strung with bags filled to their limit with an array of clothing. Dom's eyebrows rose. "Are you moving out?"

"I don't know how long I'm going to be gone, do I? And I'm going to be hiding out somewhere with a baby, which means multiple changes of clothing for both of us for each day."

"I'm not judging." He grinned and held his palms up. His smile crinkled his eyes and made Cassie feel warm.

She glanced from the bags at her feet to the large man in her living room. He got the hint. "I'll get those for you." He lifted the large duffel bag as easily as if it had been stuffed with feathers. He carried the diaper bags with his other arm. "I'll put them in your car."

"Thanks." She gave him a sweet smile and threw in a couple bats of her eyelashes.

Then she paced the living room, waiting for him to return. She paused in front of a framed still life photograph and checked her reflection in the glass. Her feminist mother might have scolded her for raking her fingers through her hair and swiping her lips with strawberry-flavored gloss. *Chill out, Mom.*

No one could accuse Cassie of not being a strong, independent woman. She was raising a baby on her own and so far, surviving. But she'd spent her pregnancy in sweatpants and baggy shirts, and these days she struggled to find time to shower. She'd recently stopped flinching at the gobs of baby spit-up that landed on her shoulder. Some days she wondered if she'd ever care about feeling beautiful again. Maybe when her maternity leave ended and she'd returned to her glamorous job as a receptionist for an accounting firm? She doubted it.

Dom reentered the house with a smile and gestured to the car seat. "I assume you're taking him with you?"

Cassie grinned. "Yeah, I'll take him along for the ride."

And just like that, she cared about feeling beautiful.

Nick stacked Libby's suitcases beside the door to the guest bedroom in his parents' house. He'd stayed there all weekend and the house still smelled stale. He flung open the bedroom windows.

"Make yourself at home. I'm going to go through the cabinets to see what I can make for dinner. Macaroni and cheese is good forever, right?" His hands fell uselessly at his sides as he looked at her. He felt as if his entire body had been starched and ironed stiff. "Why is this so formal? I feel like a butler."

"I can call you Lurch if that would make you feel better." Libby dragged a suitcase over to the guest bed and unzipped it. "But I'm not hungry. In fact, I've felt a little sick all day, so don't worry about dinner for me."

That suited him just fine, and he wasn't about to beg her to eat, or to take a list of acceptable ingredients so that he could construct a suitable meal. When they'd been dating he'd had a difficult enough time keeping track of her strange food habits. One day she was counting calories, the next day she was eating whatever she wanted as long as it didn't include wheat, the day after that she'd gone vegan and had donated all of her leather shoes to charity. He couldn't keep up with her dietary moods.

She lifted her shoulders wordlessly and then stopped. "Do you think it's okay in here? With the window over the roof like that? Couldn't someone climb in?"

She was pointing to the window leading out to the pitch roof. Nick had climbed that roof many times himself when he was younger, always at night, and never for any respectable reason. "The windows lock and my parents have an alarm. But Libby, he doesn't know you're here. No one followed us, and I was checking the entire way over." He paused. "Would you feel safer in a different room? You can sleep anywhere you feel safe."

The way she hesitated, she seemed on the verge of saying something, but then she simply returned to her suitcase. She was picking her clothes out, one item at a time, refolding each article before stacking it on the bed. All of the seams had to align, of course; her ratty college T-shirts needed those fresh-from-the-retail-chain creases on each side, just in case anyone suspected they were fifteen years old. Fifteen years old—who kept T-shirts for that long? But she folded each one with a near fondness as if she found the process soothing. Later she would dress for bed and select a perfectly folded T-shirt to sleep in. All that work just to go to bed.

She spun around and smiled, holding out a white shirt

with a faded iron-on design on the front. "You bought this for me. Do you remember?"

She was holding the souvenir T-shirt she'd selected on their college trip to Myrtle Beach—the one with the shark in swimming trunks holding a surfboard and winking while giving a thumbs up. Nick couldn't help but grin at the sight of the familiar shirt. He remembered the way she'd laughed the first time she'd seen it and the tone of her voice when she'd declared it to be "all kinds of tacky." Mostly he remembered the kiss they'd shared in the middle of the parking lot after he had bought the shirt for her, his lips lingering on her taste of dried salt water and coconut oil lip balm.

The memory stung. Somewhere, at some point after that kiss, something had changed. The girl who had once giggled about tacky souvenirs had become consumed with the grave task of constructing a tower in which to hide from the world. Libby's moods had grown dark and her life had become serious. Nick thought it may have happened during those months he was at FBI training in Quantico, but looking back, he couldn't say for sure. All he knew was that for a while, life had been better than he could have ever predicted. He was dating the girl he'd been in love with since they were children, and she seemed to love him in return. Then she'd disappeared without explanation, leaving in her place a distant woman who'd chosen to fill her free time with work.

"I remember. Admit it. I only bought you the best."

Libby laughed at that and resumed folding the shirt. Nick eyed her drawn skin and gaunt cheekbones. Her fingers had assumed the knobbiness that he knew came with working too many late nights and skipping too many meals. He'd be a lousy host if he didn't at least make an effort to get her to eat. Figuring out how to prepare soybean patties smothered in soy paste and truffle oil and resting on a bed of tempeh was preferable to watching her go hungry.

"I'm sure I could find something for dinner to tempt you," he began brightly, not fully believing it. "What are you eating these days?"

She leveled a heavy breath. "Food, mostly. You?"

He counted to ten and then tried another approach. "What if I ordered a pizza?"

She paused. "Maybe a salad?"

"Pizza and a salad, great." There. At least she would eat something. "I'll go order, but I'll be right down the hall if you need me."

"I'm sure I can handle unpacking, but thank you."

There was a quiver in her voice. She turned to him with a haunted look, as if her mind was somewhere else entirely. Then she sat on the bed and dropped her head against her hands. His jaw tightened when he noticed her body trembling with muffled sobs. He shifted first to one foot then to the other, weighing whether he should approach her or back quietly out of the room to leave her alone. He fumbled toward her to touch his hand on the back of her head. She might take offense if he stroked her head like he was petting a dog, so instead he affixed his hand like some strange hat. He'd almost forgotten how soft her hair was.

"Libby." His voice was strained. This was shaping up to be the most awkward day of his life. "No one's going to hurt you. Not on my watch."

A poor consolation. Pitiful, when what he wanted to

do was to sweep her into his arms and kiss each tear as it fell across her cheek. The ferocity of that urge alarmed him, made his gut tense reflexively as he remembered that they weren't in love anymore. Still, he sat beside her and felt her lean lightly into him as the mattress sagged under his weight. He combed his fingers through her hair. The gesture was clumsy and possibly ineffective, but he'd never been the kind of man who could stand by and watch a woman cry.

She looked at him after several minutes, after she'd cried all of the tears she'd stored and her lips were red and full. "You must hate me." Her breath rattled as she fought for control of her emotions.

Had he ever thought such a thing? He'd never felt such strong anger and disappointment toward another person as he had toward Libby. But that wasn't hate. That was anger and disappointment, and he'd felt those things because he'd been so desperately in love with her. How could he ever hate someone he'd loved so much?

"I don't hate you." He pushed her hair back from her face.

"But you did at one time."

Was that hopefulness in her voice? He stood then and walked toward the door. "I don't know what you're trying to bait me into saying, Libby. Do you want me to hate you? Would that make you feel better?" She stared in silent expectation at him. "I know this is damn awkward. I feel it, too. Would it be easier if you knew how little I care for you?" He drew his hand through his hair. He wasn't even kidding himself. "I'm trying to help you, but I don't know what to do about...*this*." He waved his hands at her, indicating her crying. Her obvious need for comfort. When they'd been dating, he knew the rules: how to touch her, or hold her, and what words to say to comfort her. Everything was different now.

"Why are you helping me? After how much I've hurt you."

"This is what I do. I protect people. It's just business." She was still searching his face. "I've moved on. I don't remember the things you said, so forget it, Libby."

He remembered every single word she'd said. He'd replayed those words a hundred times in his mind. They swarmed like gnats in his consciousness at inconvenient times, reminding him that once he'd been in love, but it had all been a joke.

Her eyes were awash with confusion. "Oh." She hadn't been expecting that, and she lifted her eyebrows as if she didn't know what to think. "Then we can start over again. As friends."

"Yes. As friends. And I'll be downstairs if you need me." He turned and walked out the door, hoping she hadn't noticed the sharpness in his voice and wishing he was a better liar than he was.

Libby's head reeled as Nick left the room. She remembered every hurtful word that had passed between them the night they ended the engagement, and he'd forgotten. Moved on, as he put it. She swiped her fingertips beneath her eyes, catching a streak of mascara. There was some relief in knowing that maybe he didn't hate her, after all. At least his assurance had gone some way toward quelling the guilt that had gnawed at her gut all day.

She smoothed her fingers over the worn material of the surfing shark T-shirt. The night Nick had bought it for her, she'd worn it to bed and curled right up next to him, draping herself over the hard edges of his body. After their vacation they'd returned to their separate homes, and she'd brought that shirt to bed with her because traces of his scent clung to the fibers. But that was a long time ago, when being away from Nick had felt like losing a part of herself.

A frown pulled at the corners of her mouth as she remembered showing her father the T-shirt. She'd wanted him to find the humor in it. Instead, he'd pulled his eyebrows tight, looked at her and said, "If you ever want to make something of yourself, you'll stop wasting your time on these antics and these *people*." Dad didn't laugh at many things. He respected hard work.

She stroked the cotton between her fingers and stopped when she saw the small hole in the side seam; she'd have to fix that.

Libby rose from the bed and inhaled deeply, stretching her arms and legs, trying to loosen the tension that had been collecting in her muscles. She'd finally given back the engagement ring, and this was her chance to smooth things over with Nick once and for all. To move on, just as he had.

She reached for her cell phone and dialed her sister's number. "I wanted to check up on you." She paused when she heard a man's voice in the background. "Who's that?"

"It's Sergeant Vasquez. He's going to escort me and Sam to a hotel."

"Good. Listen, I'm not going to keep you, but I'll have my phone on me. You'll call me if you need anything?"

"Yes. You do the same."

Libby paused to blink back the tears that had started to sting her eyes again. She couldn't believe that this was her life, that she was hiding in her ex-fiancé's parents' house and her sister and nephew were forced to hide in a hotel. "Cassie, I'm so sorry."

The line was quiet. Then Cassie's voice came through softly. "You didn't do anything wrong, Libby. You just be careful."

She swallowed her breath, trying to tamp down the ache in the center of her chest. "Give Sammy a kiss for me. Sleep well." She disconnected the call.

Libby slid the empty suitcase under the guest bed. Nick's mom had decorated in flowery prints and lace. Frilly things hung along the bottom of the duvet in layers of fabric that resembled swirls of frosting. Little end tables were covered by long floral tablecloths and a layer of lace before being topped with matching brass lamps with floral shades. She found the decor sentimental and overwhelming and longed for her bed in her own simply decorated bedroom.

She wandered into the kitchen, where Nick was typing on his BlackBerry. He was so preoccupied that he didn't look up when she entered. Without a word he poured her a glass of water and went back to typing.

That was fine with her if he didn't want to talk, because she didn't have anything to say. His kindness today had been a little too much for her to take. He'd assured her that he was only doing what he'd do for anyone by protecting her, but he must have an ulterior motive for taking a leave from work. Some self-serving motive. She couldn't imagine suspending her own life like this without a damn good reason.

He paused with the BlackBerry and she seized the opportunity. "You must be exhausted. You must have driven all night to get here."

He shook his head and turned back to his phone. "I came in for a long weekend. I left Thursday night and was supposed to have been back tonight." His response was mumbled, spoken more to his BlackBerry than to her.

"Oh? Visiting anyone?"

She'd just been trying to make pleasant conversation, but he froze and looked at her with a gaze that reminded her of a cornered animal. "Some friends." He dropped the answer and looked away again.

Nonsense. Libby knew that look instantly. When you knew someone for twenty years, you got to recognize all of their tells: what they do when they're lying, or angry, or jealous. Nick rarely looked the way he did now, but when he did, there was only one feeling behind it: guilt. Guilt, she supposed, that he'd been in town and hadn't attended her father's services. Well, he *should* feel guilty about that. He'd sat with her father at countless family dinners, and maybe they didn't always see eye to eye, but he should have paid his final respects. If she was being honest, she'd found his absence offensive.

Libby took a sip of her water. Perhaps Nick had his reasons, and what did any of it matter now? He'd taken a leave from work to be at her side; the least she could do was spare him a lecture on funeral etiquette.

"Dad's funeral was on Friday." She sighed. "I don't blame you for not attending. I know you had a difficult relationship with him." She gripped her drinking glass between both hands. "Anyway, it's okay with me that you weren't there. You shouldn't feel badly about it."

He'd put his BlackBerry away and was leaning against the counter. His short-sleeve T-shirt clung to the curves of his biceps. Yes, he'd definitely been working out more since they broke up. She wondered if he'd been doing it to impress another woman and was startled at the stab of jealousy the thought provoked.

"Your dad never liked me. He used to pull me aside when we were dating to cut me down, try to humiliate me. He'd quiz me on obscure political events or books just to prove I wasn't smart enough. I think you knew about that. There was no stopping him, anyway." He released a deep breath. "At the time I was angry. I imagined marrying you would be the best way to stick it to him. To win. But I've spent a lot of time thinking in the past few years. I tried to understand how a father would feel about his daughter, and how your father had wrapped up his dreams in you. Now I see that if he never thought I was good enough to be with you, it's only because he saw how brilliant you are. Every man would fall short."

She felt her throat tighten and her eyes stinging again. "Nick."

He looked down at his feet, suddenly seeming far away. "I meant it when I said I was sorry about your dad. I know how much he meant to you. That's why I was at the funeral."

If she'd been standing up, she would have fallen over. "Wh— You were?"

"In the back. Where you wouldn't see me."

The weight of the confession pressed Libby against

the back of her chair. And here she'd been on the verge of lecturing him...maybe he'd avoided her on Friday for a good reason. "I didn't know." The image of him paying his respects to her father anonymously touched something raw and painful. "Thank you. That means a lot to me."

He avoided eye contact as if the subject was painful for him, too. "I've tried to understand him and why he thought I was so wrong for you. Maybe when I have kids I'll understand. Revenge is the wrong reason to get married, anyway," he continued. "That's not how I want to live."

He didn't elaborate and she didn't bother replying. There was nothing more to say.

They ate dinner at the small table in the dining room, exchanging pleasantries they would have exchanged with any other casual acquaintance. Libby inquired after Nick's family, and he inquired after hers. "Sam is adorable," he said. "He has your dark hair and blue eyes."

She couldn't help but smile. "Nick, all infants have blue eyes."

"They do?" He shrugged. "I just learned something new. But he does look like you. I remember seeing your baby pictures. You were a cute baby."

She clenched her napkin in her fist. "Thanks."

"So the father is completely absent? I can't imagine. Even if it was an accident, I'd step up. I'd want to be a part of his life."

Libby dragged a slice of wilted tomato across her plate. "Not accident. *Surprise.* And that puts you in a better league than some other men. Poor Cassie. She hinted that it was a one-night stand. She was inconsolable when she found out."

"I can imagine. I wouldn't know the first thing about taking care of a baby. I'd be so lost." He shot her a small smile. "You're a natural, though. How'd you know how to do that?"

She froze. "Do what?"

"Get him to sleep like that. Is that maternal instinct?"

Her heart flipped. Was he really complimenting her mothering skills? No, she was not having this conversation now, and not with Nick of all people. "I guess." She put her fork down. "It's been a long day." She stood and cleared her plate.

Nick looked at her with alarm. "Did I upset you?"

"No." He would have no way of knowing that she couldn't have children, and she couldn't be angry with him for giving her what he considered to be a compliment. But the conversation could lead them to a place she didn't want to tread, or stir up emotions she'd settled already, and the day had been too long for any of that. "You didn't upset me. And I appreciate everything you've done today. I mean it."

She washed her dishes and set them in the drying rack. She was aware of Nick watching her from his seat at the table, but she didn't give him any indication that she was even aware he was in the room. Instead, she turned and walked out of the kitchen after uttering a good-night that sounded much more chipper than she felt.

Nick was not frustrated. Maybe he was a little surprised at the way Libby had just picked up and left in the middle of dinner, but it's not like he'd prepared anything fancy or special. He wasn't disappointed by the abrupt end to the evening, either. Disappointment would imply that he'd anticipated spending more time together, which would in turn suggest that he'd wanted to see more of Libby. He scrubbed too roughly as he washed his dinner plate. *Had* he actually wanted to spend more time with Libby?

Something nameless was clouding his thoughts, hovering just out of his grasp. He'd stayed in town because he'd have to be a bastard to leave Libby alone now, even though he'd done just that for nearly three years. He didn't *want* to see her again, or to be dragged back down that road. All of this was chance. Duty and chance but not fate, because fate would imply that something would come of their reunion.

He washed his plate four times before he realized it was clean, then he set it in the drying rack next to Libby's plate. Her plate. Her fork and her knife and her cup. He dried them himself, wondering why the action felt so intimate. It wasn't as if she'd infused the utensils with an essence of herself. Once that fork went back into the drawer, he'd never be able to guess which one her mouth had touched. But now he knew. Maybe that was the difference.

He leaned against the counter and reached into his pocket to pull out the velvet case she'd returned earlier. Nick had been so proud to present her with that diamond solitaire and all that it represented: marriage, a house, children, maybe a dog. A shared future. He pulled the ring from the case and studied the little scratches on the gold band. How many of those impressions had been made when he was with her, he wondered? Maybe one was made at their favorite restaurant, another when they spent that weekend in New York City.

He snapped the case shut and placed it back into his pocket. Three years had passed, and every woman he'd been with had fallen short in some regard. Libby had rejected him, told him after years of being together that she didn't love him. She'd coldly slid the engagement ring across the table today.

The awareness struck him like a blow to the gut. She'd done all of those things, and he'd rearranged his life for her at a moment's notice. God help him, but he still had feelings for Libby.

A chill came over him as he thought about how it would feel to taste her bee-stung lips again, or bury his face in her thick black hair. To palm her breasts and feel her chest rise against him as she arched in pleasure. One of the greatest discoveries in his young life had been that beneath her elegant composure Libby hid a passionate streak that flowed as hotly and unpredictably as molten lava. More than once, she'd kissed him chastely on the cheek when he left for work in the morning only to greet him at the door on his return wearing only a coy smile. He didn't bother fighting his body's response to the memories. She was hot, and the repressed sex goddess thing still drove him out of his mind. He still wanted her.

That didn't mean she wanted *him*. He may have some paleolithic impulse to drag her back to his cave, but that didn't matter. In a few short days he'd be back in Pittsburgh and Libby would be back to her normal routine, which didn't involve him. The sooner his primal brain got the message, the better.

His BlackBerry rang. It was Dom. He'd escorted Cassie and Sam to a hotel two towns over. "No one followed us. I think they're safe, and Cassie will feel better this way." Nick heard him clear his throat.

"Thanks for doing that, Dom. Libby will be relieved to hear it."

"They're close, huh?"

"Very. Especially since their mom died." Libby had only been sixteen when her mother was killed by a drunk driver after working the overnight shift at Arbor Falls Memorial, where she'd been a nurse in the E.R. "Anyway, thanks for letting me know. I'll tell Libby."

"I put an officer in an unmarked vehicle outside your house. Officer McAdams. He's in a black Taurus, parked across the street."

Nick pulled a curtain aside and squinted into the darkness. "I see him. Thanks."

"He'll be there until the morning. I also called because we got an ID on the victim. Her street name was Rita, but her legal name was Mary Parker. Seems she worked as a court reporter during the day but liked to have a good time after hours, if you follow. The preliminary lab work turned up positive for methamphetamines."

Nick's hand ached, and he realized how tightly he was clutching the phone. "A court reporter? I'm more interested in that. Where did she work?"

"You sitting down? She got fired about a year ago after being picked up for drug possession, but before that she worked in Arbor Falls. And she worked closely with Judge Andrews."

"Libby's dad." His pulse kicked up a notch. "We assumed that the first victim had been selected at random and that Libby was the real target."

"Yes, we did."

"But maybe the first victim was hand-selected, as well." He rubbed at his forehead. "Judge Andrews's court reporter, and now his daughter."

"You know what this means, right?"

"Someone's mad at the judge." His gut reaction was relief because he knew that Libby could stop blaming herself for having done something to put her sister and nephew at risk. But the moment passed as quickly as it had come when he thought about the implications of this discovery. At least Libby was available to assist him and Dom in the investigation and to help narrow their list of suspects. At least Libby could give them a list of persons whom she might have angered.

"He's mad at the judge," Dom repeated, and then continued, as if reading Nick's mind, "and a dead judge isn't going to tell us who he's pissed off."

Chapter 5

Libby couldn't say for sure whether she slept. Sleep eluded her for hours as she tossed and turned in the guest bed, the flat sheet twisting between her legs as she tried to find a position that would slow the frenetic thoughts in her mind. At some point she blinked and opened her eyes to fragments of morning light beaming through rose-patterned drapery. The bedside clock read five-thirty. Plenty of time to get to work.

She carried her toiletries into the tiny pink-tiled guest bathroom and showered for far too long, trying to scrub off the residue of yesterday's events. The photograph in her files. The awful suppression hearing. Her sister and her nephew in a hotel. Nick complimenting her maternal instincts. She wanted to emerge from the steamy cocoon of the shower stall a new person with a new life—a life that wasn't filled with such painful memories. A person who wasn't living a nightmare and fighting to hold herself together.

Libby wrung out her hair and heard a gentle knuckle rap on the door. "Just me," said Nick. "I'm making coffee. I don't have tea."

"Coffee's fine. Thanks."

Nice of him to remember that she was trying to reduce her caffeine intake, although she didn't see what difference a cup of coffee would make in her anxiety level. Her jaw already hurt from grinding her teeth all night.

She didn't have a court appearance that day, so she dressed in a simple floral print skirt and a short-sleeve cotton blouse that revealed just the top swell of her breasts. Business casual cleavage. She shook out her hair but then decided she'd let it air-dry. Her waves looked more like ringlets as she walked out of the bathroom, greeted by the smell of pancakes.

Nick was standing with his back to the kitchen doorway. He was barefoot, dressed in black mesh shorts and a gray T-shirt. He turned his head as she entered. "Coffee's ready, and I took out the cream and sugar."

Libby lurched gratefully toward the coffee, taking one of the mugs Nick set out and filling it to the brim with the hot black caffeinated goodness she needed to fully clear her head. She tasted it before adding cream and a little sugar. "This is really delicious," she murmured.

"That's because I bought it," Nick said matter-of-factly. "Enjoy a decent cup of coffee. My treat." He turned his head and gave her a broad, easy smile, flashing the dimple in his left cheek. "I hope pancakes are on your diet. I ordered groceries last night, but they won't be here for another hour. This is all I could find."

He paused, and Libby caught his gaze wandering up and down her frame. She didn't know why, but the subtle appraisal sent a rush of pleasure through her. "I told you, I don't have any special diet. I'm trying to be better about that. No more food rules, no more chewing on my nails. No more coffee, except for this cup. I'm making changes."

About a month ago Libby had decided she was ready for a change and set about methodically fixing all of the things she didn't like about herself. She'd made a list and had placed each item into one of three tiers. Tier one represented the bad habits, such as nail biting and coffee drinking. Tier two represented her more compulsive tendencies, such as her need to organize her bookcase alphabetically by author. All of the elements in tiers one and two would be easier to fix than those in tier three, which contained things like her fear of social gatherings, or her inability to generate charming small talk. Moving through one tier at a time, Libby reasoned, she would become a less anxious person, less of a control freak.

Less of a tight-ass.

"As long as you don't change too much." He said the words breezily.

She froze. "That must be a joke. You told me when we broke up that I was difficult to love."

His shoulders tensed. "I don't remember saying that."

"You said I was uptight and that you'd always found it difficult to love me. And now I'm trying to…change things." She inhaled. "I'm not angry about what you said. Not anymore. But I want to fall in love some day, and I want someone to love me, and it seems that for that to happen I will need to be less like myself. Wouldn't you agree?"

Nick was facing her, the spatula hanging limply in his hand. He winced at her words. "That was a rotten thing for me to say to you."

She started. She hadn't expected that. "We both said rotten things that day."

He appeared to reflect upon her words and then turned back to the stove. Libby studied him as he prepared breakfast. Yesterday at Coffee On Main, Nick had been a tight coil of masculinity: hard, strong and poised to erupt like a spring gun if tripped. Now he seemed so boyish, with his bed-rumpled hair, bare feet and shorts, that Libby fought the urge to run up and bite him playfully on the neck. He turned then and gave her a smile. "Breakfast is ready."

They sat at the little breakfast table to eat, and after they were finished, Libby cleared the dishes. "So you're going to drive me to work this morning?"

He looked surprised. "You're going to work?"

"Uh, yeah. Did you see the way I'm dressed?" She gestured to her outfit. "And what else would I do?"

He paused. "But how is that supposed to work? I'm trying to protect you."

"You could come with me to the D.A.'s, I guess. Look, I'm not putting my life on hold. I'm not living in fear. I thought this was the plan." But even as she said it, the reality came back to her: someone wanted her dead. She'd be trying hard to feel normal today.

Nick's face looked stormy, and his mouth pulled

tightly shut as he thought. "I'd prefer that you keep a low profile."

"Fine. I'll go to work, not talk to anyone." The usual.

"No, I mean that I'd rather keep you in a controlled environment. Like here, where you're guarded. He doesn't even know we're here, and the less you go out, the less chance you give him to find you." His eyes darkened. "Six signs over six days, and he strikes for the final time on the seventh. We don't know where the next sign is going to be delivered, or what it will entail. For all we know, sign three is an attempt on your life. And there's always the possibility that he gives up on the signs entirely and attacks you. This individual is clearly unstable."

She rubbed down the hair on her arms as it stood on end. "But maybe he won't even come near me today. He planted the first sign near that poor woman he killed, and I wasn't anywhere near that crime."

She felt like a prisoner. He had a point and he was only trying to help, but the thought of sitting in the house all day, hiding out from a bogeyman, made her nearly frantic. She'd go stir crazy. "Nick, you can't lock me in the house all day. Please. What if he sees me at work and that flushes him out of hiding? You'll be right there to protect me—nothing is going to happen. Right?"

But he didn't look too sure. "I need to think about this. I'm going to take a quick shower. The groceries will be delivered soon, but don't open the door. Got it? I want you to sit right here and be bored for twenty minutes."

She rolled her eyes. "Fine, I got it. Geez." And he'd called *her* the control freak.

She plopped on the overstuffed couch and pretended

to flip through a coffee table book on tropical birds, but she watched Nick as he left the room. Specifically his muscular legs and firm backside. Not bad at all. Her pulse jumped slightly and she turned back to her book.

He'd checked her out, too. Fair is fair.

"I've decided I can't let you go out," Nick declared as he carried the bags of groceries that had been left by the door into the house. "It's too risky. We don't know what his third sign might be, and I don't want to give him any help. We need to throw him off his little game, make it impossible for him to succeed."

She groaned loudly, sounding more like a frustrated teenage girl than the professional adult she was. "You can't do this to me. I thought I was free to go about my day as long as you were with me!"

"What part of hiding out in my parents' house makes you think that you're free to go about your day?"

She was sulking in response, acting spoiled and petulant. She was even slamming the groceries into their proper place. A bag of carrots landed with a thud in the vegetable drawer in the refrigerator, and she plunked oranges down almost forcefully into the fruit bowl. He gritted his teeth and told himself not to snap, to keep his cool.

"This is awful!" She finally stopped in her tracks. "I don't want this. You can't turn this house into a jail cell. I want you to drive me to work, or else I'm going to walk."

That last threat was most certainly calculated to press him into submission. She knew perfectly well that he'd never allow her to walk out that door, and he knew that she meant every word. She would walk the five miles to work if she had to.

Damn it.

He gripped his fists and looked out the window, avoiding her glare. Officer McAdams was still parked in front of the house. "I'm going to go talk to the officer who was out here last night," he said. "I want to know if he saw anything strange at all."

He heard her sigh dramatically as he stepped out the door and walked down to the bottom of the driveway. The sun was still sitting low on the horizon, and an oak tree near the sidewalk cast a heavy shadow over the vehicle. As Nick approached, he saw the officer in the front seat of the car, the side of his head resting against the window. He'd fallen asleep. Nick frowned and prepared himself to give the officer an earful. His blood pressure skyrocketed thinking about all the officer might have missed while he'd been catching some shut-eye.

Then he froze. That wasn't the officer's head on the window. It was blood.

He stood in the dead center of the road, paralyzed, his breath stalled in his lungs. He walked toward the front of the vehicle, keeping a distance, looking through the windshield. The interior of the vehicle was obstructed from view by light and shadow, but then he walked closer and saw it. His stomach tilted.

Officer McAdams was staring back at him, his eyes wide open. He'd been shot execution-style.

A well of rage bubbled in Nick's stomach and he pulled out his phone, releasing a string of curses. Finally Dom answered. "Vasquez."

"Dom, it's Nick. You need to get out here right away. McAdams is dead. Shot in his car."

"Son of a—!" He heard Dom slam a drawer shut.

"How did he find us?" Nick demanded. "No one followed us. I was watching."

"How the hell would I know? I haven't told anyone."

"Well, he knows, Dom. He knows where we are, and he killed one of your men." Nick paced. His face was hot; his breath was coming in spurts. He couldn't bear to look at the body in the vehicle. "He could have tried to kill us last night," he said, more to himself than to Dom. He cursed again, and this time he kicked a dent into the door of the black vehicle.

"But he didn't." Dom mumbled something in Spanish. "I'm on my way. You're gonna be there?"

Nick balled his right fist until the nails pinched his palm, and then he squeezed it tighter. "Yeah, I'll be here."

He hung up the phone and turned back toward the house. Libby was standing next to the front door. Her eyes were wide, and as he approached, he saw that she was crying, the tears streaking silently down her cheeks. "Pack up," Nick said. "And call in sick from work."

This time she didn't argue.

The road was blocked off to traffic, and a large area around the vehicle was roped off with yellow crime scene tape. The responding officers did their best to block the view of the scene from the gathering crowd of neighbors that stood on the front lawn two houses away.

In all the years he'd known Dom, Nick had never seen his face so dark. Both men stood across the street from the vehicle, side by side. Their silence spoke volumes. "You've got a leak in your department. Even if you didn't say anything, someone found out where we were. McAdams could've told the wrong person where he was going."

Dom's jaw clenched and the lines between his eyebrows deepened. "I can't say that for sure."

"I'll say it, then." He was fighting to keep himself together. The killer had found Libby. Whoever was responsible for leaking that information had better pray Nick didn't find out who he was. "From now on, no one knows where we are. I mean no one, Dom."

"No one," Dom repeated. "You have my word." The sergeant had his hands on his hips and was watching the officers process the crime scene. He had a sharpness in his gaze that Nick had rarely seen even when they were working together almost every day. He wouldn't want to be on the receiving end of that glare.

Libby was sitting on the front steps. He hadn't asked her to remain within his eyesight; she'd done that on her own. Her suitcase was packed and resting beside her. She'd called Cassie at the hotel, and she and Sam were fine, thank goodness. "No one knows where her sister is, right?"

"I'm the only one, and I plan to keep it that way." Dom stopped as a member from the crime scene unit approached, carrying a plastic evidence bag. "What is it?"

"It's a note of some kind. Looks like it's written in blood. Sick bastard." He handed it to Dom.

"'Seven tons hatred,'" he read aloud. "That mean anything to you, Nick?"

"The killer said he was giving seven days," he volunteered. He noticed that Libby was watching them. "I'll go ask Libby. All of this seems to revolve around something her father did, so maybe she'll know."

She had her knees close to her chest and a light blanket wrapped around her bare legs. Her dark hair had dried in messy waves, and the wind lifted tendrils across her face as he approached. "We found a note. Sign three."

"And?" Her throat sounded hoarse.

"He wrote 'seven tons hatred.' Does that mean anything to you?"

Her face was blank, and she continued to watch the crime scene investigators. For a moment Nick wasn't sure she'd heard him, but then she shook her head. "No. I don't know."

He lowered himself onto the step so that they were sitting side by side, her arm pressing against his. The current of fear he felt darting through her made him painfully aware of his helplessness. He'd promised to keep her safe, and he'd underestimated the monster they were dealing with. He wrapped his arm around her shoulders; he didn't know what else to do.

"I didn't tell you this, but it seems the first murder victim wasn't selected at random." He stared at the ground, but out of the corner of his eye he observed her turning to face him. "Until about a year ago, she'd been a court reporter who worked closely with your dad. We can't assume it's coincidental that someone killed your father's court reporter and is now threatening you."

Her back hunched under the weight of this development. "Someone is upset about something my dad did? You mean, he's acting out of revenge?"

"It may be, yes."

Her lower lip trembled slightly. "But why now? Dad…
he can't see any of this."

"We don't know yet. We're going to try to figure
that out."

She rested her head on the palms of her hands. "Nick,
I don't know what anyone could be so angry with my
father about. I guess it could be anything. He was a
judge and a politician, and he was…you know. He was
rough sometimes. Harsh." She paused, and when she
spoke again her tone was lined with quiet fury. "How
did he find us?"

"There could be a leak in the department. We're going
to leave and we're not telling anyone where we're going.
Got it? Not Cassie, not even Dom."

She nodded tightly. "Okay."

He leaned closer, bringing his mouth against her ear
so he could whisper. "No one is going to hurt you. Not
on my watch."

Her skin was warm and sweet smelling. Soft. His
hand was on her bare arm, his thumb caressing her in
lazy arcs. He wanted to pull her into his lap, kiss her
soundly and then pick her up and carry her far away from
here. He wanted to do anything to stop her from shaking.

His back stiffened. This was not where he was supposed to be. Touching her, wanting her, was not the same
as protecting her. She'd been clear about her feelings. He
should respect that. He removed his hand from her arm.

To his surprise she swung her legs closer to his and
brought her head down to rest on his shoulder. "Nick,
I'm so scared," she whispered.

He reflexively pulled her against him, wrapping his

other arm tightly around her. Their past hurt melted away for that moment. They were just Nick and Libby, clinging to each other against a cold reality.

Chapter 6

They left before the crime scene was cleared. Nick checked his car for a tracking device, searching the undercarriage and opening the trunk, patting down the tires and running his fingers along the edge of the vehicle body. Once he was finished, he thoroughly searched the interior of the vehicle. When he was convinced the car wasn't being tracked, he drove through Arbor Falls, taking a series of roads and then turning around, watching for following cars.

He drove them to Cassie's hotel two towns away so Libby could check on her sister and nephew and verify for herself that they were fine. She also told Cassie that the threats against her had something to do with their father and that Cassie could be a target, too. Libby reminded her to be careful. Once she was finished, Nick swapped his car for a rental and drove to the town of Great Springs. They checked into the Ascher House—

a sprawling farm estate that had been converted to an upscale inn.

"I've always wanted to stay here." Libby hauled her suitcase up the front steps after refusing Nick's assistance. She wasn't completely helpless. "There's horseback riding and walking trails through a wildlife preserve."

"We're not doing any of that," Nick reminded her. "We're staying inside, and you're going to do something quiet and boring. You know, reading or knitting."

She shot him a look. "I was just making conversation."

The ride over had been silent. They'd both been watching the road: he to check for following cars, and she to lose herself in the certainty of the white line undulating on its edge. Of course, she wasn't about to go out for a hike. She was well aware that they were hiding out. But she hadn't realized that she was now barred from talking about anything other than the threat looming over their heads.

They'd left the crime scene after someone from the medical examiner's office had conducted a preliminary review of the body. The killer had opened the passenger door to Officer McAdams's vehicle and shot him at close range. The time of death was estimated to be around midnight. He'd used a silencer. Just thinking about a murder occurring near her while she slept made Libby's body go to ice. She was glad to put so many miles between her and Arbor Falls.

This crime had effected a change in Nick, too. His demeanor had grown dark, and he'd spent the long miles on the highway clenching and unclenching his jaw and mumbling to himself.

Now he kept close to her side. For her part Libby wasn't thinking about the past anymore, or wondering what the future would bring. The past didn't matter and the future was uncertain. They had now, and survival meant putting their differences aside.

He paid for the corner suite—in cash, using a pseudonym—and she bit back a joke about trying to impress her. Of course he wasn't trying to impress her. He was thinking that they'd be spending a lot of time in the room and that they'd each need privacy and to maintain a respectable distance. It made perfect sense to get the suite, and this wasn't the time for nervous quips.

She unlocked the door to the suite and gasped. The room was painted a soothing shade of sage-green, and light filtered through sheer curtains covering a massive bay window. The suite was divided into a generous sitting area with a couch that, according to the desk clerk, folded out into a bed, and a bedroom with a mahogany four-poster king-size bed. The two rooms were separated by a heavy wooden door. "It's so lovely." She sighed.

"Your home away from home." He took her suitcase and carried it into the bedroom. "I'm calling the couch."

So he planned to sleep on the couch. She watched him with her bags and wondered why his statement made her feel so rejected. Time to come back down to earth. Nick was acting protective because he cared about her the way he cared for an old friend, but it wasn't as if they were getting back together. She almost laughed aloud. Certainly not, and that was fine. They'd agreed to start over as friends, and if it crossed her mind to behave inappropriately it was only because she was in a vulnerable state and craving a little comfort. It's not as if she *needed* to curl up against his warm body that night.

He reentered the room without his jacket, wearing a fitted black T-shirt and denim jeans. Libby had very particular ideas about the way jeans should fit a man, and Nick's fit him perfectly—pulling tightly against his muscular thighs where they should be tight but falling loosely where they should be loose. She stared at him as he crossed the room stealthily, unpacking some of his belongings as if she wasn't even there. Warm body— what was she thinking? Nick's body was *hot,* and being alone, locked in the same room with him, could lead to nothing but trouble.

But there would be no trouble because she was *not* going there. They'd gone down that road and it hadn't worked out, and she had no desire to expose herself to that kind of heartache again. She could admit that she missed Nick and the way he seemed to anticipate her needs. Like this morning on the drive to Great Springs, when he'd stopped at the hotel so Libby could run in to check on Cassie and Sam. She hadn't asked him to do that, hadn't even asked about Cassie, but seeing her sister and holding her nephew had made her feel grounded again. He'd taken her out of her nightmare, if only for a few minutes.

Her skin felt flushed as she remembered that he'd been that way as a lover, too. Patient and considerate. Except sometimes he hadn't been, either. Sometimes he'd come to her racked with need and touched her like a man possessed, locking her hips against his own. Those times he'd taken her impatiently and with a selfish despera- tion, and those were the times that made her toes curl.

He looked up and caught her watching him. He didn't smile and he didn't look away, and when their gazes locked she understood that he felt it, too. That they were both scared out of their minds and seeking comfort, and maybe a little more. Libby swallowed and turned, her face thoroughly hot and her body aching for his touch.

She still lusted after him, but then again, when had she not lusted after Nick Foster? There were other considerations and lots of reasons not to act on base urges. They lived five hours apart and often worked weekends. He'd told her that he found her difficult to love. And he wanted children and to be a father. He wanted that more than anything. And she couldn't help him there.

They would only end up hurting each other.

Libby headed into the bedroom without another word, closing the door behind her. She had a brain. She should use it.

She checked her cell phone. David had called with his number in Zurich. Thinking of him made her stomach twist, though whether the twisting was from guilt or the excitement of a new relationship, she couldn't be sure. David had been an acquaintance for as long as she could remember. His father, former Mayor Jeb Sinclair, had supported her father when he'd run for judge. She'd chanced to meet David shortly after her father had been diagnosed, and they'd gone on a few dates since. David loved to sit in the darkened corners of cozy restaurants, order a bottle of red wine and talk for hours. He'd listened patiently as she'd talked about her father's diagnosis and the turmoil it caused her. He'd never interjected his own experience or given her advice. David was a good listener.

She dialed the number and waited until he answered. "David? It's Libby. I'm just calling to say hello."

"Hello, Libby." He sounded genuinely pleased she'd called. "It's nice to hear a familiar voice. And are you on your new phone? It sounds great."

David had accompanied Libby to pick out a new cell phone on their second date. He was a gadget man who'd clearly pitied her when she'd informed him that her Stone Age phone couldn't even send text messages. As an attorney whose work brought him around the world negotiating the purchase and sale of commercial jet engines, he lived and breathed technology. He was a sensible gadget shopping companion. "I hope I'm not interrupting. Are you selling a lot of airplane parts?"

He laughed. "Enough. It's been a good trip, actually." He paused. "It's nice to hear your voice."

She should have felt some pleasure from that confession, but all she felt was her stomach working itself into a knot. "It's nice to hear yours, too, David. Hey, listen— I'm not at home right now. I won't be for a few days, so if you need to reach me, just call my cell instead."

"Is everything okay?" His voice was heavy with concern.

"Yes, fine. It's just… I'm going to be working a lot and maybe I'll stay with Cassie for a couple of nights to help her. Don't worry."

"Oh, good." He laughed lightly. "You had me nervous for a minute."

They spoke for a little longer before he excused himself, saying he was meeting some clients for dinner. He would be back on Friday, and it was already Tuesday. "Maybe we can grab dinner on Saturday," he said.

Libby felt her muscles tense the way they did when she felt pressured into something uncomfortable. David was a nice guy. Talking to him should have reinforced all of the things that were wrong about Nick, reminded her that she had options. David was the not-Nick, composed of all of the finer qualities that Nick lacked. Worldliness, sophistication and a fluency in matters of the intellect. He spoke three languages and loved French literature. He enjoyed cooking gourmet meals in his free time. David was gentle where Nick was abrasive, cool where Nick was hot. Calling him should have reminded her of the many reasons they were perfect for each other.

And there were *so* many reasons they were perfect together. Their dads had been friends, so they came from similar backgrounds. That was one. And they were both lawyers, which meant they could drop Latin phrases at the dinner table or discuss the finer points of contract clauses. That was two. And David was so calm all the time. Unflappable. Libby, on the other hand, tended to get excited about things, and she needed help reining that tendency in. Sure, she was cool on the outside, but inside she often felt like a swirled mess of emotions. She was sensitive, much as she tried not to be. David could help her to pack away that sensitivity, to truly be stoic the way her father was. That was reason number three. Really, they were perfect for each other.

Being with David made Libby see how right her father had been about Nick. They were mismatched. Nick didn't want to talk about court procedure. Oh, he'd tolerate it to a point, but he found it boring when she discussed legal strategy and the nuances of judicial precedent. And culture? He bought her tickets to the symphony once and fell asleep during the performance. Nick didn't help her thin skin, either. He talked to her like he was encouraging her to be softer, almost as if he didn't care how important it was for her to be tough. Nick made her feel extreme things—exuberance and rage and lust. Far from helping her to cultivate a more stable mind set, he stirred up that stew of emotions. David was what she needed. Someone unexciting. Soothing.

Dull as dirt.

"I think I may have plans on Saturday night," Libby lied. "Why don't you call me when you get home?"

They ended the call and she lay back on the bed. On paper David was her perfect match. He freely admitted that he was more interested in traveling the world than in having children. With their connections they could be at the top of the Arbor Falls social ladder, hosting dinner parties and political fund-raisers and shaping the future to their liking. David could help Libby to become a judge one day, just like her father. There was something to be said for quiet and predictability. David was her future, not Nick.

And for some reason, that depressed the hell out of her.

Seven tons hatred. Nick wrote it out on a piece of stationery. Whoever was leaving those signs had been clear about communicating his intentions. This had to be some kind of riddle or guessing game. He tapped his pen against the paper. It *had* to mean something.

Seven tons, and seven days. He tried to spot patterns in the message. He stood from the table and stretched his legs. Libby had shut herself in the bedroom so he couldn't bounce ideas off her. He reached for his phone and called Dom. "What do you think that means, seven tons hatred? Is that some kind of a clue?"

Dom released a sigh. "Man, Nick. I haven't even thought about it. I was at the crime scene for a while, then I had to talk to the widow." He sounded weary.

His widow. The words dropped to the pit of Nick's stomach. "I'm sorry, Dom."

"He was a good cop, McAdams." His voice was thick. "I've got a bunch of officers here foaming at the mouth. You take down one of our own…"

He didn't have to finish. Nick knew. Whoever was after Libby now had an entire police department gunning for him. "A lot of overtime tonight?"

"And tomorrow, and the day after that. Until we get this son of a bitch." His voice was a deep angry growl. "I don't know about the third sign or what this sick bastard is talking about. No prints on the photograph left in Libby's file, no trace evidence left on the victims. We even checked the surveillance video at the D.A.'s Office. This guy is careful. It's been nothing but dead ends."

"There has to be something. We just have to find it." He rubbed at his eyes, not wanting to think about what little time they had but thinking about it, anyway.

"We're all working on it. You just keep Libby safe, all right?"

They ended the call and Nick sat back in his seat, tapping his pen against the paper. He'd never been good at riddles and word games. He stood and paced the suite, and each pass of the room made him wonder if the walls were closing in. He opened the windows to admit a gust of cool spring air and paced again, this time stopping at the bookcase where the inn had stacked a few complimentary games, including Scrabble. He collected the letters to form seven tons hatred in his fist. "Hey, Libby?" He rapped at the door. "Are you sleeping?"

He heard her groan impatiently and stomp to the door. "Can't I be alone for ten—"

"You're good at word games," Nick said when she opened the door. "Puzzles." He walked past her and scattered the wooden letters on the bed. "Seven tons hatred has to mean something. Let's figure it out."

Her frown relaxed. "You think it's an anagram?"

Good old Libby, she was always up for an intellectual challenge. "That's what I'm thinking, unless you can come up with something else."

Her impatience disappeared instantly, and she seated herself on the bed and rearranged the letters. "You said this had something to do with my dad. Maybe it's someone's name?" She knitted her brows in concentration. "What about vendetta? Vendetta her son. But that leaves an extra *s*."

"Her sons vendetta?" Nick was still pacing, too agitated by the morning's events to sit down. "But whose son? What vendetta?"

"Vendetta seems right…." Libby rearranged the letters again, biting her lip in concentration. She was so sexy when she became single-minded like this. "Vendetta res nosh." She said it triumphantly and then sat back and made a face. "*Res* means thing in Latin, but that doesn't make sense."

"Maybe it's not vendetta anything. What else can we spell?"

She moved the letters around again. "Sonnet. How

about heard sonnet...." Her cheeks grew red. "No. It's not sonnet."

"Do you know, I never would have thought of sonnet?" Nick smiled. "But you did."

Her face grew redder still. "I'm just brainstorming. It was silly—"

"It wasn't silly."

He stopped to look at her. He hadn't said it to make fun of her. If he'd had those letters and a hundred years he probably never would have thought to piece together the word *sonnet*. Hell, he'd read a few of them, but he couldn't define them any better than he could explain string theory. "I like that sonnet was your third choice. This is why we're going to crack this puzzle and get this bastard. We complement each other."

She studied him as if she wasn't certain he was being serious. Then a whisper of a smile fell across her mouth and she returned to her puzzle. "It's not sonnet, though."

She was so intently focused on those little wooden letters that Nick realized she might not even notice if he fell through the floor just then. He grew excited while he watched her, aroused by the intensity with which she approached her work and the calm manner in which she moved the letters around yet again and announced, "Nest over handset. Does that make sense?"

No, it didn't, but neither did his erection at that moment, and *that* was very real. "Let's keep thinking," he said as he turned to block his lower half from view. A beautiful woman on a bed...what man wouldn't be turned on?

They arranged those letters dozens of different ways, and by the time Nick looked up at the clock almost an hour and a half had gone by. Nothing was making sense, and they were no closer to solving the puzzle. They could piece together a word or two, but the remaining letters would only add up to nonsense. Libby sat back on her haunches. "Maybe it doesn't mean anything. Maybe it's a joke and we're wasting our time trying to figure this out."

"It *has* to mean something. We just have to figure out the right combination."

She pulled her long hair back from her face. "I keep returning to the same words. It's like Einstein's definition of insanity, where I keep doing the same thing and expecting a different result. I need to take a break."

He stood so she could lie back on the mattress. She tucked her arm underneath the pillow and looked at him. "Do you really think this puzzle is solvable? Can we figure this out?"

"I know we can." His response was immediate. He gathered the Scrabble letters and walked toward the door. "I'm going to keep working on this. Between the both of us, we'll get it."

Her gaze was seeking. "You sound so sure. You don't know this person. How do you know this isn't just another game he's playing with us?"

He paused, one hand on the doorknob, and turned back to her. He hadn't considered that question before, but he felt certain that the words left at the crime scene that morning were a puzzle that could be solved. "I don't know anything for sure," he admitted. "But if he's playing a game with us, then what fun would it be for him if we dropped out on day three?"

She sat up. "So you think he *wants* us to solve the puzzle?"

"I do." He shrugged. "Otherwise why would he have left it? I also think that he's giving us a clue. I think he wants us to understand what these murders are about."

He hovered by the doorway, sensing she wasn't finished with the conversation yet. She brought the pillow to her lap and sat cross-legged on the mattress. "Okay," she said. "Let's keep going. This bastard isn't going to beat us."

Nick smiled. "Yes, ma'am. Back to work."

Cassie felt a bolt of electricity dart through her core when she heard a knock fall on the hotel door. She cradled Sam against her shoulder and approached silently, gazing through the peephole. A second electrical current wound its way through her. "Dom?"

"Cassie." He was distorted in the peephole so that his dark eyes looked abnormally large and his dark hair prominent as he leaned forward. "I thought you might be hungry." He lifted his arm and she saw a large brown paper bag.

She sniffed. Chinese food. She'd only ventured out of the hotel room to stock up on junk food from the vending machine, and she was half-starving. Then again, she was supposed to be in hiding, and she barely knew this guy. "This might sound strange, but how do I know you're not here to hurt me?"

She saw him flinch. The startled look on his face was endearing. "Because I'm the one trying to solve these crimes? I just thought maybe you'd want some company after being cooped up with a baby all day."

She pressed her back against the door. It wasn't as if she thought Dom was going to kill her, but there'd been another murder. Libby had told her not to trust anyone. She'd said there might be a leak in the police department.

Fear knotted her stomach. What if Dom was using his super hotness to cover the fact that he was a psychopath? She couldn't take that chance.

"You can just leave it there." She spoke to the door.

Silence. "You want me to leave your dinner in the hallway?"

"Yes. Please. It was nice of you to bring it, but I think you should go."

Another long pause. "So you don't trust me, but you trust the food I'm bringing?"

This was a good point. She couldn't trust the food. Neither could she muster the willpower to refuse it. "Yes, that's right. You can just leave the food and go."

She looked through the peephole and saw him shrug and set the bag by the door. "All right. Have a good night, Cassie."

She listened to the creaking of the hallway as he headed toward the elevator. "Hold on."

Cassie unfastened the lock with one hand, clutching the baby with her other and swung the door open. He came back and stood before her. His dark eyes were a shade of worn leather, and she lost herself in them momentarily. Then she remembered that she was wearing old sweatpants and a long sleeve T-shirt stained with baby spit-up. Her hair was pulled back in a messy knot and secured in place by the complimentary ballpoint pen she'd found in the hotel desk. She patted her head with her one free hand. "I'm a mess," she stammered.

"No, you're not." He was motionless, staring at her face. Something in his voice told her he wasn't humoring her. "You're perfectly dressed for Chinese takeout."

She swallowed, hoping he couldn't hear the insistent pounding of her heart. "We can eat it in the hotel lobby, where it's busy." She gave him her most winning smile to try to smooth over the awkwardness of the situation. "It's kind of like going out to dinner."

He lifted the bag and pointed to the elevator. "After you."

They rode the elevator to the first floor and selected a round table in the corner of the lobby, beside which were two striped couches. He set the take-out bag on the table. "It's nothing fancy. Some egg rolls, chicken wings, something-fried rice." With each item he lifted a corresponding white paper container from the bag and set it down. "Fortune cookies, of course."

Sam began to coo contently in her arms and she rubbed his back. "Go ahead. You help yourself first, and I'll hold him."

Dom set out some paper plates and plastic utensils. He finished opening the cartons and turned to her with his hands outstretched. "Ladies first. Do you think he'll come to me?"

She stared at him, slack-jawed. This giant man wanted to hold her baby? "I guess we can find out."

She slid the infant into Dom's arms and waited for the hysteria. Sam grunted and squirmed at the unfamiliar touch, but Dom confidently shifted him until he was against his shoulder and then paced the little sitting area. "You're a brave man." Cassie laughed. "You may want to put a burp cloth on that shoulder."

He scooped up the cloth she was extending and continued to walk while Cassie filled her plate. He'd brought enough food to feed a family of six, and she was pretty sure she could finish it off herself. She exercised self-restraint, not wanting to frighten Dom off with her raging postpregnancy appetite and well aware of all the stares they were getting from other hotel guests. She supposed it was unusual to eat Chinese takeout in a hotel lobby. She didn't care.

She sat on the couch and ate. Alone, unattached to another person. For the past four weeks, whenever Libby had come over, she'd marveled at the luxury of eating a meal while someone else watched her child. Eating a meal while a hot cop watched her child? That was more than a luxury. *That* was downright arousing. He seemed so natural, too, the way he bounced Sam and spoke softly in his ear. Sam looked quite content in his arms. "All right, Sergeant Vasquez. Time to come clean. How many children do you have?"

"None." He grinned, obviously pleased by the compliment. "But I have three nieces and two nephews, all under five years old." His face brightened as Sam squealed. "Thanks for letting me hold him. I needed this."

She watched him smile at her son. "Bad day at the office?"

Almost as quickly as his face had brightened, it darkened again. "Yes."

His throat was tense but his hands were gentle as he brought the baby down into his arms. He didn't elaborate and she didn't push him to say more. When she was finished eating the food she'd piled onto her plate she had seconds, and when she was finished with those Sam was drifting to sleep. She coaxed him into her arms and settled back against the couch while Dom ate. They talked about his job and her father and how disruptive the past twenty-four hours had been for both of them. When the conversation settled into a brief silence, Cassie said, "I'm sorry I thought you were going to kill me."

"You're smart. You shouldn't trust anyone. Not even me." The corner of his mouth rose in a half grin as he said it.

She suspected he was right, in a manner of speaking. His olive skin was an even richer shade in the dim lighting of the hotel lobby. She imagined running her fingers through his thick hair. He was several layers of heartbreaker, and she'd had enough heartbreak for one lifetime. She nuzzled against Sam's neck, listening to his uneven breaths, watching him grin in his sleep. Libby said that Sam's smile reminded her of their father, and Cassie felt a lump in her throat as she realized the comparison was apt. The pain of her father's absence was too fresh to probe.

Dom pulled two bottles of water out of the paper bag, opened one and set it in on the table in front of her. She didn't know what Dom wanted, why he was being so nice to her. She'd known several men who'd somehow gotten the wrong idea about her, who took her smiles for invitations. She wondered if Dom saw her the way the others had, as a free spirit and a good time. Cassie's face flushed with shame. Despite her reputation, she'd only slept with a few men. Then again, look at what that had gotten her.

The baby in her arms and the responsibility he required were all frighteningly new. Once upon a time she might have invited Dom back into her room, or maybe they'd have gone out for a few drinks. Whether the relationship lasted one night or ten years, it wouldn't have mattered. She was attracted to him, and she'd never worried about the future before. But now everything was different. Stability mattered, and once Dom had finished with dinner, she would politely clean up and excuse herself to bring Sam to bed.

But Dom rose first.

"I have to get back to work. I've already spent too much time here, but I wanted to make sure you were safe." He cleaned up the plates and utensils and folded up the food containers. "You have a refrigerator in your room, right?"

"A small one."

"These should fit. Do you need help getting back upstairs?"

"I can manage." What she couldn't manage was the pang that hit her square in the chest as he cleaned up unceremoniously, as if everything they'd done in the past forty-five minutes had been nothing. Had he really driven so far out of his way, brought her takeout and held her baby, for the purpose of checking up on her? Really?

He seemed unsure of himself as they both stood facing each other, not quite knowing how to say goodbye. "Thanks for the Chinese food." Cassie's tone was cordial but clipped.

"You take care of yourself. And that baby."

He gave a small smile as he nodded his good-night and turned to leave the hotel. Cassie waited for him to turn around and give her some signal as to what he was thinking, but he proceeded straight to the parking lot without looking back.

Chapter 7

"I can't figure it out." Libby practically threw the wooden letters in frustration. She was tired and hungry and now she had a headache. "I need to do something else for a little while."

Nick had been pacing the room like a caged lion for twenty minutes, and he was only too eager to switch activities. He glanced at the clock. "It's almost six. Let's have dinner."

She scooted across the bed and reached for a room service binder, wrinkling her nose. "It's a bed and breakfast. I'm not sure what they'll offer—"

"Nothing. I already checked." He reached down to touch her wrist. She swore her heart skipped. "We'll leave the room. Let's go out."

Even as she sat there with her jaw open wide, Nick was throwing a black sweater over his T-shirt and looking for his keys. "We're going out?" She nearly stumbled over the words. "But what about…"

"We're going out." He crossed the room to stand directly in front of her, their knees nearly touching. "We're miles away from Arbor Falls and we haven't eaten anything since breakfast, and I want to take you out for dinner. Somewhere dark and safe, where we can feel like normal people again for an hour or so." He bent forward slightly, almost to eye level. He was close enough that she felt his breath skim her cheek. "Do you trust me?"

Her breath halted in her lungs—not at the question, but at the close distance from which he asked it. "Of course I trust you. I'm trusting you with my life."

"Then know that I would never do anything to hurt you, and at the first sign of danger, we'll leave." He straightened and held out a hand to help her up. "But we need to eat something. Let's go to dinner."

The dark intensity of his gaze sent her heart thundering. Something about Nick had changed over the past three years. He'd always been attractive, but now he had the air of someone who was comfortable taking charge. His confidence was evident not only in the way he carried himself but in the way he helped her into her jacket, held the door for her and lightly guided her down the hall, his hand resting protectively against the small of her back. No, not just protectively, but possessively, as if he'd claimed her at some point in the past day. Her stomach sparked at the thought.

All afternoon they'd examined the words left at the scene of the murder. They'd rearranged the letters a hundred different ways, but they couldn't crack it. During those long hours Libby had marveled at Nick's focus and determination. This was a different side of him. The Nick she'd known was headstrong and impulsive. He drove fast and took risks and had trouble sitting still. He'd joined the FBI because the Arbor Falls P.D. wasn't exciting enough, and he'd joined knowing that he wouldn't be able to stay in Arbor Falls. This Nick was different. He'd managed to channel all of that raw energy into something more powerful still: a sense of purpose. In the three years since they'd ended their engagement, Nick had grown up.

They drove to the town center and walked the sidewalks for a few minutes before selecting an Irish pub called Regan's. The dark wooden bars and paneling absorbed most of the light that streaked through the stained-glass windows or out of the dimly glowing bulbs that hung from the ceiling. The booths were so broad that viewing the occupants was almost impossible without special effort. Nick ordered a burger cooked rare and a cold beer. Libby ordered a seltzer water and a salad.

"More salad. Living on the edge?" Nick gave her a playful smirk.

Her heart fluttered at the sight of that dimple in his cheek. "I like salads, and this one probably has more calories than your burger and fries."

"I did notice that you didn't order the dressing on the side. You keep me guessing, Attorney Andrews." He gave her a little wink that sent a rush of heat to her cheeks.

Being with him felt like the old days, back when their lives were uncomplicated by careers and ambition. A few times Libby even lost herself and forgot about the weight of her circumstances. Then the reality came rushing back as if she'd been doused with ice water. Her father's recent death. A stalker. Nick wasn't having dinner with her to reminisce about happier times. He was wearing his gun, and he was protecting her from a madman. A sobering reality.

"Nick," she began, stirring the straw in her seltzer water, "what do you think my father did? I feel like I should know why someone would want revenge, but I can't for my life remember ever knowing that he did anything that would drive someone to this. And why now, days after his death?"

"That's the question, isn't it? To be honest, this is one of the things I wanted to go out to talk about. I thought it would be helpful to reach neutral territory, because it could be that someone is acting out of revenge, but the timing suggests this may still have something to do with you." His brows lifted slightly. "Now, who would want to hurt your father and who would want to hurt you? I need an enemies list."

What a shame that she hadn't thought to bring her enemies list to dinner. "For God's sake. Do I look like Richard Nixon?"

"I'm serious, Lib. We need to talk about this. Let's start with you. Who would want to hurt you?"

"I've lost count of all the people I've helped to lock up. Let's start with them."

She'd intended to be dismissive, but Nick simply shrugged and said, "Okay, good idea. Let's talk about some of your big cases."

Libby rested her chin on the palm of her hand, ignoring the voice in her head that told her it was rude to put her elbow on the table. She didn't care about manners when her dinner companion was being irksome. He actually had a pen out and was poised to write on his napkin! Here she'd been thinking they were relaxing over drinks and having dinner, and he'd brought the Spanish Inquisition.

She answered slowly, trying not to look as annoyed as she felt. She worked with criminals for a living. *Lots* of people hated her. "Well, there's the Brislin case, obviously. He hasn't been sentenced yet, but he is facing up to five years in prison for corruption. I doubt the good senator is a fan of mine." She wrinkled her nose as she considered this. "But I would be surprised if he had anything to do with this. He doesn't have any connections to organized crime. He doesn't like to pay for luxury items, but otherwise, all of our investigations turned up empty."

"So, Brislin is a maybe." He drew a line down the center of his napkin and wrote Brislin's name in a column. Libby rolled her eyes at the ceiling. "Good. Who else?"

"Uh, let's talk about Officer Hawkins, who said in open court that he hopes someone kills me." She couldn't help the quiver in her voice. In all of her years as a prosecutor no one had ever said something so terrible to her—especially not a police officer. She pressed her fingers against her eyelids. "He must be out by now. Is Dom watching him?"

"His alibi checks out for last night, but my understanding is that he and McAdams were friendly. Dom thought it was unlikely, but Hawkins is on administrative leave pending a complete investigation based on his conduct yesterday in court. They're watching him closely."

Talking about Hawkins deactivated her normally hyperactive internal censor, and Libby was flooded with angry words. "Hawkins is a creep and a liar. You know, I had the impression he wanted me to help him commit perjury yesterday? He's got a reputation around our office, and there's only so many times we can save his sorry behind. A murderer was going to eventually walk because of him. It was only a question of when." She clenched her fists. "The abuse of power. When he lied on the stand, I swear, Nick, I could have hurled my pen at him."

Now she'd done it. Nick was back against the booth seat, staring at her with his mouth wide. He blinked a few times before speaking. "I don't think I've heard you get angry like that—*really* angry—in years."

She looked away, wishing she could crawl between the worn floorboards of the pub and disappear for a few days. "Sorry. I'm working on my emotions. Just like I'm working on my diet. I'm trying not to have outbursts like that. It's just that sometimes—"

"No." Nick brought his hand down to cover one of her fists. "Your passion is great. Don't change that. Promise me."

His hand was strong and rough. She imagined his hand against the bare skin on her arms and thighs. A flush crept across her chest. She dragged her hand out from under his and rested it in her lap. "Dad always told me that emotion was weakness. He said that the ideal of our justice system is the passionless delivery of punishment. He said that passion had no place in the courtroom."

Nick's mouth tensed into a line and he looked down at the table, appearing to be deep in thought. She could practically see him weighing his response. Then he spoke carefully, as if he was aware how closely he was treading to the dragon's lair. "And you believed him?"

It didn't surprise him at all. Judge Andrews was rigid and impersonal, except when it suited his needs to be otherwise. It didn't surprise Nick in the least that he'd tried to suffocate the passion that made Libby so fiery. So different from her father. This was the ideal she'd been striving for? Emotional vapidity? Nick's mind wandered to the icy speech she'd delivered that night they broke up, and how that disconnect had haunted him even more than her words. *I don't love you, Nick.* He'd spent the past few years wondering if the judge had somehow orchestrated their breakup. Libby's last words to him had sounded so foreign, as if she was delivering a speech someone else had written. But now he understood that in some twisted devotion to her father, she'd broken his heart according to her father's highest-held ideals: brutal truth, delivered passionlessly.

The hot anger was back again at his suggestion that her father had been misguided in his notion of justice. He could see it flaring in the wide pupils of her blue eyes. "Of course I believed him," she snapped. "My father was an outstanding judge, extremely well-respected. Before that he was a legendary prosecutor at the D.A.'s Office." She sat back as if that settled everything.

"Libby, how can justice be served without looking at the human beings involved? We need prosecutors, defense attorneys and judges to have a heart. To have compassion for the lives they affect. Otherwise we may as well create a computer program to administer justice."

He knew she agreed. He could see the conflict raging in her as she twisted her napkin between her fingers. She cared deeply for her profession and for those with whom she worked, but maybe not as deeply as she cared for her father. She agreed with Nick, but she was unflinchingly loyal to the man who'd raised her. "Justice is blind. The notion that we should give any thought to anything other than the facts of a case is offensive to that ideal."

He wanted to counter that human beings *were* facts to be considered in a case—their flaws, their motives, their struggles—but he stopped himself. He didn't care what she did in the courtroom. He cared about what she did three years ago when she'd decided their engagement was over. Had she considered *him* when she'd told him she wasn't moving to Pittsburgh? All of their years together, or the future they'd planned? Had she thought about why he needed to leave Arbor Falls, or how the town stifled him? Or had she only thought about herself and her career? He didn't ask, because asking would only turn this discussion into a trial about their engagement.

A coldness crept up his spine as his perspective shifted. Had *he* considered why Libby would want to stay near Arbor Falls after he'd accepted a position with the FBI? He couldn't remember, and that wasn't a good sign. He couldn't recall discussing how they could compromise for the few years he would be stationed in Pittsburgh so they could both pursue their careers. He didn't remember that ever being an option in his mind. No, he was sure that he'd expected Libby to move with him, no questions asked. As if he owned her. The chill settled in his gut. How caveman of him.

How unfeeling.

He shifted, suddenly uncomfortable in his seat. "Let's change the subject, shall we?" Libby gave a small grunt. It was assent enough. "What about your dad? Who did he anger enough to do something like this?"

She looked heavenward as she considered, and Nick imagined they were both thinking along the same lines. Her father had believed that compassion should be checked at the courtroom door. He'd probably angered more people than either of them could count. "I assume this all has something to do with a ruling he made during his tenure as a judge, since that court reporter was killed," she said.

"A fair assumption."

Their dinners arrived. Nick couldn't resist his burger—he hadn't realized how hungry he was. As they ate, Libby gave him a rundown of some of her dad's more significant cases, and he wrote down some possible names. "But I never had the sense that Dad was in any kind of trouble or under a serious threat."

Nick thought. "If he was under a threat, do you think that's something he would have told you?"

She paused, her fork hovering slightly over her plate. She wasn't kidding about her salad having more calories than his burger—it was topped with layers of cheese, bacon and avocado and smothered with thousand island dressing. Good, because she was looking too thin. "I think he would have told me if someone was threatening him. Dad and I were close like that."

Nick wouldn't argue the point, but in his mind there was no way that the judge would have upset his daughter by confiding in her. Libby had confided in her father, not vice versa. "Let's review. He angered a lot of people, but you never had the sense that he angered anyone enough that they would want to seek revenge in some way."

"Why would anyone want to hurt my dad? Most of the people he angered are in prison or on parole. And what would revenge matter now, anyway? He'll never see any of this." She pushed her plate to the side and sat back in the booth. "I don't know. I feel like we're missing something obvious."

They finished their drinks and Nick paid the bill. Walking around the block a few times would have helped to digest dinner, but that was too risky. As it was, he checked the rental car thoroughly before they climbed in, and he watched for following vehicles as they drove back to the inn.

Libby's bed was turned down when they entered the room, and two chocolate mints had been left on the pillow. She held one out to him. "Dessert." She smiled.

She was so cute when she smiled. Their fingers met when he took the candy from her. He turned it over in his hand before tossing it on the nightstand. He wanted more than chocolate.

He closed the shades and watched her as she walked around the room, pulling her carefully folded nightgown from the large mahogany dresser and digging in her bag for her hairbrush. Her actions were fluid and easy, not at all resembling the self-conscious movements from the day before. She was actually relaxing around him.

Relaxation was not foremost on his mind. As he watched Libby prepare for the evening, he was drawn to the shape of her thighs, suggested but hidden by her skirt. She had a silver charm bracelet around one slender wrist, and he had an urge to nibble at the silver, teasing the delicate flesh of her wrist with his lips. He wanted to touch her again, to feel her hot bare skin writhing beneath him. Tomorrow was uncertain. He needed her tonight. He stepped forward.

Her toothbrush had fallen into the main compartment of her suitcase—no surprise, since she'd packed in a hurry. Libby had just managed to find it when she looked up and caught his gaze. There was no mistaking the look in his eyes, as if he'd searched her for the one thing she couldn't bear right now.

"What?" she asked, trying to sound natural and hoping he couldn't see her fingers trembling.

Nick took another step. "You can't tell me you don't feel it, Libby."

"Feel what?"

"The heat that always burned between us. The attraction we've always felt for each other, even when we were pretending we didn't."

She rolled her eyes. "That's ridiculous. I thought I made it clear how I felt for you."

"You can't hide it." He straightened. "I see it written across your body."

He advanced, moving with deliberate footsteps and a gaze that made her heart thunder. She instinctively retreated but stopped as her back pressed against the wall. This elicited a rakish smile and a chuckle from the back of his throat.

"We're through," she stammered as he came still closer, bracing himself against the wall with one hand. Blocking her escape.

"Through?" His warm breath fell on her cheeks as he leaned down. "You really think so?"

Now his lips grazed her ear, sending a shiver straight through her center. She felt his light breath on her skin, felt the animal heat of his strong arm as it fenced her in. Nick curved his body to bring his free hand to rest lightly on her hip.

"Yes. It's over," she said. "I feel nothing for you." Her voice came out no more than a whisper, thick with desire.

Another chuckle, this one from deep within his chest. She stood helplessly still as he began to tease her shirt upward, exposing the sensitive skin on her belly. "So, I suppose this doesn't do anything for you, then?" He trailed his fingertips along her waistline, eliciting a soft moan.

"No," she gasped. "I don't feel a thing." Her skin was on fire, and an ache began at the juncture of her thighs.

He frowned playfully. "That's surprising. I could have sworn I felt a reaction."

"Nothing."

As she spoke, he brought his hand fully under her shirt and round her bare back, pressing her closer to him. She felt the length of his hardness against her heat and sighed, allowing her head to fall back against the wall. His hot mouth was still beside her ear, but he brought his lips to the base of her throat as she arched her body toward him.

"Nothing at all?" He spoke the words against her throat, and she trembled as a current of fire and ice coursed through her.

She moaned. "Nothing."

"This is troubling." He again spoke to her neck, and

Libby felt every hair on her body rise in response. Before she could react, he'd pushed one knee between hers and eased her legs open. She willingly complied. He kept one hand on her back but brought his other hand lower, blazing a trail down her waist to her thigh. With deft fingers he slid her skirt up, exposing her black silk panties. She moaned again as he tucked a finger beneath the leg of her panties and traced the edge of the fabric with a butterfly touch. "How about that?" he whispered against her ear. His voice was thick. "You *must* feel that."

She was too breathless to answer, but he didn't wait for a response as he guided her panties down her thighs. She cried out as he brought his hand back up to touch her, expertly stroking her until her knees began to shake. "Oh…"

She braced herself against the wall of his chest, fumbling uselessly at his sweater. She managed to lift it a few inches, enough to slide her fingers underneath to feel the tight muscles on his stomach tense with need for her. He sank his forehead against the wall as she touched him and a groan escaped his lips. A thrill at her own power shot through her.

Nick collected himself and continued to touch her, his eyes trained to hers. "Did you feel that? Was that a yes?"

He sounded so far away. She pressed herself against his hand, moving her hips rhythmically as a tension began to gather. Reaching up to grasp Nick's hair with both hands, she ran her fingers through the thick waves and brought his mouth to hers. He flicked his tongue against hers, matching the rhythm of his fingers. They were locked in that embrace until she pulled away and rested her head on his shoulder, clasping the strong arms that held her captive. Libby gasped as the tension inside of her shattered and she finally found her release, shuddering against his hand.

When the moment had passed, she fell back against the wall. Nick raised her panties and smoothed her skirt down then leaned forward and kissed her soundly on the mouth. He pulled away and allowed his breath to fall against her cheek. "How can you say you don't feel anything for me?" he demanded.

Libby swallowed. She tucked her blouse into her skirt and stepped aside. "You bastard," she choked as she smoothed her hair. Then she turned and stormed away to the bathroom, shutting the door behind her.

She sat on the tiled floor for what seemed like hours, waiting for her knees to stop shaking and her breath to steady. She'd really done that. He'd brazenly approached her, lifted her skirt and touched her, and she'd *enjoyed* it. Every second. That wasn't even worth lying about. But now she had to face him and his smugness at having brought her into submission, and that's what made her cheeks burn.

She drew a hot bubble bath and slid into the tub, watching her legs go red from the heat. The spice of his cologne hovered on her throat, and when she touched her arm, she imagined the skin on his stomach beneath her fingertips, hard and trembling. She closed her eyes to imagine his skillful touch again. Then she sat up.

This was a problem, this feeling as if she hadn't had enough of him. It's not like she'd asked for him to touch her like that. They had a history and maybe there was some lingering attraction, but he'd taken advantage. She reached for the washcloth and the soap and lathered her skin, scrubbing the traces of Nick's scent. Then she leaned back against the hot water, the tightness in her muscles melting inch by inch until she was weightless.

Perspective comes in hot baths. She'd made a mistake with Nick. They could not be involved again, they simply couldn't, and when he gloated, she'd have the satisfaction of telling him that he was not to try anything like that again. Better still, there would be no more touching. No hand on her back or fingers brushing her hair. How easily they'd fallen into those comfortable habits despite her best intentions. She could forgive herself for the lapse in judgment, since after all, she was afraid for her life and not thinking straight. He should have known better.

Libby skimmed her hand over the surface of the water that appeared as the bubbles faded. That puzzle still weighed on her. Seven tons hatred. They must have considered most options, hundreds of combinations. She thought of the woman in the photograph and the bruises around her throat. The poor girl. A steel ball of fury tumbled in Libby's stomach. They would get the bastard who'd strangled her.

Her heart stopped. Strangled. The largest case of her father's career as a prosecutor had come when she was still in diapers, when he'd prosecuted the Arbor Falls Strangler...what had that case been called?

She pulled the plug on the bathtub drain and stood as the water emptied in a whoosh. She wiped the remains of water and bubbles with a thick terry-cloth towel and then climbed into the complimentary white bathrobe, her heart pounding. The Arbor Falls Strangler. That case would be about thirty years old by now. If she remembered correctly, he'd terrorized the town for nearly ten years before he was caught.

By the time she emerged from the sauna of the bathroom, Libby felt wild with excitement. Nick was sitting on the bed, and his eyes were drawn with concern as he saw her. "Libby, I'm sorry—"

"The letters. Where are they?"

He blinked and she repeated herself. He then pointed dumbly to the table where the wooden letters lay in a pile.

"It's a case name." She was breathless as she arranged the letters. "Look! That's why we have the *v,* for *versus.*"

Nick was standing at her side now, watching as she worked. "I'll be…"

"And since it's a criminal case, it's State v. something." She stared at the remaining letters and then triumphantly reworked them. "There. That's it."

A smile crept over his face. "*State v. Henderson.* It works."

"*State v. Henderson.* My dad's biggest case when he was a prosecutor. The case that he said made him judge." She folded her arms across her chest. "The Arbor Falls Strangler."

Nick smiled proudly and reached out to hug her but stopped himself and instead pressed his hands to his waist. "You did it, Lib. The Arbor Falls Strangler, huh?"

"So you know what we have to do now, right?"

He nodded. "Research. Lots and lots of research."

Chapter 8

They stayed up into the night piecing together information on the Arbor Falls Strangler before finally falling asleep at three in the morning. They were up again early. Libby placed a few calls to the D.A.'s Office and managed to locate the Henderson case files.

"They were moved to a storage facility in Stillborough. It's a little under an hour from here."

Nick called Dom while Libby got ready, and then they headed toward Stillborough.

"Will Henderson is local mythology," Libby said, thinking about the macabre websites they'd found that were devoted to the crimes. "He stalked women and then killed them. And if this particular online account I read is correct, he left signs for his victims, too. It was an elaborate cat-and-mouse game." She turned to Nick as he drove. "Will Henderson died in prison soon after he was sentenced. He hanged himself. So what does it mean that someone is copying him now?"

"Could be a family member of Henderson's, or it could be someone who's as interested in the folklore as others apparently are." He straightened. "Between you and me, this feels more personal than a copycat killing."

"I agree." She gripped her cardboard coffee cup. She was drinking a lot more coffee than she should be, and she didn't care. Her arms pimpled as a chill went through her. "No one followed us, right? You talked to Dom, and there were no more signs?"

"None. It was quiet last night. Nothing at our houses. Everyone in the police department is on high alert now that McAdams is one of the victims."

She nodded silently but couldn't brush down her anxiety. Today was day four, which meant another sign was scheduled. The killer had already gone to horrifically impressive lengths to deliver his promised signs.

Nick cleared his throat. "Far be it from me to gossip, but I found out that my buddy Dom had dinner with your little sister last night."

Libby's eyes widened and she felt her shoulders loosen by a millimeter as Nick changed the subject. "Really? She left the hotel?"

"No. Apparently he brought her Chinese takeout, and she didn't trust him so she made him eat it in the hotel lobby with her." Nick broke into a broad grin. "She thought he might be the killer."

There was that prickle again on her arms. "Well… can we be sure he isn't?"

He looked at her. "Libby, Dom didn't—"

"We don't know anything for sure. He's the only one

who knew we were staying at your parents' house, besides McAdams. We can't trust anyone." She pulled absentmindedly at the seam of her jeans. "Maybe Cassie and Sam should go to a different hotel, just to be safe."

"He was my partner for years. He's a police sergeant." Nick's jaw was tight. "It's not him."

"Why is he showing up at her hotel, checking up on her? That's strange behavior, isn't it?"

He laughed dryly. "Maybe he likes her. Sometimes people do strange things when they like each other."

"I don't want him near my sister."

She pulled out her cell phone, ignoring his protests. "Cassie," she said when her sister answered. "Dom showed up at your room last night?"

Cassie snorted on the other end of the phone. "Nice to hear from you, Libby. Good morning to you, too. Sleep well?"

She rolled her eyes at the phone. "Answer my question."

"Yes, Dom came over last night. He brought me dinner."

"Why is he bringing you dinner?" Libby shot Nick a look as he groaned.

"I don't know. I didn't ask him that."

"It's strange, and I think you and Sam should leave the hotel and go somewhere else. Don't tell Dom."

"Go somewhere else!" Her shrill protest reminded Libby of their teenage years and of the many life-or-death arguments they'd had over who had used the other's makeup. "He's the police sergeant, Libby. He's not a serial killer."

"Don't you think it's weird that he would drive so far out of his way to bring you dinner?"

Cassie was quiet on the other end. Then she said softly, "Why do you think it's so strange that a man would do something nice for me?"

Libby's stomach tightened. "You know that's not what I'm saying—"

"Maybe he likes me. Is that so wrong? So weird? Maybe he worried that it would be hard for me to get out of the room because of Sam. That doesn't make him a serial killer."

Libby closed her eyes and took a deep breath. "This is not the time to worry about your love life. Go somewhere else and don't tell anyone."

"You sound like Dad," Cassie spat.

"Someone has to be the adult here," she snapped. They exchanged tense goodbyes and disconnected the call.

Libby sat back in her seat and exhaled loudly. "She is just impossible!"

Nick glanced at her out of the corner of his eye. "Did that make you feel better?"

She turned herself away from him and folded her arms. Nick continued the drive in silence, his jaw set firmly. Let him be angry. She didn't care if she upset him or Dom; she had to do what was best for her sister. Cassie was her family, and Nick was not.

The Stillborough storage center was little more than an enormous warehouse in the middle of a field, miles off the highway and accessible only by a narrow road riddled with potholes. Nick was quite familiar with Stillborough. The prevalence of street drugs and violence had landed him and his FBI colleagues in the old mill town more times than he could count, chasing the drug supply that fed larger surrounding cities. He hadn't even needed to consult a map during the drive from Great Springs.

He couldn't ignore the gnawing in his stomach. He took several detours along the way to the warehouse to check for following cars. Leaving the room again was a risk, but the information in those case files could help them to crack the case open. When the Arbor Falls P.D. was at a virtual standstill in its investigation, *not* taking the trip to Stillborough seemed the bigger risk.

Nick pulled his car into a spot near the entrance. He turned off the engine and looked at Libby. "Ready?"

She looked at him with those wide blue eyes and an impenetrable expression. "I'm ready."

She was angry that he'd defended Dom. She stepped out of the car and proceeded toward the entrance without bothering to wait for Nick. He watched her for a moment, admiring the way her black wavy hair caught the sunlight, cresting midway down her back. His gaze then dipped lower, and he was momentarily hypnotized by the seductive sway of her hips as she marched away from him. Her focus was almost unbearably sexy.

Last night he'd sat on the bed while she'd bathed, waiting for her to emerge from the bathroom so he could apologize. Not that he was sorry for doing something they'd both enjoyed. Just thinking about the feel of her breath on his neck made him hard again. But he'd upset her somehow. He hadn't meant to. She wasn't making an apology easy for him, though. Each time he'd tried to talk about what they'd done, she changed the subject. He kicked himself mentally for complicating things between them just when it seemed they were starting to get comfortable again.

He exited the vehicle and followed her.

They walked through a single glass door propped open to admit fresh air into the dank warehouse. There was no reception area to speak of, just aisle upon aisle of gray industrial metal shelving, stacked floor to ceiling with cardboard boxes. To the right was a small office with an open door and a man sitting behind a mound of paperwork. He looked up at them over the bifocals sliding halfway down his nose. "Can I help you?"

"I'm Libby Andrews, from the District Attorney's Office. I spoke with you a little while ago."

"Yes, John Lankowsky. I manage the warehouse." John was bald, with small brown eyes that darted to Nick. "Are you a Fed?" he asked.

Nick's gaze shot to Libby as she tried to suppress a smirk. "Not today," he replied.

The man placed the paper in his hand on top of an already staggering pile on the desk and stood. "*State v. Henderson.* I had the boxes pulled a while ago. We have thirteen of them, but there may be a couple more."

"I'm sure Libby explained that we'd like to go through them," Nick said.

"You can do whatever you want for the next eight hours," John replied. "But after that we're closing, and you'll need to leave them here."

Libby furrowed her brows. "Eight hours?" She turned to Nick. "Thirteen boxes. We're going to need more time than that."

"We don't have more time than that, Libby." Nick nodded to John. "You have everything set up in a conference room, I assume?"

He snorted. "You could call it that."

He led them down a seemingly endless aisle to the very back of the warehouse, where a brown metal door opened to a small room with a Formica table. Cardboard boxes were stacked against the walls. Nick looked at the one closest to the door. The box was labeled State v. Henderson #8.

"Here you go," John said flatly as he gestured to the room. "Make sure you keep this rubber doorstop down because the door locks automatically and you won't be able to get back in if you leave."

"Thanks," said Libby as she walked toward the boxes and began to read the labels.

Nick scanned the surrounding warehouse, looking for anyone or anything that seemed out of the ordinary. A few uniformed employees appeared to be taking some kind of inventory of the boxes several aisles away from the room, but the warehouse was otherwise eerily silent. He drew his hand toward his hip, unbuttoning his holster to have quick access to his gun. Nick turned to Libby, keeping an eye on the door.

"What do you think, counselor? Any suggestions as to where we should begin?"

"Sure," she replied as she pulled a box from the top of a stack and set it on the wobbly table. "But maybe I should defer to the Fed in the room." She gave him a slight grin as she returned to the box and opened it.

Nick looked down at his clothes. "Jeans and a T-shirt. I hardly think it makes me look like a Fed."

"It's not your clothes, it's the way you carry your-self." She thumbed through the files in the box. "Let's just say that no one would think you taught kindergarten." She pulled a stack of papers from a file. "Here, I found the index."

Libby placed the papers on the table and ran a finger down the top sheet. Nick came closer, catching the sweet smell of her perfume. His eyes scanned the typewritten list. "What are we doing with this?"

"I don't know," Libby admitted. "I sort of feel like we're looking for a needle in a haystack, but I figure I'll know it when I see it."

The index was nearly thirty pages long and listed the files in each of the boxes. Libby's eyes narrowed as she pored over the pages. "Dad was meticulous about his files. Everything in its proper place, labeled and cross-referenced."

"Sounds like someone else I know."

"Box five," she said, ignoring the remark. "It looks like that contains information about witnesses." She marched over to the stacks and began searching the box numbers. "You would think they would at least pile these things in some kind of reasonable order," she muttered.

"You would also think they would have better rodent control in a document storage facility," Nick said as he opened a box. "Here's box five, but it looks like some-one made a nest out of a notebook."

"Yeah, well, half of these boxes are warped, and can you smell the mold?" She sighed. "Why isn't anything ever easy?"

Nick was beginning to ask himself the same thing as she neared him and he was again encompassed by her smell. He didn't know what the fragrance was called, but he'd always found it intoxicating. He remembered nights in Libby's bed, when she was asleep, pressing his face against the side of her neck to inhale her scent: a heady mixture of woman and whatever this perfume was. Jasmine? Lilac? Like it mattered. Whatever the fragrance, it was making it impossible for him to focus on anything else.

He cleaned out the scraps of paper from the old mouse nest while Libby eagerly thrust her hands into the box. He watched with fascination as she removed a stack of files and took a seat at the table. The girl was unstoppable when she set her mind to something.

"Libby." She looked up at him. "About last night…" He shifted from one foot to the other.

She stopped him with a quick wave of her hand. "Forget it."

"What?" Impossible. That was the last thing he wanted to do, anyway.

She pressed her hands to the table. "Tension is high and we made a mistake. Let's forget it." She tilted her head slightly as he hesitated. "Right? Isn't that what you were going to say?"

Well, no. He was going to tell her that he meant every word he'd said and that he didn't regret a single second. He was going to tell her that she still drove him wild with desire and he could barely think straight anymore. But those words would obviously be wasted breath, because she didn't feel the same.

"Forget it. Yes, I was going to say that."

With every tick of the second hand on the large institutional clock on the wall, Libby felt her chest constrict.

She wetted her dry lips, fumbling through the documents before her with clumsy cold fingers. Would the suspect interrupt to deliver his sign? She read the words on the page over and over, not making sense of the markings.

The clock continued its steady pulse. Each second brought her closer to day seven, and here she was with less than eight hours to pore over thirteen boxes of attorney files in the hopes of finding anything to shed some light on who might be trying to hurt her. Libby tucked her hair behind her ears. She had no idea what she was looking for.

The folders she grabbed contained pages of hand-written and sometimes typed notes documenting her father's research in preparation for trial. Mostly the notes concerned witness interviews. "Interesting," Libby said softly.

"What is?"

Nick was staring at her, and she blushed, realizing that she'd been talking to herself. She pointed to the pages in front of her. "I'm reading notes from an interview Dad had with a detective. Apparently after Henderson was arrested for the Arbor Falls killings, a few mugging victims in a separate investigation identified him. Looks like he used to hang out near bus stops and rob old ladies." Libby shook her head. "Scumbag."

Nick folded his arms across his chest and looked at the wall, apparently deep in thought. "What is it?" she asked.

"Maybe nothing." He turned to face her. "But don't you think it's odd that a man would transition from mugging old ladies to playing some twisted psychological game?"

Libby blinked. "What do you mean?"

"In my experience criminals have their…modus operandi. They act in a way that works for them, and they don't tend to stray from that path."

"Sure, but there are plenty of criminals who evolve," she reasoned. "I've handled too many domestic violence cases to count, and I've seen abuse progress from verbal insults to murder. It happens."

Nick ran a hand through his thick, golden-brown hair as he thought. "I guess I don't see it that way."

"Oh? Then how do you see it?"

"In a domestic violence case, the abuse doesn't change, it just becomes progressively worse. It's a matter of degree. Here, you have a complete shift. If Will Henderson committed these crimes, we have to believe that he changed from a low-level creep who stole purses to a serial killer. And not just any serial killer, but a killer who tormented his victims and their families for days. He went from committing crimes of opportunity to becoming a calculated killer." Nick grew silent, his mouth forming a tight line. "I've dealt with serial killers before, and something isn't adding up."

She shrugged. "I suppose it's not fair of us to presume Henderson was guilty of those muggings when he was never brought to trial on those charges. Innocent until proven guilty." Something on Nick's face made her pause. "Why—what are you thinking?"

He looked down at a stack of papers in front of him, but she could tell that he was gathering his thoughts. "Maybe your dad locked up the wrong guy. Maybe Henderson was a mugger but not a killer. That could explain why someone would want revenge."

Libby's face grew hot. "Are you accusing my father of knowingly prosecuting the wrong person?" She tried without success to keep her voice from trembling.

"Not knowingly, Libby." He held up his palms. "We can't assume that. But I'm trying to explore all of the possibilities. Think about the pressure the police must have been under to find the Arbor Falls Strangler. Mistakes could have been made. Maybe they reached a dead end with the investigation and Henderson took the fall."

Could it be possible? Had her father locked up the wrong suspect in the case that made his career? Her heart flailed in her chest and her hands shook. "My father was an honorable man. This is all speculation. We don't even have any evidence."

The metal door slammed shut behind him. They both jumped. "The doorstop must have been loose," Nick said, and he stood and walked to the door. He turned the doorknob, but it wouldn't budge. "That's strange," he mumbled.

Libby's face was burning as she returned to the documents before her. She needed to calm down and remain levelheaded if she was going to get through these boxes in time. "What's strange?"

"The door is stuck." Nick twisted and turned the doorknob, but it held resolutely still. He started knocking on the door. "There must be someone out there in the warehouse who can help us."

"Wait a minute." The blood drained from Libby's face as she rose from her chair. "Are you saying we're locked in here?" So much for remaining calm.

"I'm sure someone will hear us," Nick replied, but the tone of his voice did little to reassure her. He began pounding on the door, and the sound of his fist on the metal echoed through the room.

She pulled out her cell phone. "I have John's number. I'll give him a call." She frowned at the screen. "Shoot. I don't get a signal here."

"I'll check mine." He pressed a few buttons and waited. "I have a signal, but it's spotty. My call isn't going through."

Libby's breath came in shallow gasps. Nick turned to her, his eyes wide with concern. "Libby, have a seat. I'll take care of this."

She was frozen, her chest tightening as she felt how small the room was. She eased herself back into her chair and leaned forward until her head was between her knees. Breathe, she told herself. There's plenty of air.

But then her eyes were drawn to the corner of the room, where a thin white line was trailing from one of the boxes. *Smoke.* "Nick," she whispered, her throat clenched.

He was pounding on the door with both fists now and shouting for help. He didn't hear her. Libby was frozen. The smoke was coming out of the holes in the sides of the box, gathering thickly and bouncing off the ceiling to collect at the top of the room. "Nick," she repeated, only slightly louder.

He continued to hammer at the door with his fists and then turned to throw his shoulder against the door. He bounced off and winced, rubbing his arm. Finally his gaze caught on the same spot where Libby's gaze was transfixed. His eyes widened. "Libby," he said.

"Fire!" She jumped from her seat as a burst of energy coursed like a jolt of electricity through her marrow. Her muscles twitched, and she thought for a moment that she might be able to scratch through the cinder-block walls. "Oh, God." She joined Nick and started beating on the door. "Help us!" She grabbed the doorknob, twisting and pulling at it.

Nick raced to the smoking box and threw it to the floor. Flames leaped out the sides. "We have to smother it!" He stomped on the box, but that only succeeded in sending flaming pieces of paper flying. The fire began to spread.

"Why isn't the alarm going off?" Libby was nearly hyperventilating as the room filled with smoke. *Not this way,* she thought to herself. *I'm not dying this way.* She looked around and saw a red light on the ceiling. A smoke detector. "Nick, we have to set off the alarm," she shouted.

He raced to Libby's side. "I'll lift you up. See if you can set it off manually."

Nick crouched down to wrap his muscular arms around Libby's thighs, squeezing her tightly before hoisting her toward the ceiling. The room was bathed in a thick haze of smoke, and Libby fumbled blindly around the alarm, trying to find a button of some kind. "I don't feel anything," she said.

"Keep looking," said Nick, his voice hoarse. He coughed.

She pressed her fingers against the plastic. "Nick, there may not be anything. It was just a guess." She stopped as the smoke detector cover twisted off in her hand. A strangled scream escaped from the back of her throat.

Nick tensed. "What happened?"

"I broke it." Libby started to squirm. "Put me down. Now!" He obliged and Libby tossed the cover of the smoke detector onto the table. Her eyes were stinging. "What are we going to do?"

Nick looked around the room and then pointed to the ceiling. "I think I see a sprinkler." He opened the nearest box and removed a thick stack of papers.

Libby coughed, trying to lift the weight settling into her lungs. "What are you doing?"

"I'm going to set off the sprinkler." He folded the papers lengthwise and held one end over the burning box. Once the paper caught fire, he sprinted to the sprinkler and held the flames against it. They waited.

"Nothing's happening!" She was on the floor where the air was less smoky, her breath sputtering.

The papers in his hand were burning furiously. Nick dropped them to the ground and doubled over in a coughing fit just as a bell began to ring. Seconds later a spray of dirty water streamed from the sprinkler.

Nick lowered himself to the ground and crawled to Libby, who was still seated by the door and coughing. "Are you okay?" He placed one hand on the back of her head and lifted her face with the other.

She gripped his forearms and nodded, still unable to talk. Several sprinklers were spraying now, and the floor was covered with cold water. Nick pulled Libby against him and wrapped his arms around her. "It's working," he said, and the feel of his lips against her ear sent a shiver down her spine.

Nick's hard body was warm amid the cold of the sprinklers, and the press of his arms around her shoulders felt so reassuring. Libby allowed herself to ease into the familiar comfort of his embrace as the water poured around them and the suffocating smoke began to dissipate.

They were sitting in this position, shivering, when Libby felt a rush of air and saw a figure in the doorway. It was John, the warehouse manager. "What's going on in here?" He coughed as the smoke billowed into his face.

Nick sprang to his feet, pulling Libby with him as he ran out of the room. Libby choked as clean air filled her lungs, and she again doubled over in a fit of coughing. When she looked up, Nick had John's back pressed against the wall, and was gripping the man's shirt in his fists. "Nick, stop!" She ran to his side.

"I want some answers!" Nick was inches from the man's face.

John had his hands up. "I don't know anything! Please!" His eyes were wide.

"Tell me who shut that door!"

"Nick." Libby placed her hand on his arm. "Please, stop."

He clutched the shirt tighter, but then let go. John scurried out of reach, smoothing his shirt front with shaking hands. "I heard the alarm go off and came to see whether you two were all right. The fire department is on its way. And of course, the police will follow."

"Someone shut the door and locked us in there," Libby said.

"I swear, I don't know anything. I came to help."

Nick stepped forward, approaching him until their faces were inches apart. "You mean to tell us you have no idea who could've come by here and shut us in a room with a burning box?"

"Someone must have messed with the door. It shouldn't have locked from the inside like that." He met Nick's gaze. "And I told you—I don't know anything."

They heard sirens outside the warehouse, and moments later a group of firemen streamed into the building. Nick and Libby stepped aside to let them through, and John walked toward a group of employees. Libby realized for the first time that she and Nick were soaking wet, their clothes covered in the black filth that had come streaming from the sprinklers. She shivered.

"Libby," Nick said as he tried to place a hand on her shoulder. "Are you—"

"I'm fine," she said, and then stepped just out of his reach.

She didn't know what had happened in that room, when she'd suddenly felt content to sit in Nick's arms for the rest of eternity. Adrenaline, she reasoned. Nothing more. Life and death situations frequently brought people together. Whatever she'd felt, she couldn't indulge it. Thank goodness for fresh air and clarity of thought.

One of the firemen came out of the room, holding the smoke detector in his gloved hand. "You two all right?"

"We will be," Nick replied. He nodded to the smoke detector. "You should take a look at that. It didn't even go off."

"Yeah, well—" the fireman lifted it up to show them and continued "—it's a fake."

Libby's heart froze. "What do you mean, it's a fake?"

"It looks like someone has created a fake smoke detector. See? It's hollow." He showed it to Libby. "The real alarm was connected to the sprinklers."

She narrowed her eyes. She hadn't noticed with all of the smoke, but sure enough, the smoke detector was nothing more than a hollow piece of plastic, a battery and a red light. Nick cursed under his breath.

"The police will check it for fingerprints." The fireman scratched at his forehead. "A locked door, a fire and a fake smoke detector, huh? I don't want to scare you, but..." He looked at Libby and Nick with concern. "Let's just say that it looks deliberate. You should talk to the police." He returned to process the scene, leaving Nick and Libby alone.

Nick pulled two pairs of latex gloves from his jacket and handed one pair to Libby. "Fingerprints," he explained.

She pulled on the pair of gloves and picked up the smoke detector from its resting place on the table. She turned it over in her hands, spotting something white inside. "Wait a minute," she said, and ran her fingernail on the inside of the plastic. She caught the object and pulled it through the crack. A small piece of paper.

"What is that?" asked Nick.

His question was drowned out by the pounding of her heart in her ears as she clutched the paper with shaking fingers. Nick coaxed the paper from her hands and unfolded it. His face reddened as he read the message. "Nick, what's it say?"

She took the paper back from him, her stomach twisting. There were only three words on it, a message written in a childish scrawl: *Three more days.*

Libby's mouth went dry. "The fourth sign," she whispered.

As they locked gazes she could see the fury on Nick's face. Somehow, the killer had found them.

Chapter 9

"We walked right into his trap!" Nick brought his fist down on the roof of his car. "I knew the clue could lead us into harm, but I took precautions. I had my gun, I secured the scene...." He stopped and shook his head.

"It's impossible." Libby was talking to herself more than responding to Nick. She leaned against the hood of the vehicle and crossed her arms. "It's impossible that this was the plan."

He snorted. "Seems pretty damn possible to me."

"No, this couldn't have been the plan." She looked at him. "The D.A.'s Office keeps most of its records in Ridgefield. Some were moved here temporarily when the Ridgefield unit had flooding problems, including *State v. Henderson,* but he couldn't have known that. The files were just moved two weeks ago, and I only learned about it this morning when I called over to the D.A.'s Office." She chewed on her thumbnail, which did nothing to quell the anxious energy pulsing through her veins.

"But you knew that the files had been moved."

"Yes, but only because I had access to that information through work."

Nick furrowed his brow. "He could have known where those files were if he works with you."

That was the obvious conclusion to draw, but hearing it out loud made Libby sick to her stomach. Did someone at work want to kill her? She thought of the look on Greg's face on Monday when she interrogated him about her reputation for being uptight. No one would want to kill her for being uptight or insensitive…right? She ran through her list of colleagues and tried to assign a motive to each one.

"That can't be right. No one who worked on the Henderson case works there anymore. It can't be a colleague." She took a breath. She knew she was on edge, but she didn't need to be paranoid.

Nick leaned next to her, and they watched the police officers interrogate the warehouse employees. An investigator had discovered a homemade remote controlled device in the box that had caught fire and black paint on the lens of the security camera watching the room. One of the warehouse employees had readily admitted to pulling those boxes but claimed he had no idea that one box had been rigged. Libby believed he was telling the truth.

"That device could have been planted weeks ago," Nick said. "Months, even. We don't know how long this whole scheme has been in the works."

"True," she admitted. "But the note in the fire detector? That had to have been planted more recently because the files were just moved here. And I'm wondering if it was planted today." She fumbled for her cell phone.

He shifted. "Who are you calling?"

"I know the warehouse manager in Ridgefield. I want to know what that smoke detector looks like."

When the Ridgefield warehouse manager answered, she gave him some background and asked him to check the smoke detector in the file review room. "It's a fake," she announced as she snapped her cell phone shut. "And there was a note inside that said it was the fourth sign."

He slid his palm over the stubble on his cheek as he thought. "So the killer must have been expecting us to go to Ridgefield. That's where he'd set the trap. But instead, we came here, and he *still* found us."

Libby wrapped her arms around herself. An hour after they'd fled the room, she was still damp, and the light breeze did nothing to help the chill seeping into her skin. All she could think about was getting back to the hotel and crawling into a hot bath again.

"How did he know, Nick? Are we wired? Is our room being bugged?"

"I've checked. I've checked every damn thing." He gritted his teeth.

The Stillborough police sergeant Jay Katz approached them and grasped Nick's hand. "Nick, Libby. We'll be here for a while yet, but we have your statements. You're free to go."

"What are you learning, Sergeant?" Nick folded his hands across his chest.

"Not too much yet." Katz scratched at the corner of his eye. "Seems there may have been some kind of break-in recently. We found some scratches on a back door that the manager says weren't there last night. We also found what appears to be a remote controlled device on the door that may account for it suddenly closing on you. I'll let you know if we find anything else after we've had some time to process the scene."

Libby tugged at his sleeve. "Nick, the files."

"I need the contents of those boxes, Sergeant. The ones in the room. I'm on a case."

Katz squinted into the sunlight. "I'll see what I can do. I can probably get them to you within a week or so."

"I need them tonight."

The sergeant emitted a loud laugh. "Hey, you're funny, man. C'mon, you know how it is. These things take time."

Nick leaned in closer. "Look, I don't have time. I need these documents tonight, and I'm willing to cut a deal."

Katz was still smirking. "What kind of deal?"

"Information for information." Nick kept his voice level. "You want to impress the Stillborough mayor? Be a regular hero to the Stillborough residents?"

"I'm listening."

Nick smiled slightly. "Stillborough likes its crystal. It's no secret, Sergeant. It's a little town with a big meth habit. I understand you had an incident on Christmas Day. A meth lab in a two-family house exploded and two young children were killed in the fire. It made national news."

Katz reddened, looking slightly uncomfortable. "We're following up on leads."

"Of course you are," said Nick. "But what if I told you that the Bureau is watching the person who caused that explosion closely and that I can give you some insight to his location?" He shrugged nonchalantly and stuck his hands in his pockets. "We have an informant. Your boy is a small player in a big drug ring we've had our eye on for a long time."

"Are you serious?" Katz leaned in closer. "Don't jerk me around—"

"I'm quite serious, Sergeant. You make that arrest, and you'll be a local hero, tough on crime, tough on drugs." Nick touched his shoulder and whispered, "We can work with you and make that arrest part of a larger drug bust, if you can hold out for a little while."

Katz did not move. "And you want copies of those documents in return?"

"Tonight. It has to be tonight."

Katz sucked his teeth, and his face twisted as he thought, but after a few moments had passed, he turned to Nick and said, "Deal." He extended his hand.

Nick broke into a broad smile and accepted the sergeant's handshake. "I'll be in touch, then."

Libby grabbed his arm as Katz walked away. "Nick," she whispered, "you did it!" Hotheaded Nick had just coolly negotiated a deal. In their entire relationship he'd never amazed her as much as he had over the past two days.

The corner of his mouth rose in a grin. "You didn't actually think I'd let you leave here without those files, did you?"

"I guess I never took you for a diplomat. You're full of surprises." She realized she was still gripping his arm. His biceps felt like steel beneath her fingertips— taut, barely restrained masculinity. She released him.

"It's good that we'll be able to review those documents, after all."

His face grew solemn. "You heard what he said about the break-in? The killer may have come out here this morning to set this trap."

She shivered. "No one at the D.A.'s Office knew we were coming here. I spoke to the records administrator, but I've known him for years and we're friendly. It's not him." Nick was silent, so she continued. "I'm guessing that whoever set that trap expected to destroy the files. Maybe it would be best if no one else knew we had copies. If you understand."

A shadow crossed his face. "No one in Arbor Falls will know we have those files." His voice was tight.

Libby didn't have to say anything more. Dom Vasquez knew they were going to the Stillborough warehouse. He was the only one who knew.

Dom wasn't the killer. Rationally, Nick knew that. But there were too many coincidences he couldn't explain.

Dom was the only one who knew they were staying at Nick's parents' house, and that's where the third sign was delivered. He was the only one who knew they were going to the Stillborough warehouse, where the fourth sign was delivered. Dom *didn't* know that they were staying at the Ascher House, and no threat had appeared there. Too many coincidences.

He waited in the suite while Libby took a long bath, focusing on not thinking about her, soapy and wet, only paces away from where he sat. He was unsuccessful. She was all he could think about—curled up against him in the chaos of the warehouse or moaning softly in his ear against the wall of the suite the night before. He wanted her, and he had a sizable amount of evidence below his belt to prove it, and it was all damn inconvenient.

Regret settled in his belly. Nick had moved too quickly last night, scared her off. She wouldn't talk about what had happened between them, which was a relief because he didn't know. He hadn't been looking for a relationship when he'd made that advance, he'd been thinking about getting relief for the raging desire that had plagued him almost from the moment he saw her again. He shifted, painfully aware that he hadn't succeeded on that front, either.

He didn't want a relationship. He knew that much. Everything about Libby and their shared history warned him off. He'd trusted her with his heart and she'd dumped him. Crumpled him up and thrown him out. Then again, last night at dinner Nick had started to understand for the first time why they'd broken up. It wasn't because Libby had met someone else and had betrayed his trust. Maybe it was because he'd betrayed *her* trust by asking her to give up a career she loved so he could pursue a career *he* loved. Maybe he'd demanded too much.

He paced the room, still chilled from his damp clothing and eager to get into the shower himself. He'd demanded too much…but that didn't excuse the iciness of that last conversation, or the way she'd informed him that despite all of their years together, she didn't love him. She'd delivered the message with measured cruelty. The memory still cut.

He'd chosen to protect her knowing that she'd been disturbingly unaffected by their breakup. He'd expected her to be icy, stringent and uptight, exactly as her father had groomed her to be since she'd entered the legal profession. He hadn't expected her to show him glimpses of the softer, more sensitive Libby, the girl he fell in love with when they were twelve years old. The smart, tough girl who wasn't afraid to cry or fuss over babies. The woman he'd wanted to marry and have children with. The woman he'd wanted to devote his life to.

She'd thrown him for a loop.

Nick brought his hands down on the table by the bay window and looked outside at the bright afternoon. She seemed to be the old Libby, but he'd be foolish to get involved again. He'd given her some of the best years of his life and then asked her to marry him, and none of that had been enough to win her love in return. Loving her had left him vulnerable. He wouldn't let his guard down again.

The sooner he accepted this opportunity with Libby as the chance to smooth over old hurt before moving on, the better. They were over.

He sat in the chair by the window, picked up his BlackBerry and checked his inbox. He had an email regarding his transfer that stated he would be relocating to Washington, D.C., that summer. This was the assignment he'd wanted, and yet his first thought was that he'd be ten hours away from Libby instead of five.

He shook his head. *Snap out of it*.

Nick looked out the window, strumming his fingers on the table. He considered calling Dom. He should tell him about the latest threat, maybe gauge his response. His shoulders knotted against his neck. If Dom really was the killer, wouldn't he suspect that they were on to him if Nick didn't maintain contact? Shouldn't he continue the charade?

He dialed Dom's number. "Dom. It's Nick. Thought you should know we received the fourth sign today. Bastard locked us in the file review room at the Stillborough warehouse and rigged one of the file boxes to catch fire."

Dom mumbled something in Spanish. "When did this happen? Just now?"

"A few hours ago."

"And you didn't bother to call me?" His voice pitched. "I could have been at the scene! Now I've gotta go piece things together with the Stillborough P.D."

Nick gripped the phone. "We spoke with Sergeant Katz. They were well-organized and methodical, and I'm sure they'll cooperate with you."

Silence. He heard Dom breathing and shuffling around. "Nick, I need you to tell me where you are. I can't protect you and Libby unless I know that, and this guy is always a step ahead."

He tensed. Nick had trusted his partner with his life for years, but he couldn't trust him any longer. "I can't tell you that."

"Why the hell not?"

He rubbed at his forehead. "It's safer this way."

Dom let out a string of curses and then lapsed into a long silence. When he spoke again, his tone was ominous. "You call me from now on if there are any developments. Got it?"

Nick hesitated but then hung up without responding. He felt queasy. Dom had done little to settle his suspicions.

* * *

Sergeant Katz called Nick late in the afternoon to tell him that the documents were ready. "There was a lot of damage," Nick explained to Libby. "We'll have to do what we can to piece it all together."

They drove to meet one of the Stillborough officers at a neutral location in the center of town because Nick didn't want anyone to know where they were staying. Libby noticed that he was on high alert—his body was tense, and she caught him stealing furtive glances at their surroundings. After they received the boxes of documents, Nick drove to a grocery store and they picked up nonperishable snacks and dinner.

"No going out tonight," he said. "We can't risk it. Tomorrow morning we're packing up and heading somewhere new."

They used to sit in a companionable silence when dating, but now the silence felt like another person in the room as they avoided a discussion of the night before and what it had meant. Nothing, she told herself. The encounter couldn't mean anything because she and Nick couldn't be together. She couldn't deny that her heart still warmed every time he smiled, or that he had a unique ability to make her feel safe under this most trying circumstance, but she couldn't pursue those feelings. Not when she knew how much Nick wanted children. She'd only be setting up heartbreak for both of them.

As if he could read her thoughts, he reached over and took her hand carefully in his. "I'm going to make some hotel coffee when we get back, and we're going to go through these boxes and do our best to figure out why this guy is after you." He gave her hand a squeeze.

Libby brought her other hand on top of his and held on to him.

Half an hour later they'd cleared an area on the floor of the suite and were going through the boxes. Intermittently they searched leads on the internet to see what they could uncover. They worked through dinner, silently reading the files and making notes. Libby rose to draw the curtains long after the sun had set and noticed Nick looking at her. She gave him a wan smile.

"So, are you finding anything?" she asked.

"More than expected. I keep coming across all of these campaign flyers for Jebediah Sinclair." He picked one of the flyers up and handed it to her.

"Of course." Libby nodded as she read the flyer. "Jeb Sinclair. He and my dad were good friends. David, my boyfriend, is his son."

Nick flinched. So he was her boyfriend now? He noticed her giving him a furtive sidelong glance before she continued.

"Gosh, I remember going door-to-door with Dad for Jeb Sinclair's re-election campaigns when I was a kid. We had campaign materials everywhere in the house, piles of flyers and mailers stacked in the hallway. Dad told me that he would take a bunch of flyers when he left in the morning and hand them out after work. And now that I see them in his files, I guess he wasn't kidding." She smiled. "I collected his campaign buttons. I think I had a few shoe boxes filled with them."

"Sinclair," Nick said thoughtfully. "I remember him. I never knew David, though."

"David went to private schools. I knew him when I was much younger but only recently met up with him again. Jeb was the longest-serving mayor of Arbor Falls. I think he was elected thirty-seven years ago, and he was one of Dad's biggest supporters when he ran for judge." She turned her gaze to a stack of papers, making a face as she looked at them. "I found copies of letters that Henderson sent his victims. They're similar to the one found beside the body of that poor girl. Sign one."

Nick glanced over the letters. Sure enough, the content was similar to the first sign and contained open threats and political nonsense. He frowned. "Henderson wrote this?"

"Well, yes. He committed the crimes. Why?"

"Because the handwriting on these letters doesn't look like the handwriting on his confession." Nick lifted the confession from its place on the top of his documents and put them side by side. "See? I don't think the same person wrote these letters. I'm going to ask to scan these at the front desk and send them over to an expert at the Bureau to see what she thinks. I'll ask her to put a rush on it."

Libby pursed her lips as she studied the confession. "He signed a confession? But there was a trial…." She traced her finger along as she read the scrawl. "Oh, I see. He only confessed to breaking and entering to plant the signs but not to committing the murders. The state had to try him for the murders."

"Six signs over six days. There was a pattern to them." He reached for a notepad and began reading. "Sign one is 'firing a warning shot.' He would send the victim a picture of themselves in the ordinary course of their day."

Libby's skin prickled. "That was the newspaper photo

he left at the scene of the murder. And of course he dressed the girl to look like me." She felt ill at the memory.

"Sign number two, he 'makes entry.' It seems Henderson liked to let himself into the victims' homes to plant that sign. Just like he did with your case file."

"Yes, I remember." Libby curled up with her back against a chair and drew her knees to her chest. All of a sudden she felt very cold.

"Sign number three, he sends a gift." His face darkened. "Is that what this bastard considered McAdams to be?"

Libby tucked her fingers beneath her knees and her teeth chattered. "God, Nick. It's like when cats leave their prey on the front steps. But maybe the gift wasn't McAdams, but the clue? That led us to these documents, and maybe it will give us a fighting chance to stop him."

His brow was knit tightly and he didn't respond, except to continue. "Sign number four was 'contact from afar': leaving threatening notes for the victim, just like the one he left in the smoke detector today. Which leads us to sign number five: 'the trap.'"

"A trap?" Libby pulled her knees closer.

"What the police learned during the investigation was that all of the victims escaped some kind of life-and-death situation before their actual death. One was mugged on the street, one was in a car accident." Nick's brow creased as he thought. "There were six victims total, and they were all a little different."

"Six victims," repeated Libby, clutching her hands together to stop her fingers from trembling. "God."

"Yes, but Henderson was only prosecuted for three

of them. The evidence on the other crimes wasn't strong enough."

Libby's stomach turned. "And do I even want to know what sign six is?"

"That's the thing." Nick spread his hands wide. "I can't find it anywhere. Henderson didn't say, and the victims never lived long enough to tell anyone about it."

"It all fits. He's following the pattern of the Arbor Falls Strangler." She felt hot as a wave of nausea churned her insides. She brought her trembling fingers to her mouth. "Does that mean he's going to try to kill me tomorrow?"

"Libby, no. Don't go there." Nick was at her side immediately, his arms wrapped tightly around her shoulders. "Tomorrow is another threat, but it's not the end. This is why we have these files, so we can anticipate what he's going to do and then try to stop him."

His arms felt strong and his body warm, but she couldn't stop shaking and she couldn't bring herself to speak. Images streamed through her mind. The murder victims. The fire in the warehouse. The photograph of her. She couldn't move, and she couldn't stop her mind from racing. Her chest felt as if it was being squeezed in a vise.

"Come on."

Nick lifted her gently as if she were weightless, tucking one arm underneath her curled legs and the other behind her back. He carried her to the bed and placed her on the mattress. Then he smoothed her hair back from her face. "No one's going to hurt you."

He held her hand and stroked her hair, and his eyes never left her face. Minute by minute, breath by breath, her breathing deepened, the shaking slowed and the pain in her chest subsided. She tightened her fingers around Nick's, and when he squeezed her hand back, her heart swelled in response. "Don't leave me. Please promise me."

He swallowed and his eyes softened. "I'm not leaving your side, honey. I promise."

She stroked the back of his hand with her thumb but didn't say any more. The promise only went so far because if she survived this ordeal, Nick would be gone again in a matter of days. A heavy sadness fell across her, pressing her further into the mattress. Closing her eyes, she attempted to memorize the feel of his hand wrapped around hers, to give her something to think about when he was gone and she was alone once again.

Chapter 10

Once Libby felt recovered, she and Nick continued to read through the Henderson files. He'd urged Libby to go to bed, but she was insistent.

After reading for a while, Nick looked up. "I'm learning more about this Will Henderson. Seems the police only began to suspect him after receiving a tip from an anonymous source. Until then, despite frequent brushes with the law for petty theft, he was never even on their radar. In terms of his criminal past, nothing I've seen suggests that he should have been considered for these crimes."

Libby didn't look up from the document she was reading. "We've been through this already. Lots of serial killers begin as petty criminals."

"But the crimes that serial killers begin with are more antisocial in nature. They set fires and torture animals.

Grabbing purses or stealing cigarettes doesn't seem to fit the profile."

"But Henderson told the police about the signs, right?" Libby sat back. "That's compelling evidence of his guilt."

Nick turned to her. "What are you thinking?"

"Let's assume the police had a bunch of evidence from the crime scenes, including a lot of things they didn't understand or view as significant. Let's also assume that they never told Henderson about this evidence. Wouldn't it be strong evidence of Henderson's guilt if, as part of his confession, he was able to explain the significance of evidence the police never told him they had?"

Nick nodded. "Yeah, sure. False confessions are common, so we hold back details all the time. If the person confessing to a crime can explain those details, it's an indication that the person is telling the truth."

"And Henderson explained the signs in his confession. He gave the police additional information about the cases." Libby gave him a triumphant smile. "So you see? Henderson *must* have been the killer. Even if it doesn't make absolute sense for a petty thief to become a serial killer, this is great evidence that in this case, it happened that way."

"Libby, I understand why you would be relieved about Henderson being the Strangler," Nick began slowly. "After all, that means your dad prosecuted the right person. But if Henderson was the real killer, that doesn't tell us who is threatening you now, or why. There must be something else going on with this case."

"Did he have a wife?" Libby asked. "Kids? Maybe we should talk to them."

"No kids, and the wife died while Henderson was in jail. She took her own life shortly after her husband was sentenced."

Libby winced.

"There's one other problem with Henderson being the killer. I found a note about an eyewitness who was interviewed early on in the investigation. She claimed to see someone lurking around the second victim's home. According to this witness, she saw this person leaving the scene of the crime, his clothes covered in blood."

"Eyewitness testimony?" Libby's eyebrows rose. "I'm confused. I thought there hadn't been any eyewitnesses to the crime."

"I thought the same thing. But then I saw this note. Clearly there was an eyewitness, but she was never called upon to testify at trial."

Libby frowned, her whole face a jumble of confusion. "Well, why on earth wouldn't Dad call an eyewitness to testify at Henderson's trial?"

"From what I can figure, it's because the eyewitness would have sworn that Henderson wasn't the one she saw that day."

Libby paled. "Wait a minute. Let me get this straight." She leaned forward. "Will Henderson signed a confession. Not only did he confess to planting the signs, but he gave the police reliable information about the evidence they had collected, further strengthening his confession. And now you're telling me that there was an eyewitness who would have testified that Henderson *wasn't* the person she saw leaving the second victim's house, covered in blood?"

"Here, you can see for yourself." Nick handed her a file.

Libby sifted through the file, which contained several newspaper clippings about a victim's neighbor who claimed to have seen the killer brazenly leaving her house in broad daylight. "'Harriet McGovern,'" she read aloud. "Oh, shoot—she was seventy-three at the time."

"Yeah, seventy-three forty-one years ago. We're not getting an interview."

Libby continued to sort through the papers in the file, coming across handwritten notes on sheets of yellowing paper. "Looks like Dad had the opportunity to sit down with Harriet." She squinted. "Is this even written in English?"

"Here, I've always had an easier time reading your dad's writing." Nick took the paper. "This says that Harriet was having tea on her porch at three o'clock in the afternoon when she saw a man leaving the victim's house, covered in blood."

"Did she say what the man looked like?"

"It looks like she did, if I'm reading this correctly." Nick had his finger against the paper as he focused on the barely legible writing. "She said he was extremely tall, well over six feet. Light brown hair. Does that say red?" He showed the paper to Libby.

"It looks like ruddy. Ruddy face." She sat back. "That's an interesting description. So she saw an extremely tall man with light brown hair and a ruddy face. I found a few pictures of Will Henderson on the internet, but I didn't see anything about his build."

"I did. Henderson was no taller than five foot eight,

with fair skin and dark hair. Here." Nick showed her Henderson's mug shot.

"It doesn't seem likely that Henderson would be confused with an extremely tall man with light hair." Her tone was quiet.

"No. It doesn't."

She brushed her hair behind her ears. "It doesn't add up. Maybe Dad made a mistake, after all."

She looked down at the floor, staring silently at nothing. His body tensed. The past few days were more than anyone should have to deal with.

"Hey," he said, touching her arm lightly. "Why don't you go to bed. Get a good night's sleep."

She paused, trailing her gaze across his face. "Is that really what you wanted to say?"

Nick's stomach tensed. That was one of the things he wanted to say, but he had a hundred more to add. He wanted to know what had happened between them, how they could have gone from best friends and lovers to virtual strangers.

"I'm trying to make this better, Libby. I'm trying to fix this so you can go back to your normal life." He brushed his fingers through his hair. "I really do want you to sleep well tonight. You need to get some rest."

She was quiet. "What if this is all I have, Nick? What if tonight is it?" Her widened pupils were surrounded by her brilliant blue irises.

"It's not," he replied, feeling the words catch around the tension in his throat. "You'll live to be a hundred."

"But you don't know that. All I have is today." She paused before rising and walking to the arm of the couch, where she perched like a small bird.

"Libby."

He said it without knowing what would follow. There was nothing more to say, and he didn't want to lie to her. All of his professional training and preparation had taught him that she was right. Nothing was guaranteed. If he was honest with himself, he'd have to admit that this could be their last night together. But he couldn't face that honesty. Not now.

Libby pulled at the charm bracelet on her wrist. It chimed softly when she moved. "This was my mom's. Dad gave it to me the Christmas after she died. He took me and Cassie to Sarasota. He told us that Christmas was canceled." She twisted her mouth as the pain of the memory rose in her throat. "It was miserable."

Nick shifted. "I can imagine."

"When Christmas came, it was like we spent the whole day avoiding it. I had this giant book that I was reading so I didn't have to talk to anyone. Cassie was angry with Dad about something...I forget what." She shrugged. "It was easier for her to be angry with Dad than with God. I can't even tell you what we ate for dinner. We were thousands of miles from home, isolated in a beachfront hotel, and we barely spoke a word all day. And then, after dinner, Dad wanted to take a walk on the beach."

Nick studied her. "You never told me about any of this."

She tightened her fists against the ache of the memory. That Christmas, night had fallen early, but the remains of dusk clung to the horizon. Libby had taken off her shoes and walked on the sand, not caring that it was too chilly. In that place, so vastly different from home, she'd been haunted by thoughts of her mother—the way she'd held Libby's hand while she'd napped during chemotherapy treatments, or the way she'd hugged her after school and asked about her day. Her mother had been the most constant presence in her life, and Libby had visualized the pain in her chest that Christmas Day as a cavity filled by the bottomless depths of her absence. Everything else had felt numb.

Her mother was supposed to have had more time. She was supposed to have been at the breakfast table the morning after she kissed Libby goodbye. She should have been there to pick out her prom dress and to send her off to college. Libby pulled the bracelet tightly against her wrist, allowing its sharp edges to pinch. *You were supposed to have been there when the doctors told me I couldn't have children. You were still supposed to be my mother.*

"We stopped at a spot on the beach near a palm tree strung with white lights. That's where Dad told us about Mom." Her throat ached from holding back the emotion, and she swallowed before continuing. "He told us to remember that her favorite color was blue and that she wore a perfume that smelled like lily of the valley. He told us to remember that she hated the snow and liked to be barefoot and that she would have wanted us to be somewhere warm for that first Christmas without her. Then he gave Cassie a locket, and he gave me this." She fingered the charm bracelet. "It was Mom's. He told me that he used to watch me sit on her lap when I was a toddler and play with it. I liked the treasure chest and the piano. See? Because they both open and close."

He smiled faintly. "I see."

Libby dropped her wrist to her lap and frowned. "Then he told us that Mom was gone and that we should bury her there, on that beach." Her chin trembled. "He said that we had to be strong. Emotions were signs of weakness, and he would never talk about her again. And he never did." The tears welled in her eyes, and blinking sent them streaming down her cheeks. "But Cassie and I talked about her all the time, in secret. She was our mother."

Nick had grown strangely quiet. His jaw was set firmly and his body was tense.

Libby stuttered a sigh, her breath jagged. "I've never been good at emotions. I've never been comfortable with telling people how I feel or what I want." She folded her hands and unfolded them, then rubbed her fingers together. "I've led a...measured life. I plan for the future. I meet my goals. I don't like surprises. And all of that was fine when I assumed there would always be a tomorrow."

"There's going to be a tomorrow, Libby."

"We can't know that. If you hadn't stayed with me this week, there may not have been a now. I can't assume there's a tomorrow. Not anymore. And there's so much left to do." She slouched her shoulders and stared at the floor, which was nearly covered in white photocopied documents. "Nothing is how I wanted it to be. I thought I'd be married or at least in love. I thought I'd be on my way to being a judge. I thought...I'd be a mother." She swallowed tightly as her eyes began to water.

Nick shifted to his knees. "Don't talk this way. There's going to be time for all of those things."

"No."

She looked straight at him. The life-or-death situation her stalker was supposed to put her in tomorrow could end in death; nothing was certain any longer. She should tell him the truth, right now. Tell him about that doctor's appointment that had changed both of their lives. Ask him to forgive her for breaking up with him before he could break up with her. Maybe show him that when she'd set him free, she was only trying to be noble. Even if it didn't seem that way.

She blinked back the tears. Who was she kidding? She couldn't tell him any of those things. If he wasn't angry with her, he'd think she was pitiful, and she couldn't bear either. "There's no more time," she sniffed. "I only have tonight."

He spoke slowly, as if he was weighing every syllable. "And what do you want, then? What do you want if tonight is all you have?"

She looked into his dark eyes. "I don't want to be alone." The words came from some deep place that she hadn't known existed. "I want to be with you."

The minute she said it, her pulse went wild. She couldn't believe those words had come from her. She'd never been so honest. Not in an emotional way. As she sat on the arm of the couch waiting for Nick to digest that last statement, she felt as if all of her clothing had been suddenly stripped away. She trembled against an unseen current.

But he was quiet. She watched him watch the floor as he weighed his response, hesitating and deep in his own head. Her heart thundered in her chest as the silence stretched, continuing into uneasiness. She'd opened herself up, and she'd made a terrible miscalculation. "Say something. Please."

A shadow crossed his face as he turned to look at her for the first time since hearing her confession. "You know I'm not going to leave you tonight. I promised you that already."

Her heart plummeted to the pit of her stomach. He was rejecting her. A hot flush of shame smeared her cheeks. She'd practically asked him to sleep with her, and he was rejecting her. She was a complete fool. When she spoke, her lips trembled. "I'm sorry." She didn't know what else to say.

She stumbled to her feet, feeling unsteady. He rose and tried to take her hand in his, but she pulled it out of his reach. "Libby, I confused things last night. I shouldn't have—"

"Forget it. I have."

"Wait." He reached out to grab her by the arm. "Please wait. Let me explain."

There was a rushing in her ears. She didn't want his explanation. She didn't want his pity. "You don't need to explain anything." She tugged at her arm. "Let me go." He released his grip.

She walked toward her room, stepping around the piles of documents on the floor. All of that information and hours of research, and they weren't any closer to finding out who was after her. Someone wanted to kill her, and would it have killed *Nick* to be a little more sympathetic?

He ran in front of her to stand in the doorway, blocking her retreat. "I don't know what you want. You rejected me." She was startled to hear the still-raw pain in his voice. "You told me that you didn't love me and that you never had."

Libby paused as a resounding pang struck her square in the chest. She recognized her own words. Hard words, designed to hurt Nick, to punish him for wanting to join the FBI and move her away from Arbor Falls. To punish him for wanting a family, because that hurt more than anything. They were words designed to make him hate her as much as she'd hated herself when she said them. Even now, almost three years after she'd uttered them, they packed a punch when thrown back at her.

"I really hurt you." She saw it in the tension between his brows and in the way his mouth was shut tightly. The evidence was all over his face. "Nick, I'm sorry."

"I adored you, you know that? I would've done anything for you. I worked hard to establish myself so we could have a future together. A nice house, little Nicks and Libbys running around." He wavered slightly. Then he slid his hand to the back of his neck. "I don't think you know how much I loved you. I don't think you ever knew."

Her chest was tight. She knew that he'd surprised her with flowers on her car when she'd had a bad day at work, or brought her to sit beside the bench at Arbor Falls when she needed to talk. She knew that Nick had discovered a million little ways to make her happy. No one since Nick had ever come close. Maybe she'd taken him for granted.

"I think I know now," she said softly.

His shoulders relaxed by a fraction. Libby was emboldened to continue. "But we couldn't have had a future together. You didn't accept me and my goals. Not really.

You wanted me to give up everything. You wanted me to leave my family and my career so that you could get what you wanted from your career. It wasn't fair to me."

Even as she said the words, she realized she was talking about much more than their careers. Maybe they could have eventually reached a compromise with their jobs. But fundamentally he needed her to be someone she wasn't. She could only disappoint him.

His shoulders tensed again. "I should have known better than to listen to your father."

She started. "My father? What in the world does he have to do with this?"

Nick folded his muscular arms across his chest. "He never approved of me, told me that he didn't want you wasting your time with some low-level cop. Then one day he let it slip that he admired FBI agents and that if I wanted to marry you, I should better myself by becoming one."

Libby's stomach dropped. "He told you to be an FBI agent."

"I expressed an interest and he encouraged me, indicating that this would be the way to win his approval. And I wanted his approval. I wanted him to approve of us." Nick paused and shook his head. "He knew full well that I'd be relocated once I was admitted. New agents aren't stationed in Arbor Falls, it's too small. He told me that he'd help in whatever way he could and that after I completed my rotation, we'd be able to return to Arbor Falls and he'd pull strings so that you could pick up right where you left off with the D.A. Now let me guess—while he was encouraging me to join the FBI, he was encouraging you to stay in Arbor Falls. I'll bet he told you that you deserved better than that and that I'd be stealing you away from your family and ruining your career."

Yes, that was pretty much exactly what her father had said. He'd said that Nick was selfish to even consider such a dangerous line of work, that he was only thinking of his own need for excitement. He'd told her that he knew for a fact that once she left her position with the D.A., it would be nearly impossible to come back. Tension drew her brows closer. Her father had encouraged their breakup. All of those nights she'd missed Nick, all of those years lost, and her father told her that she'd done the right thing and deserved better. That Nick was selfish and incapable of putting her first. She'd never told her father about her infertility, but he'd convinced her that Nick would never let Libby stand in the way of something he wanted. And Nick wanted a family.

And yet her father had lied to her. Nick had joined the FBI thinking that career would be better for *them,* not just for him. He'd thought he was putting their future first. Her stomach spun. Her father had exploited Nick's devotion to her. She'd been all wrong about both of them.

He continued. "So I was supposed to give up my career? To stay in Arbor Falls so that you could stay at the D.A.'s Office?"

"I don't know!" She threw her hands into the air. "I don't have any answers, either. But what's done is done. It's clear that we didn't belong together. That we still don't. Otherwise it would have been easy." She folded her arms.

His laugh rose from deep in his chest, but it was

edged with a gentleness. "Is that what you think? That it should have been easy?"

"Yes. Love should be easy if it's love."

He paused. "And is that why you said that you didn't love me? Because things between us weren't perfect and easy?"

No. She'd said it because she wanted him to leave without asking questions, and hadn't that been the perfect thing to say? But she supposed she had *also* said it because their relationship was so damned complicated. Perfect and easy would have been nice.

"Yes."

She couldn't read Nick's response—relief? Understanding? His face was softer now, although she didn't see what there was to be so relieved about. She'd explained why she hadn't loved him, not told him that she'd been wrong to say such a thing. "Maybe you didn't love me, either. Not really. You told me that I was difficult to love."

His mouth tensed into a thin line. "I was hurt when I said that."

"You said that I was uptight. Obsessive-compulsive. That I lived for control and that was an absurd way to live, that I can't expect to control every aspect of my life." She paused. "I'm trying to change that. I'm trying to loosen up a little."

He sighed. "I never had trouble loving you, Libby. Sometimes your quirks were annoying, like your wacky diets. But you were always easy to love. I hate that you'd want to change because of something I said."

"Not just because of something you said. Because I don't like who I am sometimes."

Like now, when she was an emotional mess. Her insides had gone to puddles, as if there was nothing holding her up. How many times had she rehearsed this moment when she gave Nick a piece of her mind? She hated that when that moment came, her voice trembled.

"I wish I was the kind of person who lit up the room and made other people laugh. I wish I could kick back and enjoy a few drinks without thinking about a vehicular homicide case I've got sitting on my desk or the first-degree murder that started with a backyard cookout. I wish I could...*lighten up*." To be more like Nick, who could be spontaneous and angry and passionate without giving a damn about what others might think.

"Lighten up?" His eyebrows shot upward. "You're idealistic. You dream of a better world. That's serious business, and I've always loved that about you. Your focus, your drive. Hell, I've worked hard to be more focused."

She looked away from the gaze he fixed on her, and she felt a warmth creep up her neck. This was all too much exposure. "Well, now that this is all cleared up, I'm going to bed."

"Libby." Her name on his lips was a statement in itself, filled with any number of unspoken words. "Don't leave like this."

"Why not? We're both tired. I see no point in dwelling on the past." She couldn't help the way her voice pitched, revealing her hurt. It was all wrong. She'd told him too much, and everything was all wrong.

He walked forward, took her hand and brought it to his lips. His mouth was soft as it crested the knuckles of her fingers then lighted on the sensitive skin on the underside of her wrist. Libby sucked in a breath, unable to take her hand back and not wanting him to relinquish his control over her.

Nick came closer still and tucked a hand around her throat, cupping her jaw. She parted her lips without thinking as he stroked her mouth with the pad of his thumb. "I told you," he whispered, "I'm not leaving you alone."

He lowered his mouth to hers, pressing softly at first, testing her response. She reached her arms around his waist, pulling him closer as the room slid away in that moment. His mouth was warm and his kiss skillful but reserved, familiar but brand-new.

He broke the contact gently and slipped his fingers between hers to lead her into the dark bedroom, flipping on the soft light of a table lamp. Even in that dim lighting Libby could make out the impressive outline of his arousal. Her knees felt soft, and her stomach went to knots. She'd never wanted anything as much as she wanted this moment with Nick.

He tugged at the strap of his leather belt, clicking metal, pulled it through his jeans and tossed it to the floor. He began to undress, lifting his shirt off and balling it before throwing it across a chair. She didn't even think of wrinkles—her focus was drawn to the ripples of his abdomen. He unbuttoned his pants, and Libby realized that she was fully dressed, watching him with her mouth slightly agape. "Nick, what—"

She'd been about to ask him what she was supposed to do. It wasn't as if she was a virgin. He'd been her first, but that was years ago. Still, she felt a newness in the experience, an uncertainty about the steps in the dance ahead.

"Last night I was in charge. Tonight it's your turn." There was no humor in his voice as he stood before her, fully naked and fully aroused. "Take control, Libby."

He climbed onto the bed and stretched on his back. Libby froze in place. "I don't…usually…"

"You know what to do." He tucked his hands behind his head. "Anything you want or nothing at all."

"What…is this some sort of weird therapy?"

"Yes. Didn't I tell you? I'm a psychotherapist now." Nick smirked good-naturedly. "For God's sake, Libby. It's sex. This is where you get to loosen up if you want, though to be honest, I've always preferred a stern mistress."

She approached him tentatively, then boldly reached out to stroke his side. The muscles tensed and quivered, and Nick sucked his breath through his teeth. "Go ahead. I won't even tell you to hurry up and take off your clothes."

"Don't rush me," she scolded him with a smile as she trailed her fingertips down his abdomen. Every square inch of him had pulled hard and tense, though some spots were evidently harder than others. He really was beautiful, composed of sharp angles and straight lines, his skin soft and smooth in the light of the lamp. And he wanted *her.* She grasped his length in her fingers and felt a shiver at the groan her touch elicited.

She disrobed slowly, teasing him, feeling her own arousal intensify as he watched her with a longing that she'd never seen before. She flung her shirt at him, and he reached up to catch it in one hand. She tossed her camisole at him and laughed as it bounced off his chest. He never took his eyes from hers except to trail his gaze down her body with a combination of pain and admiration. She'd never felt so powerful in her life.

"I'm not going to beg you." His eyes were half-closed as if he was in some kind of delightful agony. "But I wouldn't mind if you sped up a little."

"I don't have any such intention," she replied as she lowered her lips to his and slid her tongue into his mouth. His kiss had been chaste. She wanted to taste him fully, to satiate the hunger for him that nothing else satisfied. He responded with a growl from the back of his throat and arched up to thrust his tongue against hers. Libby pushed him back against the bed with a gentle hand. "Not so fast."

She was going to savor him, to enjoy the way he needed her. Watching him shiver at the slightest of her touches filled her with awe. He desired her in spite of who she was, or maybe because of it. She wished she could save this feeling, put it in a bottle and carry it with her.

"You're beautiful." Nick's voice was strained as he watched her. As she straddled him and leaned forward to run her tongue teasingly along his neck, he released another agonized groan. "Please."

"Now, now. You said I was in charge." She proceeded down his chest with soft, tantalizing kisses.

Her long hair swept across his skin as she moved, and he reacted with a series of gasps. "Libby. I can't take much more."

She sat up, and he reached for his pants. He removed a condom from his pocket and tore the wrapper.

"Please tell me you don't just carry those things around with you."

He shook his head. "Believe me, honey, my sex life is about to get much better than it has been in a long time."

Hers was, too.

He stretched onto his back and she mounted him, taking him inside of her with one slick movement. She moved slowly, teasing both of them as their bodies met, then parted. He palmed her breasts, squeezing them gently, and then pulled her down toward him so he could take the tight bud of one nipple in his mouth. She continued moving, feeling the tension inside of her build as he bit the side of her breast lightly and moaned into her soft flesh.

"I'm sorry. I can't take it."

He didn't need to apologize. She didn't mind that he gripped her hips and turned both of them over onto the bed. She certainly didn't mind as he claimed her like a man possessed, with hard fast thrusts and a thin layer of sweat coating his skin. Moments later she was lost. She dug her nails into his muscular shoulders and arched her back as wave after wave of pleasure rolled over her. When she was finished, she collapsed with a sigh as Nick stiffened and groaned his own release into her ear. He fell beside her on the bed.

He stroked her hair back from her face as they lay side by side, their limbs intertwined. "Libby, I'm sorry."

"For that? You have nothing to apologize for."

"No, not for that. For everything before that. For asking you to give up everything for me. It wasn't fair."

She traced his face with her fingertips, lingering on the rough stubble on his chin. "I'm sorry, too. In my own way, I was trying to get you to give everything up. I resented that you were joining the FBI, and I wanted you to stay. I just didn't know how to come out and say it." She brushed her thumb across his cheek. He took her hand and kissed her palm.

She shoved aside the thoughts of the world outside of that bedroom even as those worries crept up. For once in her life she wanted to be happy in the moment she was experiencing, to let the what-ifs fall away. Nick was warm beside her. Perfect moments were hard to come by.

She pulled closer to him, flinging her arm across his side and tucking her face into his neck, inhaling his spicy scent. "I feel safer with you around."

Nick kissed her forehead and stroked her hair. Within minutes they were both asleep.

Chapter 11

Cassie stomped around the hotel room. She'd woken that morning after having slept better than she had in months. Sam had slept for six hours straight, and consequently, so had Cassie. She couldn't remember the last time she'd slept so well, but it was certainly before pregnancy, which had given her insomnia and disrupted sleep for at least six of the nine months. Cassie had been in a good mood that morning. No, she'd been in a damn *glorious* mood. And then Libby had called.

Leave the hotel and go somewhere else. That was so typical of Libby to order her around. She could be such a know-it-all. And when she insinuated that Dom was under suspicion because he had the nerve to bring dinner to her last night…Cassie had almost hung up right then. He'd gone out of his way to bring her a meal, knowing she was locked in a hotel room with an infant and cut off from the rest of the world. He'd held her baby while she ate and talked with her about his day. And to her brilliant, socially inept sister, that spelled serial killer.

Cassie huffed. Well, if Libby was such a genius, she should have clued Cassie in as to where in the world she was supposed to go, because she was *not* moving every other day. Not with an infant.

He was a cranky infant at that, having missed his afternoon nap. He balled his hands into little fists and wailed from where he lay on a blue-striped receiving blanket. Cassie stopped her packing and sank down to the floor, resting her head in her hands. All of this because Dom had brought her Chinese takeout. If a gentleman paid her any attention, it must be because he was a psychopath or a scoundrel—was that Libby's reasoning? Cassie heaved a sigh. Libby thought Dom could be the killer, and Cassie knew he wasn't, but she was packing up her clothes and fleeing all the same. Because Libby always got her way.

But the more she thought about it, the more she resented her sister's order. Dom had escorted Cassie to a hotel and made her feel safe while Libby and Nick ran off to a secret location. She couldn't accept the thought that he would hurt her when all of her instincts told her that she could trust him.

She rolled her clothes loosely and tossed them into her duffel bag. She was tired of living in a hotel and hiding out. She was tired of being bossed around by her sister. Cassie lifted Sam and shushed him, cradling him against her chest and rocking him until he began to settle. She would not be spending another minute at a hotel, sleeping on a lumpy bed and eating food from a vending machine. She was going home.

She had to make three trips to the car before she'd finally packed everything. She grumbled with each round, stewing about how everything in the world seems that much closer to impossible when you're hauling an infant around and doing things one-handed. Libby had given Cassie some kind of baby carrier when Sam was born. Well, Libby called it a baby carrier, but it was nothing more than an endlessly long piece of fabric that Cassie was supposed to use to wrap Sam against her chest. This way, Libby had explained, she could have both hands free. Of course it was organic cotton, too—just another yuppie accessory. Cassie would need a college seminar and six months to figure out how to use it. At some point, it was easier to hold the baby with one hand and work with the other.

She checked out of the hotel and drove back to Arbor Falls, but as she drove, she began to second-guess her decision to go home. She pulled over and used her cell phone to look up the address. The directions were easy enough. He'd probably be home from work by now, and if he wasn't, she'd just turn around and head to her own house, no harm done. But she was relieved to see the lights on as she pulled in front of the condominium. Truth be told, she felt safer in the hotel room than she did now that she was back in Arbor Falls.

Sam was sleeping. She plucked his car seat out and carried him to the front door. Then she rapped three times, firmly.

Her pulse quickened at the sound of his footsteps. The porch light came on and the door swung open. "Cassie."

Dom was standing in a white T-shirt and gray sweatpants. His eyes looked tired behind his wire-rimmed glasses. She didn't know he wore glasses. They were sexy. "I'm sorry for showing up like this," she blurted out. "I left the hotel and I want to make sure it's safe to go to my house. Libby says I could be a target, too. That this is about something our father did." An unfamiliar anxiety tumbled around her stomach. "Is this a bad time?"

He looked confused for a split second, and then he looked from her to the baby and back to her. "No. Come in." He stepped aside.

Cassie entered the unit and placed Sam's car seat gently on the beige carpet. This was no bachelor pad. Dom's house was meticulous and the decor was carefully selected, from the Chinese silk screen standing in the corner, to the comfortably overstuffed couches, to the ornamental sword hanging above the fireplace. He'd placed large potted plants in strategic locations, and Cassie's eyes widened to absorb the complementary array of reds, blacks, light browns and greens. A large vase decorated with cranes and waterfalls rested on a black wooden coffee table. She never would have guessed that Dom Vasquez had a passion for Asian art.

"This place is like a museum," she breathed, and then thought about how she'd shoved her clothes into her duffel bag.

He waved a hand. "It's my home. Make yourself comfortable."

She knelt to unfasten Sam from his car seat. "I'll only stay for a minute. I don't want to impose. I thought I'd go home, but now that I'm back in town I'm a little nervous about it." She frowned. "Do you think it's safe?"

"Your house?" He shook his head. "No, I don't. You

need to be somewhere different. We don't know yet whether you're a target, too."

She groaned. Her gut told her he was right, but the thought of locking herself in a hotel room again was enough to make her want to cry. "I guess...can I use your computer, then? I need to find somewhere to stay."

He studied her for a beat before sighing. "It's late. You can stay here for the night, if you'd like. I have a guest room, though it's not as nice as the hotel you were at." He gestured to Sam. "And I don't have a crib. I can't promise to be a decent host, either. I worked all night and into today, and I should be sleeping but I can't get my mind to slow down." He raked his fingers through his hair to emphasize the point.

"I don't need anything. I...Libby thought I should go somewhere else, and I don't know where else to go."

Dom's eyes narrowed. "She told you to go somewhere else? Why, did something happen at the hotel?"

Cassie patted Sam on the back as she held him. He was still sound asleep. "Don't get mad. They think it's strange that you brought me dinner last night. Suspicious."

Dom ran a finger across his brow. "I got the feeling there was something like that going on. So Nick and Libby think I'm a killer?" He shook his head, visibly frustrated. "They're paranoid. That's why they're not telling me anything. How am I supposed to help them if I don't know where they are?"

His neck had taken on a corded appearance, and his cheeks were flushed with anger. Poor Dom was right. Libby and Nick were locking him out of his own investigation. They thought they were so smart.

Cassie sighed. "I agree they're being paranoid. It's understandable to some extent, but I think they're wrong to suspect you."

Some of the anger on his face receded. "Thank you." He released a frustrated sigh. "So that's why Nick is returning my phone calls with text messages. He's not even talking to me."

"You know," Cassie began, "I could find out where they are, or at least draw them out of hiding. Then you could confront them." Her chin wavered. "I don't want anything to happen to Libby. She's the only family I have left, and I think she's being...*stupid* to keep you in the dark like this. You're trying to help her. I know that."

Dom nodded slowly. "What are you thinking?"

She lifted one shoulder. "I'll ask her to meet me somewhere tomorrow. She'll come out, especially to see Sam. Then you can be there waiting to talk to her. You can clear your name. Tell them you brought me Chinese food because you have some kind of fetish for all things Asian."

"A fetish?" A slow smile spread across Dom's mouth. "You know, I hadn't thought about that. I just like Chinese food."

"And Japanese art." Cassie beamed. Her heart somersaulted when he smiled at her like that. "I would've guessed you'd live in more of a bachelor pad. Worn leather couches, old movie posters taped to the walls, stuff like that. My ex-boyfriend lived that way. I thought all bachelors did."

He eyed her. "Ex-boyfriend? As in, Sam's father?"

Now she'd gone and stepped in it. Cassie shook her head. "No. Sam's father and I were never dating. He was a guy I knew in high school. It was one time. Stupid." She turned from his gaze and ran a finger along Sam's tiny palm as he slept. "He doesn't know. He lives in North Carolina, anyway. It's not like he can…help anything."

Dom was leaning against the doorway, propping himself up with one hand. He was studying her. "He might surprise you. Maybe he'd step up and be a real father to Sam."

Cassie's back went rigid. She was not interested in hearing a lecture—especially from someone who could never possibly know what it was like to walk in her shoes. "You think so? Because when I told him I was pregnant, he handed me a wad of cash and told me to 'take care of it.' As far as he knows, I had an abortion. He doesn't know I gave the money to a homeless man and had the baby." She pulled Sam closer. "I'm pretty sure he doesn't want to be a father, and I'm not looking for advice."

"I was wrong to give it." Dom straightened. "Forget I said anything."

She nodded stiffly. "Okay. Forgotten."

He lifted the corner of his mouth in a smile and looked her in the eyes with a frank, open gaze that made her pulse respond. Shoot, she'd never stand a chance in an argument against him. "Come on," he said. "I'll show you to your room."

Nick had been up for over an hour. He'd showered, dressed and prepared the complimentary coffee provided by the inn while Libby stretched languorously in bed, soundly asleep. She lay on her side with her bare back exposed by the drape of the white linens. Her long black hair presented a strong contrast to the sheets, and the subject herself was of course a study in contrasts, running hot then cold then hot again. Each element of the image fit together like a perfectly staged photograph.

Nick closed the door to the bedroom and considered the slew of documents on the floor of the sitting area. Today was day five, and if the killer stalking Libby was following the pattern of the Arbor Falls Strangler, her life was going to be put in danger today. His stomach roiled. Time was running out.

His BlackBerry vibrated on the table beside him, jarring him from his thoughts. He grabbed the phone. "Nick Foster."

"Nick, it's Molly," came a woman's voice.

He'd managed to track down a supervisor at the inn the previous night and convince him to allow Nick to use the office scanner to make electronic copies of Henderson's handwritten confession and a letter he'd allegedly sent to one of his victims. Nick had emailed the handwriting samples to his colleague at the FBI, Molly Ericson.

When he'd first moved to Pittsburgh, he'd been eager to get over Libby and find someone new. He'd taken Molly to dinner one night and enjoyed her company, even offering to take her out again the following night. She'd laughed kindly and patted him on the arm. "Nick, all you did was talk about your ex-fiancée tonight. Frankly, you can't afford to hire me as your therapist." Instead of dating, they'd become good friends.

"Molly. Good to hear from you. Thanks for responding so quickly." He glanced at the clock. It was only eight in the morning, but Molly had probably been in the office for hours.

"You said this was urgent. What's going on? I thought you were supposed to be in the office this week."

"Something came up. A family emergency."

She was silent on the other end as she read the cues from the tightness of his response. "You take care of yourself, okay? If you decide you want to talk, you know I'm here."

"I will. Take care of myself, I mean."

He heard her sigh. "These samples you sent over are interesting. The threat letter displays narrow, tense handwriting, oddly shaped letters that defy any convention I know and extreme height differentials." She paused. "I'm disadvantaged because I'm not looking at the original, so I can't comment as to the pressure of the writing on the sheet. But I think it's fairly safe to conclude that the letter was written by a person with a schizoid personality."

"A schizoid personality? As in schizophrenic?" Nick felt his muscles tense.

"No, schizoid is different from schizophrenic. This is what I would expect to see from a serial killer's handwriting. This indicates a person who is emotionally cold or even emotionless. Secretive. A loner."

No real surprise there. "All right."

"I can also tell that the individual who wrote this letter is highly organized and intelligent," she continued. "The confession is much different. Were these samples said to be written by the same person? Because they sure don't look like they were."

Nick sat on the edge of the chair and leaned forward. "You don't say." If Molly was correct, then Henderson hadn't written the letters to the victims' families, which meant he may have confessed to crimes he hadn't committed. Nick's thoughts were swirling around his head at light speed. "Tell me about the person who wrote the confession."

She cleared her throat. "I'd say this was a male with a grade school education at best, based on the formation of the letters and the language being used. I wouldn't guess he was a schizoid personality, but I wouldn't be surprised if he was involved in some criminal activity. You're probably aware of the studies suggesting a correlation between poor education and criminal activity."

Nick's pulse pounded in his ears as she paused. Henderson seemed to have had a proclivity for petty theft.

Molly continued. "If we compare the confession with the letter you sent, I would say there's a significant disparity in education and possibly social class. If you look beyond the handwriting style and consider the vocabulary being used, the letter appears to be written by a highly educated individual, whereas this confession looks like it could have been written by a kid in middle school."

Nick tapped his fingers against the table and leaned forward in his chair. "The person who wrote that confession is dead. So if we were looking for the person who wrote that letter, or for someone like him, we would be looking for a person who would be considered a loner, right?"

"Well, not necessarily," she replied. "That's often how a schizoid personality will present itself, but sometimes people are very skilled at hiding their antisocial tendencies. You may be looking for someone who is quite charming."

Nick groaned. "So a loner or the life of the party, then? I thought you were supposed to make this easier for me."

Molly laughed. "Sorry, Nick. People are complicated."

His forehead was tense. "I'm kidding. You have no idea how helpful that was. Thank you."

"Glad to help. This stuff does get the pulse racing, doesn't it?" She sounded breathless.

"Yeah, I love violent crime," he said wryly. "Hey, I don't know if you heard, but it looks like I'm going to be stationed in Washington, D.C., in a few months. I just found out yesterday." Bureau policy dictated that he was required to spend three years in an office in a major city, after which Nick would have more flexibility in choosing the office he worked in.

"I hadn't heard. We'll miss you here in Pittsburgh. I was stationed in Manhattan, but Washington will be great. Will you be living in Virginia or Maryland?"

"Too early to tell. I have to start house hunting." He caught a movement out of the corner of his eye and turned. Libby was standing in the doorway. "Molly, sorry, but something came up and I have to go. I'll talk to you later," he said, watching Libby. "Thanks for your help." He disconnected the call and turned to Libby with a smile. "Morning, sunshine."

"Morning." She rubbed her eyes and yawned. She'd thrown on a bathrobe, but she hadn't bothered to smooth her sexy, disheveled hair.

"I ordered up breakfast. I hope you don't mind muffins and eggs."

"That sounds perfect." She seated herself on the couch, tucking one leg beneath her. Nick tried not to think about whether she was wearing anything beneath her robe.

"I sent those handwriting samples to an expert at the Bureau. That was her on the phone just now."

"And? What did she say?"

"I gave her two samples. The first was a letter sent by the Arbor Falls Strangler to one of his victims, and the second was the confession written by Will Henderson." He paused. "Libby, they were written by two different people."

"Oh, my God." Her brow knit and she stared at the floor, deep in thought. "That means Henderson wasn't the Arbor Falls Strangler. He confessed to crimes he didn't commit."

This was the news she'd feared. Her father had locked up a potentially innocent man. She picked absentmindedly at a frayed thread on the terry-cloth robe. It didn't seem possible that Dad would have known he was prosecuting an innocent man, and yet she'd learned only last night that he'd slyly helped to orchestrate her breakup with Nick. The coldness of that betrayal unnerved her. Could anything in his past surprise her anymore?

"My dad prosecuted the wrong person," she whispered. "The wrong man went to jail—died in jail—for those crimes while the real murderer went free." Her own words left her feeling numb. She looked at Nick. "What else did the handwriting expert say?"

"I figure we're looking for the original Arbor Falls Strangler or someone like him. Molly's a psychologist, and she said that the person who wrote that letter probably has a schizoid personality, which would make him antisocial and a loner. Or conversely, he may be extremely charming."

Libby raked her fingers through her hair. "Well, okay. A loner or a charmer. That doesn't seem to help very much. Do you think that this is payback for a wrongful conviction?"

"Could be," Nick said.

She knitted her brows. "But the timing still doesn't make sense. Why now? Henderson's been dead for years."

"Maybe someone else just learned about the wrongful conviction, too. Who else would know that your dad made this…mistake?"

She flinched at his words. "A mistake? Do you think he made a mistake?" He didn't move except to look away, confirming her suspicions. "No, you don't think that at all. You think my dad knew about this, don't you?"

He rubbed the bridge of his nose. "You're the one suggesting that something deeper was going on. I would have no way of knowing that."

He was right. Libby had a gnawing suspicion that her father may have knowingly done the unthinkable, but she couldn't explain it. Maybe that suspicion stemmed from the peculiar animosity she sensed from certain people who'd worked with her father. Judge Hayward, for instance. She'd been a public defender when Libby's father had prosecuted Henderson—did she somehow know? But Libby also found it difficult to accept that her father, the very man who'd taught her right from wrong and fostered her unwavering faith in the justice system, would have knowingly prosecuted the wrong person for a crime. This wasn't any crime, either: her father had prosecuted the wrong person for a series of murders and requested multiple life sentences. Her father had helped to lock away an innocent man for the rest of his life.

She felt a rush of heat. "I think I'm going to be sick," she mumbled.

Nick rose. "Can I get you something? A glass of water?"

Waves of heat and nausea passed over her, and she took deep breaths to steady herself. After a minute or two the nausea receded and she was breathing easier. "I'll be all right."

Nick was behind her, and his hands were on her shoulders, kneading her muscles. "You're so tense."

She sighed at the sensation of his touch. His warm hands were heavy and reassuringly strong, and his grip was firm but gentle as he worked his fingers into the knots on her upper shoulders. She sat up and leaned her head back, relaxing against his tight stomach. Her shoulders were tinged with slight achiness as her muscles softened, sending a dizzying rush of blood to her head. She moaned softly. "That feels amazing."

The compliment only served to encourage him, and soon his fingers were tracing slow, firm circles to the base of her neck. His touches on her shoulders and her neck stirred memories of his touch on other parts of her body. Her breathing became shallow as she fell under his trance, her head tilting softly this way and that as he commanded her body. She was utterly under his control, and she wouldn't want it any other way.

He stopped, resting his hands on her shoulders and whispering, "Feel better?"

"Oh." She sighed. "You stopped."

There was a knock. "That's breakfast."

Nick opened the door, and Libby heard him explain quietly that she'd just woken and he didn't want anyone entering the room yet. She pulled her bathrobe tighter as Nick reentered the room with a cart draped with a white tablecloth and towering with croissants, muffins and Danish. A pitcher of orange juice and a carafe of coffee rounded the breakfast display, which was punctuated by a single pink rose in a glass vase. "How lovely. You ordered breakfast for fifteen."

He smiled at her. "I wanted you to find something you'd enjoy." He handed her coffee in a porcelain cup. "I think that we need to talk to someone who may have some insight. Someone involved with the Henderson trial."

She considered the question. "Who do you have in mind?"

"Henderson's defense attorney, Christopher Henzel. He's near seventy, but I looked him up and he's got a small law practice in the center of Glen Hills."

"What's he practice?"

"Real estate."

Libby blinked. "He's no longer a public defender, huh?"

"He hasn't been for a long time. In fact, it seems he opened this firm less than a year after Henderson went to jail."

"In other words Henderson was the last criminal he represented before he decided he wanted to practice real estate?"

"Exactly."

Libby laughed dryly. "Yeah, I agree. We need to talk to Attorney Henzel."

"After breakfast we'll pack up our things. I've found a different hotel for us to stay in, and Henzel's office is on the way."

Nick tugged at the door of Christopher Henzel's law office, located on the first floor of a small office building near the center of Glen Hills. "Remember—no details about what's going on with you. The police are trying to keep certain elements out of the media."

Libby nodded. They'd been fortunate that Attorney Henzel had an opening to meet with them that morning. The last thing she wanted to do was to make him regret the visit by burdening him with the gruesome details.

The receptionist pointed them to a small waiting area furnished with comfortable leather chairs. The office itself was drenched with sunlight and decorated in a cheerful mix of yellow, green and brown. Libby settled into a chair and watched the brightly colored fish dart around the saltwater aquarium on the far wall. Nick sat beside her and reached over to grasp her hand. She drew herself closer to him, enjoying the warmth of his skin against hers. Savoring the moment for a change.

"Sorry to keep you waiting." They heard the voice from behind and saw an older but still sprightly man in a white polo shirt and khaki pants. "I was reviewing the results of an especially hairy title search and I lost track of time.

"We just got here," Nick said.

Henzel's frame was thin, and his brown eyes contained a warmth that Libby found reassuring. "An FBI agent left me a message wanting to talk about William Henderson," he said. "It piqued my interest."

"I left you that message. Special Agent Nick Foster." The men shook hands. "And this is Libby Andrews."

"My father prosecuted Mr. Henderson."

Henzel seemed unsurprised. "You have your father's eyes."

He led them into a modest conference room and library. Libby and Nick pulled up chairs.

"I would offer you something, but I don't know how to use our coffee maker. Would you like some milk or orange juice?"

They both shook their heads. "Thank you, Attorney Henzel," said Libby. "We're fine."

"Well, then, what brings you here? You know I haven't practiced criminal defense in almost thirty years, and I haven't looked over the Henderson files in nearly as long."

Nick said, "We've been reviewing some old files, and we've noticed some…discrepancies."

"You've been reviewing the case files?" Henzel looked interested. "For what purpose, if I may ask?"

Libby and Nick exchanged a glance. "We're writing a book," Nick replied.

Henzel replied with a short "Hmm" before sitting back in his chair. "Please continue. I didn't mean to interrupt."

"As Nick said, we've noticed some discrepancies in the files. A handwriting expert at the FBI compared the letters the Arbor Falls Strangler sent to his victims' families with the confession Henderson wrote. She concluded that Henderson didn't write those letters."

"You've involved a handwriting expert at the FBI? This must be some book." Henzel's face remained still, and he pressed the tips of his fingers together. "What kinds of discrepancies did she notice?"

"The person who wrote the letters to the victims' families was highly educated and showed signs of having a schizoid personality. The person who wrote the confession had a grade school education at best," Nick said.

"We know that Henderson wrote the confession," Libby continued. "What we don't know is why he would confess to crimes he didn't commit. We're here because we're wondering whether Henderson may have said something to you." She noticed Henzel flinch in hesitation. "Henderson is dead, so there's no longer an attorney-client privilege to preserve."

"Of course," Henzel replied, folding his hands in front of him. He paused to scratch his eyebrow, and he seemed lost in thought. "I must have looked at those letters and that confession dozens of times, but the truth is I never noticed a difference in the handwriting." He raised his gaze to meet Libby's. "If I had, I would've raised that question at trial."

She leaned forward and lowered her voice, speaking to Henzel kindly. "That must have been quite a trial for you. You were charged with defending someone who'd practically confessed to being a serial killer. That couldn't have been easy."

"I received death threats for defending him," Henzel said, his voice calm. "I became a criminal defense attorney out of a sense of…obligation, I suppose. I had ideals. I believed in 'innocent until proven guilty,' and I thought that by putting forth a strong defense I would protect all of society from overzealous prosecution." He looked at the table and assumed a faraway expression. "I was a fool."

The statement thrust Libby back against her seat. "Why were you—"

"Henderson was arrested at work," Henzel continued as if she hadn't spoken. "He was a dishwasher at the country club. Someone spotted what appeared to be bloody clothing in his duffel bag and reported him. The police later identified that clothing as belonging to the sixth victim. Of course Henderson told me he was innocent. He swore the clothing had been planted in his bag, said he'd never killed anyone. You know how it goes." He directed that statement toward Libby.

"They're all innocent." She smiled. "At least I'm not the only one who hears that."

"In that way, at least, he was just like all of my other defense clients."

"But something made him different," Nick prompted.

"Quite a few things, really. I realized early on that Henderson had a benefactor of some kind. I don't know who he was. I just know that Henderson was receiving lots of money from someone. His wife was, at least."

"Did this benefactor pay your legal bills?" Nick asked.

"No, I was the public defender assigned to the trial, so I was paid by the taxpayers. But Henderson didn't have a penny to his name. He'd never been able to hold down a steady job in his life. Suddenly his wife was buying fur coats and going out for fancy dinners." Henzel shook his head. "I remember Will telling me about the job at the country club, and he would talk about it like it was the funniest thing in the world. He was washing dishes to feed people who could, as he put it, 'buy and sell him twice before sunset.' I always got the sense that he hated those people, the upper echelon of Arbor Falls, so to speak. But he also wanted to be accepted by them. He desperately wanted their approval."

Libby rested her chin on her palm. "Do you think that's where he met this benefactor, at the country club?"

"Could be," Henzel said. "We never talked about it. I didn't want to know. But at the beginning, when he was first arrested, he was desperate to get out of jail. He said that he needed to work and that his wife needed his support. Then he changed."

"Changed? How so?" Nick asked.

"He wasn't as desperate to get out of jail. He seemed untroubled by the usual court delays." Henzel frowned. "Then one day he told me he knew who the real killer was, that he was...how did he put it? 'Negotiating a price.'"

"Negotiating a price? With the Strangler?" Nick leaned forward over the table.

"Yes. That's the way I understood it."

"Henderson was in prison this entire time, wasn't he?" Libby asked.

"Yes. He was being held without bail."

"So if he was having visitors," Libby said, her brow creasing as she thought, "then the prison would have a record of that."

Henzel shook his head. "Except that there was no such record. I checked. Henderson's wife came to see him every now and again, and that was it. If he was negotiating something with the benefactor, then that benefactor had friends who didn't make him fill out the visitor paperwork."

"So if I understand this correctly," Nick began, "Henderson professed his innocence and seemed impatient about being held in jail, but then he received a lot of money from an anonymous benefactor. Later he signed a statement confessing to have played a part in the murders." Nick sat back against his chair and stared out the window as he thought about this. "You think that he was paid to take the fall?"

"I do. I think that the Strangler was a very powerful person in Arbor Falls, and I think that he must have cut some kind of a deal with Henderson. If I had to guess, Henderson was promised the things he'd always wanted. Money. Respect. Notoriety. In return, Henderson would sign a confession, plead guilty to lesser offenses and suffer through the trial. There had to be a murder trial. The mayor wanted his pound of flesh. In return Henderson would be treated well in jail and his wife would be cared for." Henzel's face darkened. "But his wife wasn't cared for. Not for long, anyway. Shortly after Henderson was sentenced, she was found dead in their home. Strangled."

Libby felt a wave of coldness wash over her. "Was she killed by the Strangler?"

"The police never made that connection. If they had, they would have had to admit they'd locked up the wrong person. No, the medical examiner ruled her death a suicide by hanging. But Henderson told me she'd been killed. He was certain of it." Henzel was quiet. "That's when Henderson started telling anyone who would listen that he was innocent, that the Strangler had paid him to take the fall. As soon as Henderson started talking, of course…"

"He was killed," Libby finished in a whisper.

Henzel nodded. "Whoever did it made it look like a suicide, but I never believed it."

"We found newspaper accounts of a woman who claimed to have seen the Strangler walking from a victim's house, covered in blood," Nick continued after a brief silence. "Why didn't you call her to the stand? She could have introduced reasonable doubt."

"Yes, Mrs. McGovern was one of the first people I tried to contact when I received Will's case." He sighed. "Unfortunately she'd died a year or two earlier. Natural causes. I suppose that can happen when it takes ten years to arrest a suspect." His tone was bitter. "I offered those newspaper articles into evidence, and I even called the reporter who interviewed her to the witness stand. The state countered with evidence that Mrs. McGovern had been legally blind, and the reporter admitted he didn't know whether she'd been wearing her glasses or not. It was a disaster."

"But someone must have known something," Nick said. "Henderson was talking, people were being bribed to look the other way when a mysterious visitor came calling at the prison—"

"Believe me," Henzel replied, "even if someone knew something, no one was willing to *say* anything. It was a death sentence. And for what? A sense of justice?" He snorted and shook his head. "No one ever said a word."

He was quiet for a moment. "No, I take that back. There was a prison guard who approached me once, telling me that Henderson had been receiving a strange visitor, that all kinds of rules were being broken to protect this visitor's identity. The guard told me that something was going on, but he wouldn't get more specific than that. He said he was going to speak with his superiors about it." Henzel closed his eyes. "He was found dead in his home a few days later. Shot in the head."

"Oh!" Libby covered her mouth with her hands.

"The police report said all signs pointed to an apparent burglary. I knew better."

Libby shivered as a silence fell across the room. Then Henzel continued. "Henderson only confessed to planting the signs. That was the arrangement, I suppose. I think he thought that he would have some leverage with the Strangler if he didn't confess to all of the crimes, that he could turn state's witness if the Strangler stopped making payments. Will Henderson wasn't the smartest client I've ever had. Some people took advantage of that."

Libby bit her thumbnail as she thought. If the Arbor Falls Strangler was a powerful, well-connected person in the community, there could have been a vast conspiracy to convict Henderson. She felt sick to her stomach. What had her father done? What had her father *known* when he went to trial? Her mouth was dry as she said, "Do you think my father knew about this?"

Henzel's eyes narrowed slightly. "I would have no way of knowing that."

"I'm only asking your opinion. I would ask my father directly, but he passed away last week."

"I'd heard. I'm sorry for your loss." Henzel remained unmoved.

"We need to know what Judge Andrews knew," Nick said.

"For your book, I suppose?"

Libby swallowed and tucked a strand of hair behind her ear. Based on his icy response, she suspected that Henzel knew something about her father, something that made him think less of him and of her. Guilt by association, just as she'd experienced with Judge Hayward.

"Look, I don't know what my father did. I've learned over the past few days that you can know someone your entire life without ever actually *knowing* them." The words brought tears to her eyes, and she blinked them back. "I just want to understand what happened. That's all."

Henzel's face softened, and he took a deep breath. "Your father was a complicated man, Libby. He had many sides, and he was capable of things that surprised me."

A tear rolled down her cheek, and she wiped it away. Nick placed his hand on her knee. She let him.

Henzel sighed. "I believe that your father knew everything. I believe he knew that Henderson was being paid to do the time for someone else, and he knew that he was prosecuting the wrong man."

Libby brought her hand over her mouth. Her head reeled to hear those words.

"Someone had to take the fall. *Some*one had to pay when the public was in a panic about a serial killer." Henzel's voice was low.

"Why Henderson?" Nick asked. "Was it because he needed the money?"

Henzel smiled tightly. "I've wondered that myself. Unfortunately he never told me."

The nausea was back, rolling over Libby in another wave. She rested her hand on her stomach. "Really, Henderson was another victim." She felt hot again, as if there wasn't enough air in the room.

Nick was watching her. "I think we've taken enough of your time, Attorney Henzel." He stood and extended his hand. "Thank you. This information has been invaluable."

Henzel shook his hand mutely, but his eyes were fixed on Libby with an expression of concern. "I've upset you."

"No, you haven't." Libby stood and pressed his hand warmly as she tried to force a smile. "You had nothing to do with this."

She tried to take her hand from his, but he was clutching it, staring at it. She was alarmed by the expression on his face: a haunted, fearful look. "Attorney Henzel?"

He looked up at her with hollow eyes. "Not a day goes by that I don't think about that trial and wonder what I could have done differently."

Nick approached them. "Like Libby said, this wasn't your doing. You didn't know what was happening."

"I could have talked to someone. I could have done something." His lips were shaking. He dropped Libby's hand. "I knew the killer had gotten to the prosecutor. I was afraid that he had also gotten to the judge, or even the jurors. I didn't know who the good guys were anymore."

"You could have ended up like that prison guard. No

one could blame you for keeping quiet." Libby bit her lower lip. "It would be easier if the good guys dressed in white."

A sound like a short laugh escaped from Henzel's lips, and he wrapped his arms around himself as if he'd caught a chill. "Isn't that the truth." He brushed a hand over his face. "Yeah, that would be almost too easy."

Chapter 12

Nick wrapped his arm around Libby as they walked to the car, darting his gaze right and left. They were miles away from Arbor Falls, but the killer had found them in Stillborough yesterday, and today he would be looking to put Libby in a life-and-death situation. More life-and-death than a fire in a locked room or a bullet fired outside her window as she slept. Nick pulled her closer.

"Hey, I can't walk like that." Libby shuffled a few steps off-balance.

"Sorry." He loosened his hold, but only slightly.

When they reached the car, Nick performed what had become a routine examination of the vehicle carriage, checking for strange marks and wires—anything that might have changed since he'd parked. Finding nothing different was a relief, but it quickly turned to a burning in his stomach. "Nothing" meant they were still waiting for the sign.

He'd just turned the key in the ignition when Libby's phone rang. She frowned as she read the number. "Hello, Cassie?"

Nick waited while they talked, hearing only Libby's end of the conversation. "I can't tell you where I am… Now?…Is everything okay?…We're about half an hour from the center of town…I can meet you…Okay, see you then." She hung up and looked at Nick. "I told Cassie we'd meet her at the diner in the center of Arbor Falls."

"Why? What's wrong?"

Libby took great care in placing her phone into her pocketbook. "Nothing. I don't know. She just said she wants to see me."

"And nothing's wrong?"

"You want a reason?" She pulled her seat belt across her lap. "We just lost our dad. She just had a baby. I'm being chased by a serial killer. She could be a target, too. Take your pick."

"Arbor Falls isn't safe."

"No place is safe. But I want to see my sister, and she's in Arbor Falls."

They locked gazes like bulls locking horns, and then Nick backed the car out of the parking space and made the drive to Arbor Falls without further argument. "Is she going to be waiting inside the diner?"

"Yes. She wants to have lunch. Just to talk." Libby reached over to stroke his forearm lightly. "Thanks."

Even now, with his shoulders tight and his mind racing, her touch triggered a response. Her fingers were warm, but he knew that already because the smell of her perfume filled the car, fleeing from the heat of her skin in waves of jasmine and musk. He gripped her hand and brought it to his lips. *Mine.* He'd found her again. She was *his,* and no one was going to touch her.

A lunch crowd was gathering at the diner, but Cassie wasn't among them. "She said she might be late," Libby explained. She glanced around, obviously uncomfortable to be back in town.

A waitress approached them and reached for menus. "Table for two?"

"Three," Nick said, and waited for Libby to pass in front of him.

They sat in a booth with duct tape on the seats and permanent coffee rings stained into the Formica. They didn't open the menus, but when a waitress came to the table, Nick ordered a coffee.

"Just a water for me, thanks," Libby said.

The coffee arrived in a brown ceramic mug with a chip on the lip. It was lukewarm and tasted as if it had been sitting on the burner for hours. Nick sipped it. Libby didn't touch her water. They both watched the door.

The diner hadn't changed since the first time her parents had brought her here. The blue-and-white gingham wallpaper was pulling from the walls at the edges, but who would notice those details amid such a distracting amount of kitsch? The ceramic animals lining the randomly placed wooden shelves had to be at least fifty years old—perhaps the only items in the diner actually older than the booth cushions. An entire wall was decorated with old dented license plates collected from around the country. Old advertisements for corn flakes and white bread cluttered another wall. The Main Street

Diner was simultaneously unique and exactly like every other diner Libby had ever visited or passed by. The familiarity offered little comfort as they waited for Cassie to arrive.

Something was wrong. Libby had heard it in the tone of Cassie's voice as clearly as if her sister had made a confession. Her hands were clammy, and she wrapped them around her glass of water and reminded herself to breathe. *Cassie is safe. Sam is safe. Breathe.*

She saw her hair first. The blond curls caught the sunlight as she bounded up the steps. Cassie was carrying the car seat, and Sam was covered to his chin with a blue receiving blanket. Libby nearly choked with relief as she rose to embrace her sister.

"I'm sorry I'm late." Cassie swept a hand down her curls. "I'm still figuring out the timing with an infant. Everything takes longer."

Cassie sat down opposite Nick and Libby and rested Sam on the bench beside her. "I was worried when you called and wanted to meet like this," Libby said. "Is everything all right?" Cassie looked down and away, and Libby's pulse quickened. "What's going on?"

"Don't be mad at me." Her gaze shot to Nick. "You, either."

Nick sat forward. "Cassie—"

"Mad at you? Why? What happened?"

Cassie ducked her chin slightly to make her large gray eyes appear even larger. This was a remnant from childhood that Libby was certain still served Cassie well with some people. Not her.

"You can't be mad at me. You have to promise."

Nick mumbled a curse. "Stop playing games!"

"Cassie." Libby's stomach sickened. "What did you do?"

She twisted her lips as if she was deciding whether or not to ask for more assurance. Then she cocked her head to the side and said, "I'm staying with Dom."

"What?" If the table hadn't been bolted to the floor, Nick would have knocked it over. Instead, he struck his legs against it before landing solidly back in his seat.

Cassie looked at Libby imploringly. "He's not the… *guy,* Libby. It's not him! He's been nice to me, and I *like* him—"

Libby's stomach heaved. "Cassie." She stopped, unsure of where to begin. "You have no idea. You have no *idea!*" She tensed her fists and struck her upper thigh. Then she caught the look on Cassie's face and her heart stalled. "Oh, my God. Is he here? Did you actually set me up?"

She had the decency to look guilty. "It's not like that. He's trying to *help* you, and you won't let him do his job! He said there was some kind of fire yesterday and you didn't tell him about it until hours later! You're hiding information from him."

Libby's eyes were drawn to the large windows that lined the side of the diner. A tall figure was heading to the front door. *Dom.* She clasped her hands across her mouth.

Nick saw him at the same time. He touched Libby on the shoulder as he rose, reaching under his jacket to unfasten his holster. "Stay here."

Libby ducked lower and watched as Nick stopped Dom at the front door and led him down to the sidewalk. Conversation in the diner stalled when Nick grabbed

Dom by the lapels and pushed him up against the wall. Two officers ran up behind Nick and pulled him away from Dom, but Nick pushed them off and advanced again. Libby heard the clinking of silverware striking the tables and the muffled shouting outside.

Cassie's jaw was open. "Geez. Nick's pissed off." Patrons were gathering by the window now, fixated on the scene. "I'm going to watch." Cassie jumped up, leaving Sam asleep in his car seat, still on the bench.

Libby rubbed at the tension in her forehead, not completely aware that she was one of the few people left inside the diner as the conflict outside escalated. She heard the shouts but couldn't make out the words. She didn't care. She wanted to crawl under the table.

"That your boyfriend?"

She hadn't seen him approach, but now he stood beside the table: a man in a black jacket and a New York Yankees baseball cap. He gestured to the fight scene with a tilt of his chin. "What, he get a parking ticket or something?" The man chuckled at his own joke.

Libby edged farther into the booth. He was standing too close. "I don't know," she mumbled.

"Someone should tell him he ain't winning." The guy smirked, revealing the bottom edges of a row of pointed teeth. "All those cops."

She rose to her feet to look out the window, but a crowd blocked her view. "I can't even see anything."

"Your guy is taking swings at cops. That's gotta be a crime, isn't it?" He shrugged. "I mean, you would know."

A chill shot through her. "What—what do you mean?"

He turned his dark eyes to her, and Libby's pulse went jagged. She tried to step away from him but only wound up stepping farther into the booth. "You're Elizabeth Andrews. Haven't you memorized the penal code?" He shook his head again. "All those cops out there, fighting with each other."

Her vocal cords felt paralyzed as she tried to formulate a response. He chuckled again, but this time there was no forced warmth. "We should get out of here." He pointed to his pocket. "I have a gun."

Her lips trembled. "No." She stole a quick glance at the car seat as Sam squeaked and sighed.

"I know you don't want him to get hurt, so let's make this easy." His mouth tightened as he chastised her. "It's not time yet, Elizabeth. Got it? It's only day five. Don't make me break the rules. Now," he flashed the pistol, "let's get some air."

By the time the junior officers pulled the two men apart, Dom and Nick were doubled over, breathless. Dom had the beginnings of a black eye, and Nick's mouth tasted like copper. His ran his tongue across the cut on his lower lip.

"Damn it, Nick!" Dom rose to his full height and rested his hands on his hips. "We were partners for four years, man! You know me!"

Nick broke his arms free from the officers who'd restrained him. He knew them both; they'd been rookies when he'd left Arbor Falls, and that was probably the only reason he wasn't in handcuffs. "You set us up. That's low. How the hell am I supposed to trust you?" He was tired, but he still had adrenaline to burn.

Dom ran a hand over his face, avoiding a spot on his cheek that was starting to swell. "You're so damn hotheaded. I'm on your side—how many times do I have to tell you that?"

"You're the only one who knew!" Nick advanced, then halted when he saw the officers prepare to restrain him again. He held up his hands to them. "Explain it. You knew we were at my parents' house, and that's where McAdams was killed. You knew we were going to Stillborough, and we were locked in a burning room. How is that possible?"

Dom's face remained tight. His neck was corded with effort to restrain his rage. "I can't explain it. Because I'm not the guy. You think I'd kill one of my own men?" His eyes glistened. "You ever tell a woman her husband just died? The father of her kids?" He broke off and turned away with a dismissive wave of his hand. "You're crazy, you know that? I'd never hurt one of my men, and I'd never hurt you or Libby."

Dom walked over to where Cassie was waiting on the cement steps to the diner. She had one hand on his forearm while the other rubbed his shoulder affectionately. They looked awfully cozy for having met only a few days before.

Nick didn't see Libby. He shouldered his way through the crowd and back into the diner. They were getting out of this town, and they were going to go somewhere far, far away. He'd drive straight through the night if he needed to, maybe straight to Canada. He glanced through the diner. She wasn't in the booth.

He walked closer and then froze. The car seat was still there, with Sam in it.

A chill brushed over him. "Libby!" She'd never leave her nephew unattended. Not by choice.

His heart rocked in his chest as he checked under the tables and behind the counter. She wasn't in the kitchen or the restroom. "Libby!" He pulled out his BlackBerry and dialed her number. She didn't answer.

He picked up the car seat and pushed his way through the crowd of patrons who had filed back into the diner. Dom and Cassie were still on the sidewalk. The steel in their glares didn't register. "She's gone. Libby's gone."

Cassie's eyes narrowed, and she reached for the car seat. "She didn't leave. She's probably in the bathroom."

"She's gone. I checked everywhere."

Dom's swollen face darkened. "What are we looking for, Nick? Have you figured out the signs?"

His stomach tensed. "A life-and-death situation." He glanced at the officers milling about the scene. They were listening with interest. "I need your help, Dom."

Dom didn't hesitate. "All right." He raised his voice to the officers standing in wait. "Ask around, see if anyone saw a woman with long black hair leaving the diner. Someone must have seen something."

Nick sprinted up the stairs and into the diner. The officers were talking to patrons one table at a time. Someone had to have seen her leave.

And what if no one had?

A man tapped him on the shoulder. "Hey, you looking for that girl?"

Nick spun around to face a middle-aged man with the haphazard beginnings of a salt-and-pepper beard. He was dressed in dirty old blue jeans and a red flannel shirt. "You saw her?"

He ran his index finger against his temple. "Yeah, I seen her. She left with a man wear'n a Yankees hat. She didn't want to go with him." He pointed to the back door. "They left out there."

"And you didn't see them again? Were you watching?" The frantic tone of his voice startled even Nick.

"I didn't see them."

That meant they hadn't walked past the windows on three sides of the diner. Nick gave the man a quick tap on the arm and a hurried thanks before he darted back out the front door. He didn't slow except to say, "They went south!" as he ran by Dom and turned the corner.

He didn't stop to think about where he might be going or what he had to do. There was the pounding of his feet on the cement sidewalk and the sound of his breath in his ears. The rest of the world had fallen away.

He pushed her through a wooden gate into a narrow alleyway. The nozzle of the gun was shoved painfully against her spine, and Libby had difficulty walking straight. "You can relax the gun," she snapped. "You've made your point."

She heard him laughing—a low, dry laugh. "And what do you think my point is?"

"You're some sick bastard who has a twisted fascination with a serial killer. You copy him because you lack the imagination to do anything original."

She saw sparks as he cuffed the side of her head with his fist. "Watch your mouth," he growled against her ear as she stumbled forward, "or next time I'll use the hand holding the Glock."

Libby's vision blurred as she righted herself. He was walking her down an empty alley blocked from view by windowless brick buildings. Her chest constricted and she fought to breathe. "What are you planning to do?"

A stupid question, and one she didn't want the answer to, especially when he responded with another deep chuckle. The sound alone made her feel as if she were covered in filth. Then he turned her and pushed her back up against the side of an old factory building. The back of her skull knocked into the bricks with a sickening thump and a thrust of pain. Then his breath was hot against her ear.

"I know everything about you," he panted as her stomach heaved. "The roads you take to work. The time you wake up. The meals you cook."

The words slipped through the sides of his mouth as he gritted his teeth tightly. "I know you're all alone." He snaked a hand around her thigh and cupped her bottom. Then he pinched her, hard. She cried out, but the breath snagged in her lungs. "I thought I could be your date."

He released his grip and brought his hand to his waist. Bile rose in her throat as he fumbled for his belt buckle, his knuckles fluttering across her belly. He grunted and the movements continued. He was having difficulty with his belt. He lowered the hand with the gun and backed up just a little.

Just enough.

Libby brought her right knee upward with a quick jab to his crotch. When he gasped and stepped back, doubled over, she lunged forward, landing her right shoulder squarely against his sternum, knocking them both to the ground. The gun crackled across the asphalt, sliding just out of her reach.

She was straddling his waist. He shifted to throw her

off, but she bore down on him with all of her weight and knocked him back against the pavement. "Bastard!" She felt mad with rage as she dug her nails into his face, releasing trails of crimson. Thrusting the palm of her hand against his nose, she heard a dull crunch as the cartilage broke. He screamed and his hands flew to his face. Libby rolled away to grab the gun that still lay only inches from his arm. She started to wrap her fingers around the cool metal grip when the gun flew out of her grasp.

He had reached it first.

Libby took off running, hearing him cursing behind her as her feet pounded the pavement. A bullet ricocheted, zipping past her ear. A bloodcurdling scream escaped her throat, and she heard her own breath coming in shrill spurts. There had to be a way out of here.

Another shot rang out, this one puncturing a metal trash can as she ran by. He was shrieking in pain as he pursued her but gaining ground. Libby approached a gate that seemed to lead out of the alley, and she crashed her shoulder up against it. She could hear him coming, and a bullet shattered the top of the board on the gate, too close to her head. "Help me!"

With clumsy fingers, she clawed at the latch on the gate. It was locked, or jammed—she couldn't tell which, but it didn't matter because the result was the same. She was trapped, and a killer was quickly closing in.

"I've got a few patrol cars circling the block," Dom said as he and Nick continued down Marbury. "They want to get this SOB as much as you do. He killed their brother."

Nick glanced down an empty alleyway but didn't respond. This bastard had Libby. No one wanted to get him as much as Nick did.

A few other witnesses had confirmed that Libby had left with a tall man in a black jacket and a baseball cap. No one had seen them get into a car, but that didn't mean they hadn't, and it sure didn't stop the gnawing in Nick's gut. The downtown area was vibrant on this spring afternoon. They could have disappeared into the crowd. They could have walked, unnoticed, into any number of buildings. Some of the old industrial spaces were boarded up and dilapidated, an eyesore and a nuisance. A magnet for criminal activity.

"There," Nick said, pointing to the site of the old Sterling Textiles Company. "We should check out that area."

They entered the alley by way of a gate in a six-foot white picket fence. The gate opened on rusty hinges that creaked at a pitch that felt like a finger down Nick's spine. The dried-out skeletons of last summer's weeds littered the cracks in the pavement. The bricks on the old building pinched under their own weight to the point that Nick wondered if the building had ever been built straight, or if it was warping under the stress of time. In the middle of a bustling area, the textiles factory was a forgotten place.

"No windows," Dom mused quietly.

"There are windows around the corner, in the front of the building. He could have taken her in that way." The hair on the back of Nick's neck rose.

"I'll check in here," Dom said. The rotted green boards he pointed to barely classified as a door. "You go around the front."

A gunshot shattered the desolate silence of the alley, followed by a desperate scream.

Nick and Dom drew their weapons and sprinted down the alley. Another gunshot. More screams for help. "Nick!" Dom pointed to a slick spot on the pavement and a short trail of drops.

Blood. Nick's muscles went to ice. Each second down that alley stretched to a year, and when they turned the corner of the building, the alley before them was empty. "Keep going!" Nick said it, but neither of them had hesitated.

More gunshots, and this time they came in rapid succession.

He fled down the alley past the front of the textiles building, his lungs burning and his body heavy with dread. If he lost Libby now...he couldn't bear to complete the thought.

He neared the corner of the building and looked to his left, where the alley continued back to the main street. He saw another wooden gate, and his gaze rested on a figure on the ground—a body, twisted and bleeding. "No!"

He hurled toward the gate. A person hovered over the body, standing in a shadow, holding a gun. Nick stopped in his tracks and raised his weapon. "FBI! Drop your weapon!"

He heard the metal hit the ground. "Nick!"

His body shuddered with relief as she stepped into the sunlight. *Libby.* He ran to her, sweeping her into his arms, kissing the soft black waves of hair that fell across her cheeks. "Oh, God, Libby. Honey, are you all right?" He stepped back an arm's length, looking her over. Her shirt was bloody and her clothes were ragged. "What did he do to you?"

She shook her head. "I'm okay." But her teeth rattled as she tried to answer him. "I think I killed him," she said, and pointed to the body.

Dom came up behind them and dropped down to inspect the man on the ground. His nose was broken and bloody, and his jacket was riddled with bullet holes. He turned to Libby, his eyes wide. "How did you—"

"I fought him. Nick, I think he was going to…" Her voiced splintered, and she brought a shaking hand to her mouth. She didn't complete the thought. "I broke his nose like you taught me one time, and I tried to run away but he kept shooting at me. And then I reached this gate and I saw that." She pointed to a black bottle of wasp spray on the ground. "They must have it because of the trash cans. The can says that it sprays up to thirty feet, and so I tried it and I got him in the eyes. He dropped his gun."

Nick's jaw was slack. "And then you shot him?"

She shook her head. "No. I was going to hold him there, but then he lunged at me again and I shot him." She looked at the body with contempt. "I kind of enjoyed it, too."

Nick's eyebrows shot up. "Well, we'll strike that last comment from the record."

Dom gave a low whistle and placed his gun back in his holster. "You ever thought about being a cop, Andrews? Maybe a vigilante?" He shook his head with visible admiration and lifted his two-way from his belt. "I'm in the alley by Sterling Textiles, off Marbury. I need backup."

Libby settled her head against Nick's heart. She trembled against him, and he pulled her tighter. "It's all over. Breathe, honey, it's over."

She inhaled a breath that rattled her entire body. "Does this mean I'm safe now?"

He brushed his lips against the top of her head. "Yes, sweetheart." He reached up to touch a hand to her cheek, to press her closer to him. "You're safe now."

Chapter 13

"We don't have the official ID yet, but looks like his name was Reggie Henderson," Dom announced as he slid a photocopy of a driver's license across the table. "At least that's what the driver's license we found on the body says."

"Henderson?" Nick said. "Must be a relative of Will Henderson's. A nephew or a cousin, maybe."

"Nephew," came Dom's quick response. "Run-of-the-mill dirtbag. He had a couple of arrests for driving under the influence. He did time a few years ago for armed robbery. Ballistics is running a check on the gun, but it looks like a potential match in McAdams's death."

"Good. Sounds like we got the guy." Nick nodded to Libby. "Maybe I should say, sounds like Libby got the guy."

Libby turned away from the picture. They'd been in the precinct for several hours. She was tired and sore, and as the reality of the afternoon seeped in, she was exhausted. She'd given a statement, and she and Nick had told Dom their theory on the case, which was that Libby's father had knowingly prosecuted an innocent man in return for political favors from the Arbor Falls Strangler, and someone who knew was seeking revenge.

"I still don't understand," she said. "Dad died without knowing about any of this. I didn't do anything wrong. I was in diapers when Dad prosecuted Henderson. Why would someone want to hurt me?"

Dom's face softened. The poor guy had taken a beating from Nick—a dark purple bruise was still developing under his eye. "It could be some twisted logic, or some need to right a cosmic wrong. Will Henderson was innocent and your father took his life, in a manner of speaking."

She sat perfectly still. Dom's voice was gentle, but the truth of his words cut deeply. She reached for the bracelet on her wrist and fidgeted with it, clicking the little piano open and shut. Ever since that morning in Henzel's office, she'd been thinking about what her father had said on that beach in Sarasota all those years ago when he'd told her that he'd watched her play with the charms while sitting on her mother's lap. He'd even choked at the memory. How was it possible that at the time he'd fondly observed Libby playing with her mother's charm bracelet, he'd been cutting a deal with a murderer? She couldn't reconcile these two truths.

Nick slid his arm around her shoulder and pulled her closer. "It doesn't matter why anything happened. What matters is that the guy who was after you is dead and that all of this is over."

Libby's shoulders tensed. "It *does* matter. My father had a past that I couldn't fathom three days ago. I knew he was stern, but I'd always thought he was *just*. I thought we shared that ideal." She leaned forward, away from his touch. "It matters to me that my father was a stranger with these terrible secrets. He sold his ideals for his ambition."

Dom and Nick eyed each other silently as Nick pulled his arm away. A knock on the door split the heavy silence, and Cassie entered the room with paper take-out bags.

"My turn to bring dinner." She smiled easily, but her smiled wavered when she looked at Libby, and then she looked away. "It's nothing fancy, just sandwiches and chips. I bought some chocolate chip cookies for dessert."

She fluttered about with an energy that Libby hadn't seen in years, taking special care as she arranged the plates, utensils and food. Cassie had never been one to be so concerned about neatness, but she stacked the sandwiches with an almost exaggerated attention to detail, tucking the corners of the butcher's paper in which the meals were wrapped. Libby glanced at Dom, who sat watching Cassie with rapt attention and interest. That's when Libby understood.

"Here, I can help you." She rose and walked over to where Cassie was stacking the sandwiches. "Maybe we can pass these out so you don't have to go to all of that trouble." She touched Cassie's upper arm. "Thanks for bringing dinner."

Cassie paused, looking as if she was searching for a response. She looked down and swallowed, and then she surprised Libby by throwing her arms around her.

She turned her face to speak into Libby's neck, suddenly seeming much younger than her thirty years. "I'm so sorry."

Libby reached her arms around to return the embrace. "For what?"

"I brought you to the diner. I thought I was doing a good thing."

"You were. I was lucky to have all of those cops around." Libby tightened her arms. "And I'm safe now."

She sniffed. "What would I have done without you?" Cassie shuddered. "I have no one else left."

"You don't need to worry about that. I'm still here, and so is Sam." She paused. "Hey, where is he?"

Cassie pulled away. "I left him with a neighbor. She used to run a daycare, and she's been offering to watch him since I was four months pregnant."

Libby squeezed her arm affectionately. "Don't blame yourself for this. Any of it. I don't blame you."

She bit her lip and nodded but didn't say anything more.

The four of them picked at their dinners, punctuating the meal with dashes of almost cheerful banter before settling back into the heavy fatigue they shared. When they were finished, Nick rose and said, "If we're done here, it's been a long day and I'd like to take Libby home."

They said their goodbyes, and she clutched Nick's hand as they walked out of the precinct, through the parking lot and to the car. He drove directly to her house and pulled into the driveway. She sat staring at the house. She loved everything about it: the flower gardens, the cherry tree that was only a few weeks from erupting in delicate pink-and-white blossoms and the fact that inside those walls, everything was arranged to her liking and comfort. *Home.* But her heart was beating too quickly and her body felt too heavy to move.

Nick opened his door and stepped out. She watched him walk along the front of the vehicle to her door. He opened it.

"I can't," she said. "I can't go back in."

His brows knit, and he rested his forearm on the roof of the vehicle and leaned closer. "It's over, Libby. Henderson's dead. It's safe to go home."

Her thumb flew to her mouth, and she chewed on the nail. "What if he left something inside? He's been in my house before."

"We're not sure of that. But would it make you feel better if I went inside first?"

She nodded and handed him her key. "The pass code to the alarm is the same."

She waited while he walked around the outside of the house, then went through it, turning on lights as he checked the rooms. He came back outside with a smile. "All clear."

She stepped onto the driveway and walked to the house on shaking legs. Her breath came in shallow gulps as she reached the front door. She entered. Her house smelled faintly floral, the way it always did. Clean and untouched. She felt ill at the thought that Reggie Henderson had ever seen the inside of her home—how she decorated or how it smelled. She tried to clear the thought from her mind.

"See? Nothing to be afraid of." He carried her bags

inside and dropped them beside the front closet. "Home sweet home."

Her gaze swept across his bruised face. He had a split lip and another cut on the left cheek. All for her. He'd promised to stand by her until she was safe, and he had. He hadn't left her side, and that made her stomach flutter. She liked having Nick around.

Yet they hadn't discussed what would happen once she wasn't in danger. He had a life and a home hours away from here. He had no choice but to leave again, and now as he stood by the door, he looked as if he was bracing himself for something painful.

She swallowed. "You're going home."

His figure was frozen. "You're safe now."

She nodded and looked at his feet. His black shoes were filthy. He'd tracked mud all over her house when he'd checked it; she could see the specks on the floor. Her eyes began to sting. "I don't feel safe."

He sucked in his breath. "Do you want me to stay? Just…one more night?"

"Yes." Her answer was too quick, but she didn't care. "Please."

He seemed to relax and just like that, the fear dissipated. She lifted her bags and carried them up the stairs to her bedroom. A dull ache had wrought itself through her muscles. She dropped the bags in the middle of her bedroom floor. She was tense and tight and exhausted, and she didn't want to unpack.

She stood in the frame of the bedroom door and listened to Nick walking through her home. He opened cabinets and closed them, then he opened her refrigerator to pour himself something to drink. She remembered hearing him make these same rounds years ago, when they were still together. Strange, to feel nostalgia at the sound of someone walking around a kitchen.

She moved easily around her bedroom now that she knew he was downstairs. She didn't hesitate to open her closet, and she didn't check under her bed. Reggie Henderson was dead. She was safe. She realized with a thump of her heart that the fear she'd felt before entering her home wasn't a fear that Henderson had left a sign here or that someone else was lying in wait. No.

What she'd feared was entering her empty house and being alone once again. No amount of checking under the bed would alleviate that concern.

Cassie curled up on her couch and hugged a pillow against her stomach. Weeks after giving birth, the elastic waistband of her favorite sweatpants still felt tight. She slid them down around her hips. That was better.

Sam was asleep in his crib, which meant that she had a few short hours to sleep herself. She should take advantage, but she couldn't slow the thoughts in her mind. The image of Nick and Dom fighting on the sidewalk like young boys brawling over a girl. The thought of Libby nearly being killed because Cassie had lured her back into Arbor Falls, right into the lion's den. She shivered and felt a wave of nausea. *What if...?* She'd never have forgiven herself.

She jumped at the sound of a knock at the door. "Who is it?"

"It's me."

Dom.

Cassie pulled up her sweatpants and brushed down

the front of her old long-sleeve blue T-shirt, pausing to examine a new stain on the front. She'd tied her hair back in a ponytail, but she tugged a few tendrils loose. She caught a glimpse of herself in the mirror and paused. She was a mess. An ashen-faced, bloated mess. She'd lost her chin somewhere at around thirty-four weeks, and it still hadn't fully returned. She was forty pounds heavier than she'd been eight months ago, and she felt frumpy in every extra ounce.

Her heart twisted. She'd never felt this flutter in her stomach about any man before. What a cruel joke, that he would keep appearing and seeing her in this state, at her absolute lowest. She almost wanted to drag out old photos, just to show him that—look!—she used to be cute, and maybe if he came back in three months, she would be again. Cassie sighed and opened the door.

Dom had changed. Showered. He smelled like soap and spicy aftershave, and he was dressed in a black button-down Oxford shirt and denim jeans. He broke into a broad smile when he saw her. She couldn't believe the way her traitorous heart sped up at the sight of him, or the way it urged her to offer to put something on that swollen cheek of his. Ice? A steak? She didn't even know, and she didn't have either.

"What are you doing here?"

"Hi, Cassie." He stepped closer, saying the words in a low voice that made her insides quiver. "Do you want some company?" He didn't wait for a response before he stepped into the house, closing the door behind him.

"Well, come right in." Cassie inched backward as he approached her. "Can I get you something?"

A devastating smile curled one side of his mouth. "I just wanted to see you."

"Oh." She stepped away from him, walking back into the arm of the couch. She sat on it and he inched closer. "Do you always visit people at this hour?"

"Fair's fair. You came to my front door last night with an infant. I'm at least empty-handed."

He held up the palms of his large hands, and Cassie lost her breath for a moment as she imagined what they might feel like working across her skin. She wiped her hand across her forehead. "No secret babies. Yes, we've covered this topic."

He paused, leaving only inches between them. Her nose was level with his broad chest. It was all she could see. He brought his head down. "My house was quiet tonight."

She smiled. They'd stayed up talking nearly the entire night before, telling each other stories about their families and their jobs. She'd told him the name of Sam's father, and he'd joked that he'd be sure to put him in a special database in case he was ever pulled over for a traffic violation. She felt comfortable with Dom. At the same time, he made her want to do sinful things, and such things had only gotten her into trouble recently.

"My house is quiet, too," she said. "But it won't be in two hours when Sam is up."

He hesitated. "Do you want me to leave?"

She ran her gaze from his dark, almost black irises to his full mouth and powerful jaw. Running the tip of her tongue across his lips had entered her mind. Asking him to leave had not. "That would be rude of me. You didn't kick me out last night."

"I promise I'll be a gentleman." He inched closer and took her hands in his. "But I can't stop thinking about you." His gaze dipped to her mouth.

"You don't mince words," she breathed.

"It's not in my DNA." He pulled her hands to his chest, placing them so that she could feel the steady thrust of his heart. He brought his gaze back to her eyes and his face softened, almost as if he was in pain. "Cassie, you're so beautiful."

The laugh that erupted was loud and unladylike and poisonous to the mood he'd set with his heartbeats and gentle words, but it was how Cassie felt. "Beautiful? In my sweatpants and T-shirt? I just gave birth, Dom. You have no idea how un-beautiful I am right now." She dropped her hands. "You're making fun of me, and I don't like it."

"I say what I mean." His gaze was intense as he tucked his forefinger under her chin and lifted her face toward his. "You're smart and you're strong. This past week has been one of the worst of my professional life, and you still found ways to make me laugh. You don't know how radiant you are." He smoothed his palm against her cheek. "You're beautiful."

He brought his mouth to hers and tasted her gently, as if he feared she might break. His lips were soft and warm, and his kiss was tinged with the faint suggestion of moisture. Cassie responded by wrapping her hands behind his neck and pulling him closer. She teased his lips open with her tongue and delighted in the way he drew nearer still, deepening the contact between them. When he broke away, they were both breathless.

Dom smoothed the loose tendrils of Cassie's hair back

and then grew still, framing her head gently with his hands. "I know you're tired, and if I stay any longer I won't trust myself to leave. Besides, I'm old-fashioned. Can I take you out to dinner tomorrow?"

"Yes." She was amazed she found the breath to respond. "I'll get a babysitter."

He stepped away with a tilt of his head that may have been a nod. "I'll pick you up at seven, then?"

"Seven-thirty is safer." She stammered. "You know, with Sam's schedule."

He smiled. "Seven-thirty. And I'll take you somewhere nice this time. No Chinese takeout."

She followed him to the front door and watched as he climbed into his car and drove away. Then she locked the door and pressed her back up against it, trying to catch her breath. She had a date with a man who thought she was beautiful in sweatpants.

Her heart pumped a warm pleasure through her veins. Dom thought sweatpants were sexy? A small grin twisted her mouth as she thought of the elegant black dress she'd purchased early in her pregnancy. She ran to her closet and pulled it out, holding it in front of her before the full-length mirror in her bedroom. The fabric was stretchy and soft. The dress would fit.

She smiled at her reflection. He didn't stand a chance.

Chapter 14

As tired as she was, Libby contorted into a hundred different positions, failing to find one that was comfortable. All the while Nick slept soundly beside her. She'd watched him sleep, attempting to lose herself in the steady rise and fall of his chest. Then morning broke outside her window and she gave up even trying.

She headed down the stairs and sat on the couch in her living room, listening to the silence of the morning. Last night her heart had nearly broken when Nick hadn't carried in his suitcase. He had to leave. There was no choice. The realization had knocked her sleepless. She was in love with Nick: again, still or maybe for the first time.

No good could come of these feelings. Her life was in Arbor Falls and his was in Pittsburgh. They were both married to their careers. A relationship would only mean sacrifice, which would lead to resentment and, ultimately, heartbreak. Neither one of them should be required to give anything up. Love shouldn't work that way.

She bit her thumbnail and then stopped, but only because there was nothing left to bite. So much for her plans at self-improvement. She pulled her knees up into her chest and leaned back against the side of the sofa. She'd worn her mother's charm bracelet to bed, and it chimed pleasantly as she moved. Libby toyed with the tiny treasure chest, opening and closing it, imagining the treasure that could be tucked in so small a space. Tiny gold doubloons, maybe, or a little emerald necklace. Some day Sam might like to sit on her lap and play with it, just like she had when she was a child.

Libby folded a pillow beneath her head. She was in love with Nick, and so what? Even if they could figure out a way to bridge the miles between them and reconcile their work schedules, he wanted children. Her face was hot. She couldn't enter into a relationship with him now, knowing how important children were to him and the resentment that would surely result. Much better for her to date someone who was comfortable being childless. Like David.

Her stomach plummeted. No, not like David, who was boring and passionless and liked to talk about contracts too much. She didn't want to date David. She wanted to feel fiery and alive. She wanted to feel *powerful.* She was tired of encapsulating herself in ice and measuring every word, every move and every response. She was ready to be who she was, even if she still had to figure that part out.

She swallowed. Nick should be who he was, too. He

should have the future he imagined for himself, with an exciting job and babies who had his beautiful brown eyes. A dog. And a wife who was not her.

Her hand flew to the sudden ache in her chest. This was the right thing. The good, practical thing, to let him go and to make it easy on him. But it hurt.

Nick raised the shades in the living room to admit a flood of sunlight before he realized that Libby was sleeping on the couch. She groaned and rubbed her eyes. "What time is it?"

"Almost seven-thirty. Sorry, I didn't see you there."

She stretched and then sat upright, passing a hand through her hair. "I didn't sleep well last night. Too much excitement."

He could have guessed as much from her pale complexion and the dark circles beneath her eyes. "I'll make breakfast. After that you can take a nap."

She blinked at him. "No. I'll be fine."

She stood and followed him to the kitchen, where they prepared a simple breakfast of scrambled eggs and whole wheat toast with strawberry preserves. Libby seemed to be troubled by something, but whenever Nick pressed her about it, she shrugged it off with a casual excuse. She was exhausted from the past few days, and her thoughts were clearly elsewhere. She was probably thinking about the pile of work that would be on her desk when she returned and wondering if she should go into the office that day.

They returned the rental car that Nick had been driving, and then they picked up her car from the lot at the District Attorney's Office, where it had been parked all week. They took a walk around the park at the foot of Arbor Falls in a companionable silence. Any conversation would have been drowned by the roar of the falls, anyway. They ate pad Thai at one of Libby's favorite restaurants. Then they returned to Libby's home, and a stiffness settled into his limbs.

He had to ask her. About them. About what would happen when he returned to Pittsburgh and then moved on to Washington. But Libby was bustling around the house, suddenly too busy to sit still as she straightened shelves and dusted or cleaned out anemic vegetables from her refrigerator. Then she picked up the phone to call her sister. She was avoiding the discussion, too. The realization left him cold.

He'd rehearsed his speech in the shower. "Libby, I think we should try again." But damned if he knew how; he always stopped when he came to that part. Living five hours apart was bad enough, but ten? How, exactly, were they going to manage *that?*

But they would. He knew it. Maybe he could be reassigned to Manhattan instead of Washington, and if Libby could move to a different office… He straightened. There were options. There had to be, because the only thing he couldn't imagine was returning to Pittsburgh and leaving her behind as if the past week had never happened. Now that he'd found her again, he couldn't go back to being without her.

He waited in the living room for her to finish her phone conversation. He wiped his palms on his pants and ignored the way his stomach was turning. This was no time for nerves. Libby stomped into the room and he looked up with a start. "What's wrong?"

"My sister." She put her hands on her hips. "You know that she's going out tonight? With Dom?" She paused. "Why are you smiling?"

He shrugged. "Good for them. I thought there was something going on. They'd be good for each other." He stretched out one arm. "Come sit next to me."

"No." She huffed and folded her arms across her chest, clearly displeased with his response. "What about her son? All these strange men...she won't even tell anyone who his father is!"

Nick frowned. "I'm sure Sam won't remember any of this, Libby. For all we know, they could end up married." He shifted on the couch. Her mouth was pulled tightly, her entire face set in a frown. "What's wrong? Why are you so upset about this?"

"Because she's acting like a child. Because she's being irresponsible with her son. She can't continue to do whatever she wants. She has to put him first!"

His skin prickled. Something was wrong. Libby adored her sister, and he'd never heard her stand in such strong judgment of her before. "I know how much you love your nephew, but Cassie's a good mother, Libby." He rose and approached her. "She loves Sam, too, and she won't do anything to hurt him. Dom's a good man." Even as he said it, he felt a punch in his gut about the things he'd said to Dom yesterday. He'd gotten carried away.

Libby wouldn't look at him. "She barely knows him. Sam's too young for all of this."

He rubbed her tense shoulders. "It's okay. She's a new mother. She deserves a night out." He gave her a kiss on the ear. "You'll feel the same way one day."

He felt her go rigid. Then she pulled away from his

arms and spun around to face him. Her eyes were steely. "I won't."

His gaze trailed across her features. Her chin was tilted at him defiantly, daring him to question her. He tried to laugh, but it sounded more like a cough. "Right. You'll be supermom. It's not a fair comparison."

"You don't understand." Now her chin trembled slightly, but she struggled to keep her composure. "Nick, I can't have children."

He stared at her blankly for far too long as he tried to process that statement.

"I found out when you were in Quantico. It's because of the cancer treatments." She hated the way her voice cracked. She shrugged, trying to appear nonchalant. "So, I won't ever know what it's like to be a new mother and to want a night out."

He took a step back. He was staring at the floor, but he lifted his eyes to meet hers. "I didn't know."

"Almost no one knows. I never told my dad. I haven't told Cassie." She swiped her hand beneath her nose. She was *not* going to cry about this.

"But you knew when we were together." He frowned. "You kept this from me."

A strange defensiveness pulled her straight. "I didn't want your pity."

"My pity?"

He stared at her, his eyes wide. Libby had rehearsed this moment a thousand times. In each iteration she'd imagined Nick to be angry, or dismissive or hostile. But now he was none of those things. He was hurt. "We were engaged. We talked about having a family together...."

He froze. "Wait. Is this why you broke off our engagement?"

"We both deserve to be happy. If I'd gone to Pittsburgh with you, I'd have lost a job I love and you'd have lost the family you always wanted." She balled her fists. "Anyway, it's not your problem. You don't have to worry about it."

That got his attention. He tilted his head in surprise. "Not my problem? Libby, we're…what about us? This past week?"

She braced herself. "There is no *us*. We don't make sense together. I'm not moving to Pittsburgh and you're not moving to Arbor Falls. This was a fling, pure and simple. And now it's over."

A shadow crossed his face. "A *fling?* I put my job and my life on the line for you, and that's what you think this was?" He shook his head tightly, visibly furious. "You know, you have some nerve."

Her stomach heaved as he began to storm around the room, pacing without purpose. "Come on, Nick. We both got carried away. It's understandable that two people in our position would be attracted—"

"No, it's not understandable. Not to me." He stopped in front of her. "We have something. We have the chance to make this work."

She stared at him. "How could this work? You want to be a father. You want that more than anything. You want the stable, loving family you never had. Are you really ready to give that up?"

He was silent. He was silent for too damn long. Then he said, "What if you adopted?"

The question struck her squarely in the heart. A part

of her had been hoping that he'd sweep her into his arms and tell her that she was wrong, that he didn't care about children. She'd wanted to hear that she was good enough for him. Just Libby, flawed and broken. But he hadn't said that. Because he didn't think it.

So much for not crying. She blinked back a sting of tears. "I'm not having this discussion. Not now, and not with you."

He gritted his teeth. "What's that supposed to mean?"

She narrowed her eyes. "It means I meant what I said three years ago. I don't love you. I never have. It's time to accept that."

He stepped back as if she'd slapped him. "You sure seemed to love me the other night."

"Get out." Rage pulsed through her. Her voice was shrill and she didn't care. "You have ten minutes to get out of my house. After that, I don't want to see you again."

She flew into the kitchen and set the timer on her stove to prove that she wasn't kidding. He had ten minutes to leave.

He was gone in eight.

Her head was throbbing. Every time she closed her eyes, Libby's mind replayed the scenes from the past week. The photo of the dead woman in her files. The sound of gunshots reverberating in an empty alley. The feel of Nick's bare skin on hers. The sounds of their last words.

Cassie came over shortly after Nick left. She was running errands before her date with Dom, and she looked radiant when Libby opened the door. "I just dropped

Sam off with Mrs. Cummings. She's so excited—" Then her jaw dropped when she saw Libby. "Oh, my gosh. What happened to you?"

"Is it bad?"

Libby checked a mirror. Yes, it was. Her eyes were red and puffy, her nose was pink. She was pale from lack of sleep.

"You look awful." Cassie put her arm around Libby's shoulders. "Where's Nick?"

That set off a fresh stream of tears, and Libby hid her face behind her palms. "He left. We had a fight. It's over."

Cassie pulled her sister closer and held her while she sobbed. Libby told her everything—about her infertility and the secret shame she'd been carrying for years, and about how Nick had asked her if she would adopt. "Like it was a condition of him staying with me." She sniffed. "He'd only stay if I would adopt."

Cassie's face was streaked with tears. "Lib, I had no idea. I can't believe you hid that for so long. All during my pregnancy." She shook her head. "That must have been so hard for you. Here I was, pregnant by accident, complaining about it all the time to you...." She hugged her.

They sat down and talked for hours. They talked about their father's death and how much they missed him, and they talked about their mother and how they should have objected when their father insisted they bury her memory in Sarasota. Cassie told Libby about Sam's father and how she thought she'd been in love with him, but then he'd told her that Sam was "her problem." Libby held Cassie's hand as she cried about how much she struggled with being a single mother, feeling a pang as she thought about her angry outburst earlier that afternoon.

She squeezed Cassie's hand. "You're doing a great job, Cass. You deserve to go out tonight and have fun."

Cassie's mouth turned up in the hint of a smile. "I really like Dom. He's great with Sam, and I enjoy his company. He makes me feel safe."

Libby swallowed. "And that's hard to find."

Cassie rose when she looked at the clock and realized she had less than two hours to get home and get ready for her date. She promised to call Libby in the morning. After she left, Libby closed the door and bolted the lock. She'd lived by herself for years, but suddenly the house seemed too quiet.

She watched a television movie and fell asleep on the couch. When she woke it was nearly eleven o'clock. Libby rubbed her eyes and yawned, feeling too awake to go to bed. She wandered into the kitchen to make some tea.

Her cell phone vibrated to indicate she'd just received a text message. *Nick.* Libby lunged forward but frowned when she saw the message was from David. He wanted to come over.

She sighed and dialed his number. They needed to have a difficult conversation, but now wasn't the time.

He picked up after two rings. "Hello?"

"David, it's Libby."

"Hey, you!" She'd almost forgotten how chipper he could be. "Did you get my message?"

"Yeah. Look, it's not a good time. I've kind of… It's a long story."

"I have time," he said. "And I was just on my way over."

"Now?" She glanced at the clock. "It's late."

"I know, but I was in the neighborhood and I wanted to see you. I have some chocolates from Switzerland."

She smiled feebly. "Ah, you've figured out my weakness already."

"So I can come over? I'm about five minutes away."

She thought about it. What difference did it make? Maybe hearing about David's trip would be a pleasant distraction. "Sure, why not. I was just about to make some tea."

"See you in a few."

Libby rushed to her room to change into something more presentable: jeans and a simple T-shirt. She splashed cold water on her face, but her eyes were still swollen from crying. It would have to do, she decided.

There was a knock at the front door, and David held out a small blue gift bag.

"Oh, you shouldn't have." She smiled politely. She opened the bag and removed a box of chocolates. "These look amazing."

David smiled, and Libby looked away. They were barely dating. So why did she suddenly feel so guilty?

She stepped back to allow him inside. "How's your father doing?" she asked.

David's father, former mayor Jeb Sinclair, had been diagnosed with dementia several years ago and had been in a nursing home for some time.

"He's not doing too well, to be honest. The doctors want to move him to a locked unit. He needs more care than he's currently receiving."

"I'm sorry," Libby said as she poured two cups of tea. She'd known Jeb Sinclair practically her entire life, and she'd always remember him as he'd been in her youth: a smiling, towering figure of a man. "You know, I was looking through my dad's old files and I found some of your father's campaign flyers. I can show them to you later."

David smiled. "Isn't it funny how our fathers were friends and we found each other years later?"

Something about his tone made her skin prickle. Libby brushed the feeling aside. "Funny."

He looked around the room. "Should we sit?"

She led him to the living room and he sat on the couch. She chose a chair across from him. "So tell me about your trip to Zurich."

David tilted his head slightly. "Are you okay? You look like something's wrong."

She took a breath and began to assure him that she was fine, but instead, she slumped forward and said, "Oh, God. You have no idea what's been going on this past week."

She told him how her father's former court reporter had been murdered over the weekend and a death threat directed at Libby had been left beside the body. She told him that Nick had stayed in town to protect her, and about the terrible signs the killer had left for them. Then she told him about the man who'd come up to her in the diner.

"This stalker—Reggie Henderson—David, he knew all these things about me. Where I work, what I eat for lunch, the roads I take." She shuddered. "I was terrified."

He leaned forward, his forehead creased with concern. "Tell me what happened."

"He abducted me at gunpoint right from the diner. It was awful."

He sat stiffly. "But…you escaped."

"Yes, thank God. I broke his nose and ran away, and he was shooting at me. I was cornered, and I sprayed him in the eyes with wasp spray left out near some trash cans. Then I grabbed his gun when he dropped it, and when he lunged at me I shot him." She sat up straighter. She couldn't help but feel some pride as she remembered the incident. "Anyway, it's over. I'm just rattled. It's going to take some time to get to feeling normal again."

"But you said there were six signs, didn't you? What was sign six supposed to be?"

"Oh." Libby shrugged. "I don't know. Henderson is dead, so I guess it doesn't matter. As far as I know, the police never figured that out."

David nodded and sat back thoughtfully. "Interesting."

She snorted. "Interesting? How about terrifying? Or, how about 'Gee, Libby, I'm glad to hear your stalker didn't kill you yesterday.' Is 'interesting' the best you can do?"

He stared at her, and Libby froze. There was something odd about his glare.

"Is that what you want me to say, Elizabeth? That I'm glad you made it out alive?"

She swallowed. His response made her uncomfortable. "I think I've upset you. Is it because of Nick? Don't read anything into that. We're completely over. Completely."

"Oh?" David arched a brow.

"Yes," she said slowly, glancing at the clock. "You know, I'm tired. Maybe we can have coffee or something tomorrow."

He smiled. "It's almost midnight, Libby. If we wait twenty minutes or so it will be tomorrow." He took a sip of his tea and then placed the mug on the coffee table. "Day seven."

Her heart skipped. "That's not even funny," she said, but the look on his face told her that he hadn't meant it as a joke. She stood. "I think you should leave. Now."

"Now?" He laughed, and the sound raked her spine. "You didn't even tell me the best part of the story!"

Libby's lips grew cold. "What are you talking about?"

"You forgot to tell me the part where you learned that your father, the right and honorable Michael Andrews, agreed to prosecute Will Henderson in exchange for the *real* killer's political and financial support when he ran for judge a few years later."

He had a sick smile as he spoke to her, and his eyes had grown wide. He was taking an obvious delight in her unease. Her mouth went dry. "How did you know about that?"

"I do my research, too, Elizabeth." He sneered as he rose from the couch. Libby's muscles quivered—she knew she had to run, and yet she felt paralyzed. "Can you imagine? Judge Andrews knowingly prosecuted the wrong person for political gain. He knew who the serial killer was, and he allowed him to go free. Of course, he made him promise not to kill again, but even still…" He shook his head and clucked his tongue. "You must have been so disappointed."

"Get out," she stammered.

"Get out?" He laughed. "Don't you want to know what the sixth sign is?"

"No." A chill flushed her body. "You—"

"Me, Libby. Reggie Henderson planted the signs for *me*. You killed my accomplice. Well, that shouldn't stop us from proceeding. And you've guessed what sign six is by now, haven't you?" David reached into his pocket and retrieved a long hunting knife. He smiled. "A false sense of security."

Chapter 15

After driving aimlessly for hours and taking a long walk near the falls, Nick stopped at the diner on Main Street for a cup of coffee. It tasted stale, as if it had been sitting there all night.

He sat back in the booth and stared out the window. Growing up, he couldn't wait for the day when he packed up and left this town for someplace more exciting. He'd seized that opportunity as soon as the FBI had offered it, and he admitted now that he hadn't considered how Libby might have felt about starting over. He'd thought he loved her and that he'd been acting out of love for her, but now he realized that it was a selfish love.

The past few days, however, felt different.

He'd willingly risked his life and his career to protect Libby this week, not because he would have done that for anyone, but because it was Libby, the girl he'd chased after since they were in middle school. The girl he'd loved at first sight. Nearly three years ago he'd gotten exactly what he'd wanted: a life outside Arbor Falls and an exciting career. But he'd gotten those things by giving up the woman who made those accomplishments feel significant. She was what mattered, and it took a major screwup almost three years ago to realize it.

He stared blankly at the dark coffee before him and thought about the way Libby had professed to have given up coffee and then outdrank him all week. Her funny diets. The way she folded her T-shirts and wrinkled her nose at the wrappers in his car. How she held her head high when a police officer threatened her in open court. She was quirky, strong and surprisingly sensitive at her core, and he couldn't imagine going back to Pittsburgh now, like this. With her hurting and angry and him lost without her.

The thought of her in that alley yesterday, held at gunpoint, had flooded his body with blind energy. He hadn't thought about the gun or the man holding it. He hadn't thought about his own life. At that moment all he thought about was Libby walking to school at twelve years old and all the time they'd had together since then, and he realized that those years weren't enough. He would never have enough time with Libby.

He tensed his fingers around the mug. She was right that he'd always imagined his life with children. That seemed to be the way things happened: marriage, house, kids. But she'd been wrong to assume that he wanted children for their own sake. He'd always imagined having children with Libby. He wanted to grow old with *her*, not someone else. There *was* no one else. There could never be, and if that meant they couldn't have children, he wasn't sure he cared anymore. He'd been prepared to die for her this week. Surely that meant he could live without children.

He heaved a sigh and rubbed his forehead, kicking himself for asking her if she would adopt. He hadn't known what to say, but that was the wrong response. Libby prided herself on being perfect. She must have been shattered when she found out she couldn't have children.

He lifted the mug to his lips, taking a big gulp of the terrible coffee. He wondered if he should continue to Pittsburgh or whether he should return to her house and beg for forgiveness. *She already gave you a second chance,* he thought bitterly. Asking for a third seemed like too much.

He tapped his index finger against the coffee ring stain on the Formica table. She'd told him that she never wanted to see him again. He should respect her wishes for once. And yet he couldn't bring himself to leave town.

The bell above the diner door rang, and a man came in to sit at the counter. Nick looked around at the nearly deserted diner. He was tired of drinking coffee by himself. Being alone meant he called all the shots. He was tired of calling all the shots.

His mind drifted back to the case. He was still troubled by something that he couldn't define. How was it possible that Reggie Henderson had known so much about Libby's whereabouts? He'd always been right behind them, no matter where they went, except that Nick had never seen anyone trailing them. Was it possible that Reggie Henderson had known where he and Libby were going in advance? His pulse began to quicken. That would only be possible if he'd been spying on them somehow.

Nick left a few dollars on the table and walked quickly to his car. Could Henderson have planted something before he'd swapped his car for the rental? He opened the car trunk wide, examining it by the light of a streetlamp. He didn't see anything out of place. He closed it and opened his door, checking under the seats and the floor mats, not knowing exactly what he was looking for. Nick paused and wondered whether he should check under the vehicle's carriage.

He sat back in the front seat, feeling the frustration pool in his chest. He looked up at the streetlamp, watching it flicker.

His phone vibrated. "Foster."

"Hello? Is this Nick?"

Nick pulled the phone away to stare at the number. It was Christopher Henzel, Will Henderson's defense attorney. "Attorney Henzel? This is Nick."

"I just turned on the news and saw that Libby shot someone in self-defense. Someone by the name of Reggie Henderson. You want to finally tell me the truth about that 'book' you two are writing?"

Nick rubbed at his forehead. "He was stalking her," he said. "Following the pattern of the Arbor Falls Strangler and planting signs. We didn't want to alarm you."

Henzel was quiet. "Is she okay now?"

"Yes. He's dead and it's over." There was a long pause on the other end. "Hello?"

"I'm still here." Nick heard him take a breath. "There's something I neglected to tell you."

His heart skipped. "What's that?"

"Henderson—Will Henderson—he wasn't as innocent as I probably made him sound. He said some things...he knew some details that he would only have known if he'd been involved in the crimes in some way."

"I don't understand...."

"After his wife died, Henderson told me that the Strangler hired him to plant the signs. His fingerprints were all over some of the photographs mailed to the victims. I remember Andrews making a big to-do about that at trial."

Nick's pulse quickened. "So there were two people working together on the Arbor Falls murders? Damn it, Henzel, why didn't you tell us this sooner?"

"Henderson was my client. I've never discussed my suspicions with anyone." He paused. "For God's sake, you should have been honest with me. I had no reason to believe Libby was in danger."

Nick gripped the wheel. In a true reenactment of the Arbor Falls killings, Henderson would plant the signs and the real killer would enter the scene on day seven.

He checked the time. It was nearly midnight.

"Henzel, I have to go. I have to check on Libby." He put the key in the ignition. "And Henzel—thanks."

He tried Libby's cell, but there was no answer. His pulse kicked as he tried not to think of the worst. He was backing up out of the parking space when he got another look at his BlackBerry. He slammed on the brake. *The cell phone.* They'd used a rental car and stayed at an inn, so the killer probably couldn't have bugged those places, but he could have tracked them by listening to Libby's cell phone conversations. That meant that whoever was after her was someone she'd allowed to get close. Someone she trusted.

Someone she would open the door to.

Nick sped out of the lot and called Dom's cell phone, praying he answered. He did. "Vasquez."

"Dom, it's Nick. Libby's in danger. I need you to meet me at her house, and I need backup."

"What's going on?"

"The Arbor Falls Strangler was two individuals, not one. One planted the signs, and the other killed the girls. If this is a true copycat, we only got the guy who planted the signs."

Dom cursed. "I'm in the area. I've got your back."

Nick hung up the phone. He sped along the deserted roads, feeling the car grip the sharp turns. He slowed for intersections and then proceeded straight through. He tried not to look at the clock.

Ten minutes to midnight. Ten minutes to day seven.

David sat Libby on a kitchen chair and bound her wrists and ankles with duct tape. Her hands tingled as the tape disrupted her circulation.

"The sixth sign is a tricky one," he explained calmly. "It took me a while to figure that one out, myself." Libby's mouth opened and closed, her voice frozen. "Oh, come now. We've known each other for our whole lives, practically. We have so much in common. You see, your father was a corrupt bastard, and *my* father was the psychotic bastard who corrupted him." He stood back and admired his handiwork. "It's destiny, really."

Her knees weakened. "Your father." She remembered sitting with Nick and reviewing her father's notes from when he'd interviewed the woman who'd claimed to see a tall, ruddy-faced man covered in blood walking from a victim's home. Jeb Sinclair was easily six foot four, and his complexion had always been spotted by rosacea. The witness wouldn't have recognized him because he didn't run for mayor until four years after she saw him fleeing the scene of the crime. She kicked herself for not drawing the connection when she found those campaign flyers mixed in with the case documents.

"That's right. Jeb Sinclair. The longest-serving mayor of Arbor Falls. A simply charming man, by all accounts." He stepped back to study her. "But he was also the Arbor Falls Strangler. And a vicious child abuser."

Libby winced reflexively. "I'm sorry."

"Your apology means nothing to me," he said flatly. "Your father could have saved me from years of torture if he'd been man enough to do the right thing."

She tried to wet her lips, but her mouth was bone dry. "*You* could still do the right thing, David," she said softly. "You're more of a man than either of our fathers were. If you left right now, no one would have to know about any of this."

"I'm not stupid, Libby. The second I left here you'd be on the phone to the police."

"But why now? If it's revenge you're after, it's too late. My father is dead and he'll never know about any of this."

"Actually, the timing was perfect," he said. "Your father knew what happened all those years ago. I couldn't risk taking my revenge and having him finally come out with the truth. That would have ruined everything." He smiled, sending a bolt of ice through her center. "So I

did the next best thing. When we went to visit him two
days before he died, when he was in and out of consciousness, you left the room and I told him everything.
That I was deceiving you the same way he'd deceived
this town and that I was going to kill you the same way
he'd killed me." He stared at her. "It's bigger than him
now. It's about justice. Someone has to pay. It's only fair
to sacrifice the favorite child."

Bile rose in her throat as he circled like a shark. The
hunting knife lay on the kitchen table. "H-how did you
find out about your father?" Her lips felt rubbery.

"He told me. I was fifteen. He'd beaten me up again,
broken a few bones. I threatened to call the police. He
told me that he could do whatever he wanted and no
one would care, that he was responsible for eight murders and he'd pulled some strings so that someone else
agreed to take the fall." His face darkened. "He actually
bragged about it."

As David paced the kitchen, Libby twisted her hands,
trying to loosen the duct tape. Her senses felt height-
ened. She could hear the rush of blood in her veins, the
blinking of her eyes, the flickering of the lightbulb she'd
been meaning to change for weeks now. She wasn't one
for regrets, but as she sat there, she thought of Nick.

What wouldn't she give to take back those final
words, when she told him that she never wanted to see
him again? She couldn't face the heartbreak of falling
short in his eyes or being the source of his resentment.
Still, Nick deserved the truth, which was that she loved
him and that she always had. That she loved him too
much to want him to be unhappy.

Libby sat up. She had to stay sharp. There would be

a way to escape, and she just had to take a deep breath and figure it out. She watched David pace like a caged lion, and her gaze drifted to the glinting blade. Terror collapsed across her as she realized how alone she was.

Nick didn't even remember the roads he'd driven as he pulled onto Libby's street, gripped as he was by the steel hand of terror. All he could think was that she was in serious danger. He couldn't entertain the thought that he might already be too late.

He cut the headlights and slowed in front of her house. Libby's driveway was empty except for her vehicle, but a dark BMW was parked across the street. He couldn't be sure whether the BMW belonged to a neighbor or the killer, but he knew he hadn't seen it before. His heart thundered as he called Dom again.

"Dom. There's a strange car parked across from Libby's house. I need someone to run the plates." He read the number to Dom, hung up and continued past the house.

He parked the car three houses away. The road was silent except for the faint chirping of crickets, and dark except for the stars and the bright light of an almost full moon. The police backup he'd requested hadn't arrived yet. He wasn't about to wait.

Nick made his way stealthily across the grass until he reached Libby's house. The shades were all drawn, but light filtered through. He tried to peer through a gap in the living room curtains, but he didn't see any movement. Crouching low, he darted around the house to the kitchen and felt a burst of adrenaline when he saw that

Libby had neglected to draw the curtains in the back of the house.

He crept silently across the back patio toward the window, straining to hear voices. His heart thrust against his rib cage when he heard only silence. Then he saw her, sitting in a chair, her wrists and ankles bound, her head sagging forward on her chest.

He was too late.

Nick struggled to breathe, his breath coming in sporadic bursts as he pressed his hand against the side of the house to steady himself. He was too late, and beautiful Libby—his Libby—was gone. His body went numb.

He'd only wanted one more minute with her, just one minute to tell her that he loved her, that he would give up everything he owned for her. Then he would have been out of her life forever, just as she'd wanted.

Then she lifted her head. Blood surged through his veins. She was still alive! He wasn't too late.

He saw a figure in the kitchen move through a shadow. Nick ducked and drew his weapon. She was still alive, but she had only minutes left. He had to act quickly.

Libby glanced at the clock on the wall. It was ten past midnight, and David was pacing the kitchen, peering out of the windows. "You're nervous," she observed. "David, you know this is wrong."

"Shut up."

She bit her lip. "You didn't kill those other people, did you? That woman and that cop."

"You know better," he said as he lifted the edge of a curtain covering the window. "I was out of the country."

She studied him as he stood by the window above the sink. "Have you done this before? I mean…have you ever killed anyone?" Her lips felt useless as she spoke the question.

He didn't answer at first. He placed his hands on the sink and leaned forward as if he was going to be sick. After a few moments he spoke without turning his head to face her. "No."

This was good, she thought. He was new at this. "Why would you kill me, anyway? I never hurt you. I kind of liked you."

He snorted. "That's why you hopped into bed with your ex-fiancé as soon as I left town? Because you liked me so much?"

Libby's face grew warm. "That's not your business."

She paused. Had he spied on them somehow? That could explain why Reggie Henderson always knew where they were when he planted the signs. "You got me," she said wryly. "You're clever. What did you do, bug my office? My house?"

"No, I bugged your cell phone." He said it nonchalantly, but she detected a note of pride. "You wouldn't know it by looking at him, but Reggie was a genius at technological stuff. I tapped your phone so we could monitor your location and listen in on your conversations. Kind of like a wiretap."

Her eyes grew wide. "And you heard…how did you know about me and Nick?"

His lips thinned. "I didn't. Lucky guess."

She eyed the clock and closed her eyes, praying that Nick wasn't back in Pittsburgh already. Maybe he would regret the way they'd left off and return to try to smooth things over. She opened her eyes. A quarter past midnight.

Who was she kidding? Their argument was hours ago. If he had any desire to see her again, he would have returned before nightfall.

She clenched and unclenched her hands, trying to restore circulation. He'd wrapped her wrists dozens of times, and there was no way to break free. She had to keep him talking—it was the only way she could think to buy time. She'd managed to fight off Reggie. Maybe she could convince David that he didn't have to go through with this.

"So Reggie planted that photograph in my files? You must have given him the code to my alarm, right? You hired Reggie Henderson to do your dirty work while you were out of the country. That was smart," she mused. "Of course, allowing Reggie to take the fall for your crime doesn't work anymore, seeing as he's dead. You didn't count on that, and that's why you're going to get caught."

David paused. "Reggie was a disappointment. He performed adequately for a while, don't get me wrong, but when he couldn't finish…" He clicked his tongue. "It didn't need to be any big deal. Day five. Life-or-death could have meant a lot of things. We talked about it. I thought he should keep it simple. And I was right." He looked Libby over. "What are you? Five foot six? Five-five? And you killed him?" He shook his head. "He got overexcited. He would have been a liability. Let's just say I'm glad you took care of it for me."

"You're glad? But that leaves you without someone to blame for…" She stopped.

"For your death?" He sighed. "I thought so at first.

But my alibi's airtight. I've been out of the country. I stopped over to bring you some chocolates, and I got a nasty surprise." He scratched his ear. "Or I didn't. Maybe I rang the doorbell a few times and left. I haven't decided yet."

Libby's heart skipped. "You've really thought this through."

"Well, I have to, Libby."

He shrugged, and his tone was as casual as if he was talking about priming a wall before he painted it. He was coldly logical. Emotionless, as if something had stripped him of all of his humanity. "I have to think it through, to make it perfect. It needs to be done, you understand. To right a wrong and restore balance. But I am *not* going to jail for it. No way. Even if they pick me up, there's reasonable doubt. An old flame. Maybe an argument."

Her mouth went dry. "You're going to frame Nick?"

"If I have to," he said. "Or at least use him to cast reasonable doubt on my own case."

"But the cell phone records. You texted me—"

"Like I said, I'll be the one to discover your body. I really think that's what I'm going to do." David smoothed her hair. Libby tried not to look as repulsed as the gesture made her feel. "You know, I did like you. Even when I knew I had to kill you, I liked you. I know this is scary. I don't want you to be scared." The intensity of his gaze made Libby's stomach roil. He leaned closer. "No, on second thought, be scared. It's sexier."

Libby heard a rustle outside the window. She turned her head toward the sound and then turned it back, afraid that David would see her response.

He stopped. "Did you hear that?"

"No," she lied.

He walked to the window. "Something walked past the window."

Her pulse picked up speed. Was it possible that someone had contacted the police? The thought that someone might have realized she was in danger was almost too much to hope for, but she needed a reason to keep going. "It's probably an animal. There are a lot of raccoons around here."

He spun to face her. "It's day seven. There's no reason to wait any longer."

Panic flooded her, squeezing the air from her lungs. "You don't have to do this, David."

"You don't understand, Libby," he said, leaning forward until his stale breath bounced off her face. "I'm a really bad guy. I *want* to do this."

The house was surrounded by police officers, all waiting for the lights to go out.

Dom had arrived only minutes after Nick had, dressed in an expensive shirt and pants. He'd had someone at the precinct run the plates on the BMW parked across the street. It belonged to David Sinclair, the guy Libby was seeing. When he found out, Nick had to stop himself from breaking through a window right then and there.

Nick led a team of three officers to the basement door. "Don't bother picking the lock," he said and retrieved the key from its hiding place under a planter in the garden. How many times had he told Libby that she was inviting trouble by keeping a key outside? Now he was glad she'd never listened.

The door flew open quietly, and the officers stepped

into the basement, flashlights poised above their drawn weapons. Nick ran to the gray circuit breaker panel and looked back at the other officers, giving them a nod. When they nodded in response, he flipped a switch, cutting electricity to the house.

"Go!" Nick shouted, and the police stormed up the basement stairs. Seconds later there was a crash as more officers broke through the front and side doors.

Nick felt a white-hot rage pumping through his veins. His muscles pulsed with pure energy as he pounded up the steps. He could think of nothing else but getting his hands on this bastard.

"In here!" Dom called, and his heart caught in his throat. Two officers were in the living room kneeling beside a bespectacled man, pressing him to the ground. "He tried to run."

Nick towered over the killer. "Where's Libby?"

The man was stunned. "Elizabeth," he said softly, his eyes glassy.

Nick advanced on him, but Dom restrained him.

Then he heard her. "Nick!"

Libby.

He sprinted to the kitchen and shone his flashlight on the chair in the center of the room. She saw him and burst into tears.

"Libby."

He darted to her side and cut away the duct tape on her wrists and ankles with a pocket knife. She moaned, and in the dim light he saw her rubbing her wrists. As he came to face her, she started to stand but then fell back in her chair.

"My feet are numb," she explained through her tears.

"Oh, honey." He took her into his arms, kissing her mouth, her cheeks, her lips. "Oh, Libby, I was so afraid I'd lost you."

"Nick." She wrapped her arms around his shoulders and sobbed into his neck. "I was so scared I'd never see you again." She threaded her fingers through his hair. "I thought you'd left me."

"I couldn't leave, Libby." His throat tightened. "I won't ever leave you. Never again."

The lights came on, and he stepped back to look at the most beautiful face he'd ever seen. She had her hands against his cheeks, and she was smiling as the tears fell. "Nick," she began, "I shouldn't have kicked you out like that."

"I shouldn't have let you kick me out." He fumbled at her, gripping her T-shirt in his fists. He'd just saved her life, and yet he'd never felt so inept. "Damn it. I can't leave you. Do you understand? I can't live without you."

Her chin trembled. "I know you want a family. I did everything the wrong way, but I said those things because I love you. I want you to be happy, even if it's without me."

He took her shaking hands in his and pressed her knuckles against his lips. "That's the problem. I can't be happy without you. You make me want to be a better man, Libby, and to do anything as important as to have children without you, without my other half…." He shook his head. "I can't imagine it. And I don't want to."

She leaned closer to rest her cheek against their hands. "I don't want you to, either."

He leaned in and kissed her, dwelling on the softness of her lips. His legs were shaking, and he fell to his knees. "We've wasted too much time. All of those years apart…I never realized until now how much I need you in my life."

She stroked his face softly. "I need you, too, Nick. I like to imagine I'm fine by myself, and I guess I've gotten by." Her lower lip trembled. "But life is so much better with you."

His heart grew warm. "I have to tell you something. I'm scheduled to be transferred to Washington, D.C. I have to relocate to a large office, but I'll request a transfer somewhere closer. New York City, or maybe Boston." He looked into her eyes. "Nothing else matters. You're all I've ever wanted. I love you."

Thick tears streamed down her face. "I love you, too, Nick. I've always loved you." She held his jaw in her hands, stroking her thumbs against the stubble of his cheeks. "We'll figure something out."

He slipped his fingers through her jet-black hair. "Maybe after I finish my paperwork and you've given your statement, I could take you somewhere nice for pancakes." He grinned. "Or yogurt and granola, whichever you prefer."

His heart ached to see her lips part in a broad smile. "There's nothing I'd love more."

Chapter 16

"That's everything," Libby said.

Nick closed the door to the moving van. "Beautiful day for a road trip." Libby didn't respond. She was looking back at her empty house, smiling sadly. Nick wrapped an arm around her shoulder. "I'm going to miss this house, too."

"I was so proud when I bought it. I planted all of those flowers in front, and I chose all of the room colors." She rested her head against him.

"Are you sure you're okay with this? I don't want to force you into anything—"

She nodded. "Yes. I love this house, and I have lots of happy memories of my time here. Then, some not-so-happy ones...."

Six weeks had passed since Nick had rescued her, and although she logically knew that she was no longer in danger, she hadn't slept well in the house since.

Every creak made her heart pound and disrupted her sleep for the night. Moving to Virginia would be a welcome change.

She wrapped her arms around Nick's waist. "I hope a nice couple buys it. This house is meant to be filled with love."

Nick brushed his lips against her forehead. "Your new home has a lot of white walls that need painting and a big green lawn that needs a garden."

Libby sighed. "Fresh starts are nice. And I'll still be coming back a lot to see Cassie and Sam. I can drive by the house if I miss it."

He pulled her closer. "Cassie and Sam and Dom, you mean."

She laughed. "I stand corrected." She'd never seen a couple click as quickly as Dom and Cassie had, and Cassie was right: he was a natural with Sam. "I'm already on the lookout for a wedding invitation."

She sniffed as she thought about her sister and her nephew. Washington felt so far from Arbor Falls. "It's just three years, not forever," she whispered. "I like it here, and I'm not leaving forever, right?"

He rubbed her shoulders affectionately. "Just three years, and we'll come back anytime you want to, whether it's to see Sam or to grab pad Thai." He took her hand. "Come on. We have one more stop before we leave."

Nick helped Libby climb into the large van, holding her hand so she could step up. A few months ago she might have resisted such aid and informed him that she wasn't helpless. Now she recognized the gesture for what it was to Nick: a desire to protect her, to be her hero every day, and not just under extraordinary circumstances. She'd always prided herself on being independent, but Nick's sweet little gestures made her heart melt.

As they twisted through the roads of Arbor Falls, Nick pointed out landmarks. "Here's our middle school. I saw you walking to school one morning, right over there." He slowed the car to point. "Love at first sight, Libby."

A blush warmed her cheeks. "You never told me about that. And here I thought you fell in love with me because of my vast eighth grade geography knowledge."

"It's true—you could rattle off the continents like a pro. And I remember you pointing out that North America was distorted on our world map to appear much larger than it is."

"Cold war propaganda," she mumbled.

Nick chuckled and turned the corner. "Mostly I remember getting a C in that class because I couldn't focus on anything but you."

The warmth on her cheeks crept down her neck.

"There's the grocery store," Nick continued. "I bought you a sandwich there on our first date, and we walked to the library afterward to study algebra."

"That wasn't a date!" Libby laughed. "I'm pretty sure you were just following me around."

"Guilty. But we ate a meal together. Sort of. I'd consider that a first date."

Libby looked at her favorite grocery store for the last time, bid farewell to her favorite roads and the Victorian homes she'd always admired and gave a little wave to the diner on Main Street. "Even though someone abducted me from there, I still kind of love that place," she said.

"Yeah, I think I still owe Dom a few beers for that sidewalk scuffle. Let's change the subject."

She smiled and sat back in her seat, looking out the van window. "I said goodbye to everyone at the D.A.'s Office yesterday. I admit, I cried buckets." Nick reached over and grasped her hand. "I took that job expecting to be there forever, or at least until I became a judge. It was hard to let go of that dream."

"I can understand that."

"But that was when I wanted to be like Dad," she said quietly. "I've realized that I'll never be like him. I've spent my whole life living within structures established by others. It's time for me to be Libby."

Nick was quiet. "Your dad...well..."

"He made some mistakes," she said, finishing the thought for him. "Terrible mistakes."

Her head still felt foggy when she thought of her father trading his integrity for his ambition and of all the havoc he'd wreaked as a result. He'd taught Libby to look out for victims, to seek justice for the powerless, and yet he'd failed to protect Will Henderson—a poor, uneducated man—from the powerful Jeb Sinclair. Worse, he'd used his position and his knowledge to advocate for the imprisonment of a man who was not guilty of the charges against him, knowing that his prosecution would allow a killer to go free. She struggled to rectify this image of her father with her memories of him lecturing her on the ideals of justice. The contrast left her disoriented.

"I'll always love my dad," she said, her voice trembling. "I will struggle with who he was, but for all of his shortcomings, I believe he tried to be a good father."

Nick took a deep breath. "You know your dad and I didn't always see eye to eye, but I have to give him credit for raising a hell of a daughter." He kissed her hand. "You amaze me, Lib."

She squeezed his hand. Libby had already begun using her share of her inheritance to establish a nonprofit to pair indigent persons who may have been wrongfully convicted with attorneys to appeal their case. She'd located a small office out of which to run her nonprofit in Washington, D.C. Nick would be working only a few blocks away. "I can't help Henderson, but I can help others like him. The wrongfully accused and powerless. I need to do this, Nick. I need to find forgiveness."

He swallowed. "You found a lot of forgiveness already. For me."

"And for myself," she added. "I've done a lot of thinking over the past few weeks about my infertility. I felt guilty about it for a long time. Guilty and ashamed, like it was something I had to hide. I blamed my diagnosis for making me feel inferior." She looked at him. "Then I realized that you still loved me and that all of those bad feelings were my responsibility."

"*Still* loved you?" Nick's voice tightened. "Libby, I doubt there's anything that could make me *stop* loving you, honey."

"I feel like I've taken the first step toward healing, at least. Forgiving myself for being imperfect. I don't know about adoption yet." She paused. "I think I'd like to be a mom one day."

"You think about it, and you let me know what you decide."

She sat back and looked at him. "You don't care about having a family?"

"Don't get me wrong, kids would be great." He shrugged. "But honestly? I have my family right here."

Libby felt a swell of emotion, and for the first time in a long time, she didn't know how to respond except to grip his hand tighter.

Nick pulled into a parking lot at the base of the trail to Overlook Point. He turned off the engine and faced her. "The day we hiked up this trail and looked down at Arbor Falls was one of my favorite memories with you. I'd like to hike it one more time before we go."

She looked outside at the warm, cloudless May morning. Getting some exercise before the long drive to Virginia was a great idea. "I'd love to." She beamed.

They locked the van and set out on the trail, which started out at a gentle slope but then grew steep about fifteen minutes in. Libby welcomed the vigorous hike. Her heart was pounding in a steady beat, and the air was cool and sweet smelling below the canopy of trees. The man beside her was smiling with that adorable dimple and wearing khaki shorts to show off his muscular calves. Better still, he was holding her hand. Tightly. Life was good.

They came to a clearing and hiked the remainder of the path to Overlook Point, where they could see the entire town of Arbor Falls and hundreds of miles in the distance. From that vantage point the world could be divided into colored squares and rooftops, lazy rivers and highways. From above, the world below made sense.

Libby sucked in her breath. "It's so gorgeous. I wish I could take it with us."

Standing in companionable silence, they watched as the morning sun burned off the haze in the valley below. Libby closed her eyes to listen to the stillness around her, feeling the warmth of the sun's rays on her skin and the earth under her feet. She inhaled. She was alive. She was still *alive,* and the realization made her want to throw her arms around someone, so she did.

Nick laughed and hugged her back. "Hey, what's that about?"

She wanted to tell him that it was about the way he'd brought her back from death, that he'd saved her in more ways than she could explain. She had her life, and she had Nick, and he made her life worth living.

"I'm not very good at talking about my feelings," she said. "So I'll just say I love you."

She looked at the valley and pointed to a spot where a white tent was being erected. "Oh, look! Do you think someone's getting married today?"

"Could be."

She sighed. "This would be a beautiful place to get married. I know we were supposed to be married in the chapel, but I would love to be married here."

"Libby, you know I'd marry you anywhere, but yes, this does seem like the perfect place." Nick smiled. "So let's get married."

She grinned and her eyes widened. "Really? I'll start planning as soon as we—"

"No." His voice deepened. "Let's get married today."

"I don't understand…"

Nick knelt on one knee and opened a white velvet case. Inside was a glistening solitaire diamond. Her jaw dropped. "Nick, what is—"

"A new diamond ring for our new life together. Marry me, Libby. Here. Now. Today."

Her cheeks felt hot as he took her left hand into his trembling fingers. "Oh, my..."

"I ordered everything you chose when you planned our wedding. The flowers, the caterer, even the officiate. I snuck your wedding dress out of the van after you packed it. Cassie is down there already, and she's going to help you get dressed."

"Nick, I—"

"Our friends and family will be here," he continued. "Your friends from the District Attorney's Office. Cassie found a little tuxedo for Sam."

Libby's eyes brimmed with tears. She looked down at herself and began to laugh. "I'm all sweaty! My hair is a mess—"

"Cassie's going to drive you to a hotel. I've reserved the suite, and you can get dressed there and do whatever you need to do." His eyes were intense as he gazed at her.

"Why, Nick Foster," she whispered, "you threw me a surprise wedding."

"Or an elaborate engagement party, if you're not ready. I even ordered the chocolate wedding cake you've always talked about."

She laughed, sputtering tears. "You actually listened to me."

"I've hung on your every word since we were twelve years old. I love you, Elizabeth Andrews, and it's a beautiful day for a wedding." He swallowed. "Marry me. Please."

Libby lost herself for a moment in his beautiful dark

brown eyes. "Yes." The word spilled from her mouth. "I want to marry you today."

He beamed and slipped the solitaire on her ring finger. He then stood and took her into his arms, kissing her soundly on the lips. Libby's heart swelled as she stepped away to look at Nick—the man she'd always loved and always would. "You are full of surprises, Nick." And she loved him for it.

"Hold on, Libby. You can't believe what I have in store for you today."

She was breathless as she grabbed him for another kiss. They stood in an embrace, watching the wedding preparations below. Finally Nick kissed her on the forehead and said, "I think we should go get ready for our big day."

Libby nuzzled against his neck. "I'm feeling pretty perfect right now," she said. "Do you think we can just stay here for a few more minutes?"

He chuckled softly. "Anything you want, Libby," he said, pulling her closer against his side. "Forever, anything you want."

* * * * *

REQUEST YOUR FREE BOOKS!
2 FREE NOVELS PLUS 2 FREE GIFTS!

ⓗ HARLEQUIN®

ROMANTIC suspense

Sparked by danger, fueled by passion

YES! Please send me 2 FREE Harlequin® Romantic Suspense novels and my 2 FREE gifts (gifts are worth about $10). After receiving them, if I don't wish to receive any more books, I can return the shipping statement marked "cancel." If I don't cancel, I will receive 4 brand-new novels every month and be billed just $4.49 per book in the U.S. or $5.24 per book in Canada. That's a savings of at least 14% off the cover price! It's quite a bargain! Shipping and handling is just 50¢ per book in the U.S. and 75¢ per book in Canada.* I understand that accepting the 2 free books and gifts places me under no obligation to buy anything. I can always return a shipment and cancel at any time. Even if I never buy another book, the two free books and gifts are mine to keep forever.

240/340 HDN FVS7

Name _____ (PLEASE PRINT) _____

Address _____ Apt. # _____

City _____ State/Prov. _____ Zip/Postal Code _____

Signature (if under 18, a parent or guardian must sign)

Mail to the **Harlequin® Reader Service:**
IN U.S.A.: P.O. Box 1867, Buffalo, NY 14240-1867
IN CANADA: P.O. Box 609, Fort Erie, Ontario L2A 5X3

Want to try two free books from another line?
Call 1-800-873-8635 or visit www.ReaderService.com.

* Terms and prices subject to change without notice. Prices do not include applicable taxes. Sales tax applicable in N.Y. Canadian residents will be charged applicable taxes. Offer not valid in Quebec. This offer is limited to one order per household. Not valid for current subscribers to Harlequin Romantic Suspense books. All orders subject to credit approval. Credit or debit balances in a customer's account(s) may be offset by any other outstanding balance owed by or to the customer. Please allow 4 to 6 weeks for delivery. Offer available while quantities last.

Your Privacy—The Harlequin® Reader Service is committed to protecting your privacy. Our Privacy Policy is available online at www.ReaderService.com or upon request from the Harlequin Reader Service.

We make a portion of our mailing list available to reputable third parties that offer products we believe may interest you. If you prefer that we not exchange your name with third parties, or if you wish to clarify or modify your communication preferences, please visit us at www.ReaderService.com/consumerschoice or write to us at Harlequin Reader Service Preference Service, P.O. Box 9062, Buffalo, NY 14269. Include your complete name and address.

HRS13

SPECIAL EXCERPT FROM

 HARLEQUIN®

ROMANTIC suspense

On the hunt to dismantle a deadly conspiracy, sexy soldier Nick Prescott takes a detour to rescue journalist Rebecca Parker. The stakes have never been higher as they work to stay one step ahead of their enemies…and each other.

Read on for a sneak peek of

SPECIAL OPS EXCLUSIVE

by Elle Kennedy, coming May 2013 from Harlequin Romantic Suspense.

Angry faces and moving bodies whizzed above her. Rebecca braced both palms on the hot pavement and tried to stand up, only to fall backward when someone bumped into her. Someone else stepped on her foot, bringing a jolt of pain. Uh-oh. This was bad. Her eyes couldn't seem to focus and shapes were beginning to look blurry.

The fear finally hit her, clogging her throat and making her heart pound.

She was going to get crushed in a stampede.

With a burst of adrenaline, she made another attempt to hurl herself to her feet—and this time it worked. She was off the ground and hovering over the crowd—wait, hovering *over* it?

Blinking a few times, Rebecca realized she *felt* as if she was floating because she *was* floating. She was tucked tightly in a man's arms, a man who'd taken it upon himself to carry her away to safety, Kevin Costner style.

"Who are you?" she murmured, but the inquiry got lost in

the rioters' shouts and the rapid popping noises of the rubber bullets being fired into the crowd.

She became aware of the most intoxicating scent, and she inhaled deeply, filling her lungs with that spicy aroma. It was *him*, she realized. God, he smelled good.

She glanced up to study the face of her rescuer, catching glimpses of a strong, clean-shaven jaw. Sensual lips. A straight nose. She wanted to see his eyes, but the angle was all wrong, so she focused on his incredible chest instead. Jeez, the guy must work out. His torso was hard as a rock, rippled with muscles that flexed at each purposeful step he took. And he was *tall*. At least six-one, and she felt downright tiny in his arms.

"You okay?"

The concerned male voice broke through her thoughts. She looked up at her rescuer, finally getting a good look at those elusive eyes.

Boy, were they worth the wait. At first glance they were brown—until you looked closer and realized they were the color of warm honey with flecks of amber around the pupils. And they were so magnetic she felt hypnotized as she gazed into them.

"Ms. Parker?"

She blinked, forcing herself back to reality. "Oh. I'm fine," she answered. "A little bruised, but I'll live. And you can call me Rebecca. I think it's only fitting I be on a first-name basis with the man who saved my life."

His lips curved. "If you say so."

**Don't miss SPECIAL OPS EXCLUSIVE
by Elle Kennedy, available May 2013 from
Harlequin Romantic Suspense
wherever books are sold.**

ROMANTIC suspense

CAVANAUGH ON DUTY
by *USA TODAY* bestselling author
Marie Ferrarella

Will the quest for justice lead to
unbridled passion?

When Esteban Fernandez suddenly found
himself pulled out of his undercover work and
partnered with unrequited love Kari Cavelli, he
thought his life was over. Little did he realize
that it was just the beginning.

Look for *CAVANAUGH ON DUTY*
by Marie Ferrarella next month from
Harlequin Romantic Suspense.

Available wherever books are sold.

Heart-racing romance, high-stakes suspense!

HRS27821